JUS [barcode: D0395636]

...a movie theate[r] [...] [i]n't on the screen.

(Samantha Fleskin's "A Hot Movie Date")

...a daring liaison between two women, all bought and paid for.

(Robbi Sommers's "Marie")

...a pair of strippers discover their inner lesbian.

(Scarlett Fever's "Bi-Curious Female Seeking Same")

...a phone-sex session that's pure electricity.

(Jolie Graham's "The Hot Line")

...a dance student teaches her instructor a torrid variation of the tango.

(JoAnn Bren Guernsey's "Private Lessons")

...bright lights, big binoculars—and some very naughty neighbors.

(Marcy Sheiner's "The Naked City")

...a coffeehouse where the waitress serves her own hot specialty.

(Susan Scotto's "On the House")

Penthouse:

Between the Sheets

A Collection of Erotic Bedtime Stories

by the Editors of
Penthouse Magazine

WARNER BOOKS

NEW YORK   BOSTON

This book is a work of fiction. Names, characters, places, and incidents are the product of the author's imagination or are used fictitiously. Any resemblance to actual events, locales, or persons, living or dead, is coincidental.

Copyright © 2001 by General Media Communications, Inc.
All rights reserved.

Warner Books

Time Warner Book Group
1271 Avenue of the Americas, New York, NY 10020
Visit our Web site at www.twbookmark.com

Printed in the United States of America

First Edition: August 2001

10 9 8 7 6 5

Library of Congress Cataloging-in-Publication Data
Between the sheets : a collection of erotic bedtime stories / the editors of Penthouse magazine.
    p.cm
  ISBN 0-446-67782-5
  1. Erotic stories, American.   I. Penthouse (New York, N.Y.)

PS648.E7 B53 2001
803'.01083538—dc21   2001023372

Book design by H. Roberts Design
Cover design Julie Metz
Cover photo © Lisa Spindler/Graphistock

Contents

Introduction

Begun in 1993 as a column especially for women writers, "Bedtime Stories" continued the *Penthouse* tradition of providing the best erotic entertainment for men. It enabled women from all walks of life, including some of today's most popular erotic fiction writers, a prominent place to publish their incredible flights of fancy. Tantalizing readers with images that expressed their wide-ranging sexual desires, "Bedtime Stories" helped to bring erotic fiction into the mainstream of American literature. Although no longer published in the magazine, this exciting column continues to provide an extraordinary venue for writers and readers alike on our website Penthouse.com. Here for your enjoyment is a mixture of stories from the magazine and the website. It has been my pleasure to act as editor of this column since its inception. I hope you enjoy reading these stories as much as I have.

Lavada Nahon
Penthouse Magazine
Editor, "Bedtime Stories"

Penthouse:
Between the Sheets

Heat Treatment

BY SUZANNE LICATA

*I*t burns, always burns. So few words spoken, so little needs to be said.

The air is hot and heavy, and the air conditioner is broken. We open a window facing the ocean, and a warm, wet, humid breeze reaches toward us. But we get hotter, just keep burning.

I wear a loose white T-shirt and khaki shorts, no bra. I am barefoot. My hair is tied back, and the sweat has saturated the top half of my chest. My neck drips as if cool rain is beating upon me. But it is not cool. Hot, always hot.

He lies on an unmade bed, just pants. Beads from a nearby doorway beat together, and wind chimes sing, reminding us of the ocean breeze blowing aimlessly around the room. It never reaches us, never cools us.

I stand at the bottom of the bed and wait. A surge of juices builds between my legs.

His hands reach to my head and he loosens my hair clip. My blond hair falls around my face, in my eyes—it moves as I breathe. But I don't move. My shirt is being pulled up and he is touching my stomach, just touching and burning—1 breathe harder. I need more. Wildly, I throw my head back. I'm angry, touch me. I'm so wet, hot, dripping.

He smells sweet with every breath I breathe. He has yet to kiss me, but I can taste him, his mouth so close to mine. Our eyes meet. His hands still wandering but not touching. Touch me.

The last of the sunlight has faded, and the beginning of twilight is illuminating what is left of the day, casting dark and deep shadows around the room. Three candles, fragrant and burning in the corner of the room, flicker a softer set of shadows to the far wall. A roaring ocean, so loud. Suddenly every sound and shape seems loud and sharp. But I am fucking burning. I feel weak and vulnerable and anything goes. I want so badly for him to touch me. I am so wet and hot. I want to scream—I'm angry.

He is sure of himself as he climbs off the bed. Every bit of energy that leaves my body climbs into his, empowers him, and transforms him into complete power. He possesses me. I have no control left. I am only his—what he wants me to be.

I stand in front of him now, my king, and I wait for his next command. But I find my feet moving one behind the other—I back slowly into a cool wall, afraid. The temperature has probably dropped to a cool and comfortable breeze. Probably.

I can go no further, my body completely neutral and waiting for the next move, his move. His strong hands open my shorts, zipper then button. Inside my shorts he reaches around my waist. His hands slide down each side of my hips now, down my thighs as he shimmies the shorts to the floor.

He kneels. Breathing hot breaths between my legs. I want to thrust my hotness into his face, but I know I must wait. I'm dripping, burning. He kisses my thighs as his hands massage my breasts.

He comes up quickly and suddenly. We are face to face. Tears well up in my eyes, I don't know why. He extends my arms over my head and forcefully holds them against the wall. But I dare not break free for only he can set me free.

He crashes his hips against mine, and we are moving in perfect sync. We grind harder and harder, my whole body being thrown against the wall. He rubs against me.

He is biting my mouth, my lips. Tears of pleasure roll down my face to meet the never-ending water pouring from my hair. Still so hot. I am sucking his tongue, biting, sucking hard. My hands still raised above my head. He is finally touching me. His body to mine. My eyes roll to the back of my head—my head banging against the wall.

His hands roam my body now, but I still hold my arms above my head, clutching my wrists. I forget to relax—to release.

His fingers roam into my underwear; they come up wet and find their way into my mouth. I suck them. Lick them. Bite them. I taste sweet, and he licks my tongue—we share me.

I am going crazy. He is driving me crazy. Crazy.

I turn to face the wall to get away—to regain myself. I mustn't be here. But I was born to be here. My face cooled by the cool wall, I rub hard into it. Cool. I need cool.

Our bodies never leave that sync, my ass now grinding into his penis. Moving slowly, never missing a beat.

I cry now, his fingers fondling inside me, two fingers fondling inside me. And the rest of his hand cupping my vagina and pushing my ass into his pants. I reach to undo his pants. I sense I have his permission. It is time. Somehow my shirt lies on the floor, torn.

He stands behind me naked. He turns me. I move my face along his as I fall deeper and deeper into the passion. He affixes a gaze into my eyes and lifts me, wrapping my legs around his waist. I am swept to his bed and into the night. Holding my hair in his hands, forcefully mashing it against my head as our kiss becomes wildly passionate.

Each part of my body comes to life under this touch, giving me what I need, have needed . . . and when I need it. I shiver and burn. He knows how to handle me, almost calculating but with certain unpredictability. I am the most alive I will ever be.

I run my fingers through his hair, down his back, around his waist, and, finally, between his legs. I stroke him. I breathe down his neck and kiss his chest and lick around his nipples. I move slowly and his groans edge me a little farther to his stomach, where I stop before taking him in my mouth. I lick up and down and twirl my tongue around the top of his penis. I finally send him down my throat and bob my head between his legs. I go farther below and moisten the area beneath but quickly return to his pulsating penis. Above I roll my finger around his tongue, which has just returned from being buried deep inside me.

I stop, I can't wait to kiss him. He towers over me as our positions change. He holds my ass up in the air, bringing my body to his mouth, and begins to drink me. I am so wet, and his tongue turns me inside out. He returns to me, but now the look in his eye turns from passion to savage. I sense he has gone mad with this fever, and it spawns an animalistic state of ferociousness and rage within my soul.

We fall off the bed onto the floor. We play a game of cat and mouse. I try to get away, and at every attempt, his grip tightens. I crawl backward on my hands, now sinking to my elbows. He crawls on top of me, keeping my body between his legs and increasing my drive for escaping him.

He plunges himself between my spread legs, and I fall lifelessly into bliss. He pumps my body up and down and lets the passion back in. My nails run down his spine. He pumps harder and harder as I beg. My entire body is being lifted from the floor. His teeth are clenched. We explode.

Ecstasy of this magnitude has an energy all its own. Our souls touch briefly as the climactic peak of this episode flows.

The air cools now, almost chilling. There is less to be said now than when we started. Yet his look and touch will live inside me forever.

The Bath

BY SARAH KATHERINE

I didn't mean to walk in on him—it was all an accident. I got to his apartment and found the door unlocked. I walked in and called out for him, but there was no answer. I knew that he usually did not leave his place unlocked— he would often remind me that we *are* in New York and we *should* be careful. I decided to check around; maybe he was asleep. I pictured myself walking into his bedroom and finding him dozing peacefully in his bed, sleeping off the afternoon high.

I entered his room; it was empty. I saw his clothes strewn about, the room in its usual state of disorder. I did not notice at the time the pair of silk panties and the tiny skirt clumped in the corner—it was not until later that this fact would be recalled. Now all that I noticed was the pile of boxers and socks that was forever growing on the floor until we finally went to the Laundromat together. A small smile crept across my face as I remembered him plopping me down onto the vibrating washer and kissing me passionately as the vibrations spread throughout our bodies, bringing me to near ecstasy in the public laundry.

I continued my walk through the apartment. It was not until I reached the little nook off of which there is a bath that I heard him. Muffled noises were coming from behind the shut bathroom door, and (was that giggling I heard?) the water was running for the shower.

I knocked on the door to the bath. "Gary!" I shouted to him. "It's me. Gary? Honey?" I heard a panicked scrambling going on behind the bathroom door. "Coming!" he screamed back, and (was that another giggle?) I heard the doorknob rattle as he unlocked it.

His head peered from behind the door. "Hey, what are you doing here?" he said to me.

"Just thought I'd drop in on you," I responded defensively. The door opened wider, and I caught a glimpse of someone else crouched behind Gary. "Who's there?" I questioned, and then I demanded, "What the fuck!" as the door opened wider, revealing another girl standing behind my Gary. Both of them were naked and still dripping from the shower. A blast of steam waved across my face as I stood in the doorway, aghast.

The girl was thin and blond, in contrast to my heavy frame and dark features. She looked frail and delicate, her breasts smallish and round, her little hips smoothly curved, surrounding her neatly trimmed pussy. She was wet, dripping with soapy water, leaving little puddly footprints all over the bathroom floor as she squirmed about under my glare. Her eyes were red from pot and she looked uncomfortable, as if she might be stifling a fit of the giggles.

Gary took a step back from me, his half-erect cock bouncing lightly against his left thigh when he moved. His eyes were redder than the girl's, only without the laughter behind them. He lowered them away from my stare as if in shame. I stared at his body; I knew it so well. His earlobes, his neck (now covered with someone else's hickeys), his chest (upon which little beads of water were slipping down), his small, perfect little stomach which lay flat in contrast to his wild, wiry pubic hair, out of which his dick poked limply. His legs were firm and tan, and his feet, on which I had nibbled and sucked on numerous occasions, stood in their own little puddles on the cold, hard tile.

I moved into the bathroom. I was no longer thinking, just acting. I should have been angry, and maybe I was, but I was also intrigued, and it was this that pushed me out of the doorway and into the steamy, damp bath. I forced them both back into the cheap little bathroom cabinet, lining them up side by side. I was aware of their nakedness, and I felt a certain power that went with not being exposed as they were. I was leaning against the opposite wall, regarding them with a steady stare, when a wave of peevish curiosity overtook me.

I reached out to the blonde and grabbed her nipple, squeezing it between my fingers firmly. She let out a small gasp. I grabbed her erect tit and rolled it around in between my fingers. I twisted it lightly, making her areola squinch up into a little, tight ball of pink flesh. I circled her nipple with the palm of my hand, and soon I was using both hands to stimulate her firm little breasts. The blonde was making little noises under her breath and arching her back to make herself more accessible to me.

Gary hadn't moved an inch, although I did notice that his penis had become erect. I leaned back against the wall and stared at his crotch. I could see the minute little throbbing movements his cock was making, causing it to bounce up and down very slightly. The blond girl cast her eyes down at the tile, but my gaze remained fixated on my lover's stiff cock.

My hands found my own breasts, and I began stroking them beneath the thin fabric of my T-shirt. I teased my nipples, causing them to stand out like the blonde's, making two little peaks under my shirt. I ripped my top off over my head, revealing my smooth white breasts and shocking red nipples. I pulled one of my breasts up toward my mouth, able to get a part of my nipple sucked in my teeth. My hand fumbled with the zipper on my shorts until they fell to my ankles. I freed my breast from my clenched teeth and pushed my underwear down, stepping out of my clothes piled on the floor, leaving myself naked as well.

I took a step toward Gary. Neither he nor his friend had dared to move while I stripped out of my clothes; they simply stood across from me in complete bewilderment. I kneeled down in front of Gary, surveying his cock up close from my new position. I bent down a little farther and opened my mouth to receive his right testicle. I sucked in air through my teeth, creating enough of a vacuum for his ball to slip gently into my mouth. I rolled my tongue across the bottom of it, swirling it around over the light fuzz that encases his nuts. Gary moaned, a noise that was small and meek. I then ran my tongue up his ball sac and licked the base of his cock, feeling the head bounce lightly across my eyes as I tongued the bottom of his prick. I continued to lick him, tracing the little vein that goes up the underside of his penis to the very top. It was there that I stopped, opening my mouth wide to receive him entirely.

I felt the smooth head of his penis slipping down the roof of my mouth back toward my throat. I fought back a small gag as I took the tip of his cock into my throat, making swallowing motions to help it go down. I forced my tongue to the front, sliding it over the underside of his cock as I sucked and massaged his stiff prick. I edged his penis in and out of my pursed lips, his hand grabbing my long hair and using it as a way of guiding my head back and forth. I looked up and my eyes met first his, then the blonde's. It was on her that I rested my gaze; she looked uncomfortable, uncertain. It was then that I made my next move.

I inched over to where the blonde was standing, my knees hurting on the hard tile. I looked at her for a moment, surveying her nakedness with a naughty smile forming on my lips. Suddenly, before I could change my mind, I dove my head into her pussy, my tongue parting her lips. I knew exactly where her clit was and went for it, grabbing it lightly between my teeth, nibbling and sucking. My hand crept up her inner thigh, making its way to her now dripping cunt. I inserted my finger into her, feeling my way up the slick walls of her vagina until I reached her cervix. I ran the tip of my finger along the base of it, feeling its smooth arch. I inserted another finger into her cunt and began ramming my hand in and out of her. I increased the pace at which I was licking her clitoris, and I could feel the walls of her cunt beginning to tremble. Her knees went weak and she collapsed a little, forcing her hot dripping cunt to slip and slide all over my face.

Gary moved behind me. He sat down on the floor and began to tongue my pussy. I felt his hard little tongue darting about all over my cunt, lingering a little on my clitoris and popping in and out of my hole. His mouth found my clit, and he began sucking me as ravenously as I was sucking the blonde. I could no longer keep my balance between the girl's pussy on my face and Gary's mouth on my cunt, and I toppled over sideways onto the floor of the bath.

Gary and the girl fell over with me; he never missed a

stroke of his tongue during our maneuver, although the rhythm I was keeping on the girl was interrupted. She then moved over to my breasts, burying her head in between them and sucking hard on each nipple. She pressed my tits together and took both nipples in her mouth simultaneously as Gary increased the pace at which he was vehemently lapping at my cunt.

The muscles in my body suddenly became tense and then released in pulsing motions, causing me to twist about on the floor in ecstasy. I was not moaning, but grunting and yelping, unable to stay cool in the face of this immense pleasure. I felt Gary's fingers and then his cock slide into my pulsating, orgasmic pussy, which clenched and released his prick in quick little motions. The sensation of his thick, wonderful cock pushing its way into my coming cunt caused me to come again. I noticed the blonde pulling away from me; perhaps I was being too loud, but nothing at this point could faze me.

Gary did not waste any time. He began pumping my hot, quivering pussy with quick, hard thrusts. My eyes screwed shut with the pleasure of my lover fucking me. Then I noticed another feeling. My cunt was becoming wetter, and there was something adding additional pleasure to my already hyperstimulated twat. I managed to open my eyes enough to register the image of the blonde—her head was crammed in between Gary's and my pelvises, and she was attempting to both lick my clit and suck Gary while he was fucking me. I felt her finger slip into my hole in addition to Gary's cock, and she began to stroke the head of his dick while it was in me, or at least that was how it felt inside me. Occasionally her tongue would slide over my clit, and she was moving her finger around the walls of my cunt. It was more than I could take. I had to make them stop.

I took control of the situation and maneuvered their bodies so that Gary could easily fuck the blonde and I had a clear view of his cock actually penetrating her. They were both lying on their sides, facing each other. I took Gary's cock in hand and inserted it into the blonde's cunt, which was still soaking from my saliva and her juices. The sight of my lover's stiff dick sinking into another girl's cunt at my command was strangely erotic. I found myself wishing that I had never given up Gary's dick, so in return I plunked myself down over the blonde's face and commanded her to suck me.

She did without hesitation. Gary was able to finger me and massage my body as he fucked her. She eagerly ate my cunt, occasionally stopping to moan with the pleasure that Gary was giving her pussy. I inserted my fingers into her cunt this time, being certain to stroke Gary's cock in all of the places that I knew he liked. He was calling my name, but his voice sounded far away because I was coming, too. I felt his name being formed on my lips, although I do not remember actually saying it. My cunt began to gush, and a rippling sensation ran throughout my entire self. My vision blurred, my body flailed, and Gary and I both peaked simultaneously (the blonde evidently had reached her own satisfaction a few minutes before). We all collapsed on the floor, spent, our sweaty bodies sticking a bit uncomfortably to the tile. My eyes blinked in the steamy bath. I noticed that the shower was still running and the bathroom had the steamy wet quality of a rain forest. "Kate, this is Michelle," Gary said to me. I looked at the blonde Michelle through the mist and thought, *Some introduction,* but I only smiled.

Crystal
Underground

BY JANE MERRILL

*S*ammy *understood*, thought Crystal, and she rubbed the supple cartilage of her jumbo Maine coon cat's thick fur. Sammy's golden eyes glowed. Crystal's tapered fingers caressed the rabbity fur under his chin, feeling for the vibration of his silent purr. At that instant the subway car seemed to buckle on its tracks. Big Sammy responded to the movement of the car with a second of rigidity, but quickly went limp and languorous in her arms. Only his big, round head evidenced signs of life as he buffed his cheek against the silk of his mistress's blouse and pressed his flat pink nose against the plump nipple that puckered out the silk.

The cat was crafty. Sammy did not want to be returned to the canine carrier. (At fifteen pounds he was too hefty for a cat carrier.) His sandpapery tongue flicked out in appreciation. What Sammy could not understand was that he was moistening Crystal's best blouse. She had just managed to get a very compromising stain out of it from her last trip with Sammy to the vet, and since the blouse had been such a wild success with the ordinarily aloof, good-looking veterinarian, she had worn it again today. Only today the female partner of the veterinary practice had been on duty, so there had been no following Dr. Padillo to the lavatory for a drink of water and shimmying up onto the side of the big tub to receive his kisses.

With the blouse on her mind, Crystal caught Sammy by the back of the neck and under the belly and tossed him back into the carrier. There he crouched in silent misery. A few cat hairs lingered on the rises of her full, high breasts. She brushed them off the silk with a gingerly sweep of her fanning fingers, yet even in this simple tidying up, her gesture was more sensual than was required, more than wise in an occupied subway car. She let her fingers skim her nipples, find her breasts' curving contours. She might have been in front of the mirror of the vanity in her bedroom.

Crystal's heart began to race and her breath quickened as a well-built, bald stranger wearing a black T-shirt and black jeans, with a earring in one ear, followed her with his eyes. Her hands lifted an inch away from her chest and hovered, like a lead curtain impeding his X-ray vision. The stranger gave her a thin but very cognizant smile. Crystal had really been very disappointed that the tiny escapade with Dr. Padillo had not been repeated at greater leisure, say, at his lunch hour. She consoled herself that she might have had the best of him. When the vet had stuck it into her, his thrusts had been enthusiastic, but she had sensed the kind of straight-shooter who has no technique. Thinking of Dr. Padillo, Crystal sighed. She was so revved up today she would have taken sex gratefully, any way he wanted. She laughed at herself, *I'm shameful.*

Perhaps she could wander back with Sammy as a pretext and see the vet another day soon. However, she could hardly lug Sammy nearly a hundred blocks downtown for no particular reason these days, when Fen was home so much in the daytime. Fen had been trained as a physician in Copenhagen, but he was a foreigner outside the AMA guild here in America. His various impressive medical credentials were invalid in the United States. Therefore, at forty, Fen worked nights at the hospital as a technician in the lab and studied insanely hard. When he was off, he came immediately home, and when Crystal got home from her nurse's job in a doctor's office, he wolfed down the dinner she'd prepared and returned to his books. He set a stop clock at 9:00 P.M. with six hours on it—hours when he studied between sleeping fitfully, until he had used up all of them.

Crystal forgot Sammy and her surroundings as she puzzled over Fen. Her husband had been as handsome as a Teutonic god when she met him. He was the color of tallow wax now, and his bloodshot gray eyes were ringed with blue bruises. A year ago he was jumping on her constantly, engaging her in delicious sex—too much of it, so her pelvis burned and ached. This year, as the September exam date approached, she had to waylay Fen into sex. She was resorting to being the aggressor—something new. For example, jumping on his lap in front of the television set and massaging his thing out of its torpor.

At first she had credited her escalating desire to Fen's neglect. But she felt the quiver of her sexual divining rod from a source deeper underground, more mysterious than hitherto. She dreamed of her sexual organs blowing up like balloons at the Macy's Thanksgiving Day parade, billowing and bouncing as she moved about her day. The shoulder bag she took to work was stuffed with underwear. Every time a handsome man twinkled his eyes at her, she creamed and had to change panties. And only her tighter bras cinched in the disturbingly protuberant erection of her nipples, which drenched her D-cup brassieres as well. *I'm all twat,* she thought half proudly, but wondering—a little worried, too—where her increased sexual urge would end.

Crystal had also noticed that the more wildly she thrashed on Fen's axis of love, the more needy she got. Satisfaction seemed to be losing its meaning for her. Instead, the act of sex hoisted her to a new plateau of heightened yearning. For the past week, when she and Fen made love, Crystal grew wild for an encore. And this she did not usually get. The vet had been her first infidelity. She and Fen made love in the morning when he was hyped from hitting the books. That one morning, as soon as he'd pulled out of her, she bounced out of bed and took Sammy to Dr. Padillo's. The appointment was for nine-thirty, and there was no time to crown sex with Fen by masturbating on the bathroom rug. That was probably what set things off with Padillo—her sheer, insatiable needs. But she wanted to be careful. With a doctor for a husband, so much was at stake that she was no longer seeking out men.

Crystal doted on Sammy. She liked to think of herself as a dog person, but an attractive woman—let alone a gorgeous, leggy, ripe-breasted sex siren like Crystal—could not walk a dog safely around the hospital at night. So she had decided to adopt a cat. She wanted a crossbreed, and would have gone to a shelter except that Fen was afraid of bringing in some awful disease. Instead she had heard about Dr. Padillo, this vet in the seventies on Amsterdam, who gave away homeless cats with all their shots done free. Fen hated the cat. Crystal tried to placate Fen—she knew which side her bread was buttered on—but she would not budge on wanting a cat. It always calmed Crystal to think how she had got what she wanted—Fen. She used this ticket to lower her hormonal temperature now. Crystal was a nurse whose fondest wish, like that of most of her profession, had been to marry a doctor. As soon as Fen passed the licensing exams, he would be an M.D. Poor fellow—he had delusions about becoming an Albert Schweitzer, but Crystal had more sensible plans. She was in the process of convincing him he could save just as many lives on Park Avenue. Crystal was Manhattan-born and trained, and she had a survivor's cynicism overlying her basically warm heart. Crystal was positive that a mild-mannered, towhaired Danish pediatrician would have the mothers of the East Side eating out of his hand.

Sammy looked more raccoon than cat. Crystal was proud when people asked if he was really a raccoon. She thought his lineage must contain a raccoon ancestor somewhere. Fen maintained that this was genetically impossible, but how could the science of genetics explain Crystal Fine Olsen herself? Huguette, Crystal's mother, a ballet teacher not yet in her fiftieth year, was a majestically beautiful Haitian, black as ebony, thin as a rail. Her father was a Russian Jew with an intelligent, friendly, generally dark, Mediterranean-style face and a slight, sinewy build. He sold marine insurance. He had gotten a free cruise once on a boat to Bermuda, where her mother's dance troupe had been performing. They married and settled in New York because this was the city where they could live unremarked, an unconventional, interracial couple bypassed and, because they had severed connections with family, atomized, yet neither heckled nor hurt. Then came *bebe* Crystal, their only child. Reuben Fine saw Crystal come down the slide in the delivery room. There was no questioning she was

Huguette's, or, he was confident, his. The translucent, pale-cream skin and pink-gold hair were remarkable features in themselves, but considering *bebe's* parents, a considerable shock. When Crystal's eyes lost their baby blueness, they turned such a clear light green that in some light the color fluctuated into blue. Huguette had saved a lock of that wondrous pink hair for Crystal, and in the summer, when her hair lightened from eye-catching red to that preposterous, lustrous shade of bright pink that no chemical ever provided, Crystal held up the ribbon with the fine baby hair to her own and saw they were quite identical, twenty-six years later.

Twelve weeks until those all-important exams. Fen thought he would pass them, but some foreign doctors took them again and again and never passed, remaining measly, underpaid lab technicians forever. Crystal opened the Hallmark calendar that she carried to recount the exact number of days until she would be Dr. Olsen's wife. Each day brought her closer to the life that Fen could help buy her.

Fen would try to make her declaw Sammy when Crystal got pregnant to protect the baby from scratches. Crystal's cat, Fen sensed, was what she most cherished. Crystal reached down and tickled Sammy's whiskers. Sammy hunched his fat, round shoulders and raised his raccoon face for more. "Even when I have a child [this was an absolute requirement for a pediatrician's wife], you'll come first," Crystal whispered. Then a thought picked at Crystal's heart like a knife blade, as the strange urgency rose in her again. Her mood darkened dramatically. "If I last that long," she added under her breath.

Because lately when Crystal daydreamed, her mind concocted the most shocking sexual fantasies. They were fueled by the totally unfamiliar, raging interior heat. She was a nurse trained at observation, and so she watched herself at moments like this. It was not as though she indulged the yearning and stoked her own fire. The craving was in her, crying out furiously to be slaked. Her inchoate longings threatened to engulf her sanity, to immolate her rational self. Ever since she had acknowledged these feelings and cheated on Fen (just a little bit) with the vet, the surge of heat had caught her increasingly unawares, sounding a terrifying alarm when she came within the purlieu of an attractive man.

Crystal was a pretty, smart girl who had never sold herself short because she had her sights set high. While other girls played down virginity and gave themselves away to be popular with dates, Crystal had stayed intact. She'd adhered to her elders' advice. "Keep your legs crossed, Crystal, and you'll have your pick of them"—her mother had told her this from an early age. Huguette did not mince words. She had been raped at nine and had had to masturbate a hideous and sadistic police official to get her visa to the States at sixteen, and she drummed it into Crystal that men were animals. On this, as on other issues, Huguette and Reuben, who was imbued with Orthodox Jewish thinking about the interactions between men and women, substantially agreed. Crystal, an ambitious materialist true to the wholesome American female form, had been sailing through her third year of marriage to Fen when the lightning struck. Suddenly she found herself ravaged by guilt, fear, and self-destructive fantasies. Under the thin crust of a proper matron, Crystal was turning into a rapacious nymphomaniac. And Crystal knew it, being nobody's fool.

She did not even know that her womanhood ran this

deep until, mysteriously, the physical awareness cut through her everyday surface. Here it was again, the roar mounting her pelvis, a fire curtain in her vagina. These were the strongest sensations she had felt in her life—Niagara Falls compared to sex with Fen. And the fire issued solo, from her own trembling body. She longed for the heat to culminate just as, cascading through her, it filled her with horrible dread.

A stricken look passed over Crystal's face. Thus, rife confusion ended her smug doctor's daydream. Postscripting it, the rushing yawn inside her reoccurred. She was in an airplane, watching the purple shadow of a vast cloud blanket her being. She became a cavernous space invaded by blazing golden rockets. The blood pulsed out of her brain and the upper part of her body into her vagina, until she felt herself a torrent of physical craving.

Crystal felt utterly helpless to block her perturbed emotions, and yet cannily capable of acting them out. Soon, like a milkpod, she began to send up a body language of subtle messages, like individual seeds, into the subway car. To relieve the engorged churning of her sex, she bucked her torso forward and back as if riding horseback, her misbehavior camouflaged by the motion of the train.

Her feeling surpassed normal sexual stimulation, Crystal was sure. It was like the appetency of a bloodthirsty goddess, and rendered her divinely unafraid. Lust would swallow her like a crumb of bread unless she obeyed it, but how? A tail-snapping dragon muzzled her, dragged her underground and quickly taught her. Now Crystal began a more insistent gyration of her pelvis. Surreptitiously, she desired to be seen. Recklessness was her only choice, other than being immolated from the inside out by her own strange, sexy flames. She shut her eyes, rocking to an invisible rhythm.

With Crystal's next jerking rotation forward, Sammy's carrier plummeted to the train floor. In an instant he flung himself at Crystal's shoulders like a flying squirrel before it clattered. He reproached her with a sharp cry into her right ear and caught his extended claws in a twist of her pink-red mane.

As her brain switched on again, the sensation receded. Crystal glanced around hesitantly, looking for signs of anybody's noticing her odd conduct. The cat's spill had been a momentary diversion for the dozen or so bored fellow riders in the car, but their faces quickly resettled into deadpan. The car heaved and doors smashed open. Crystal put her gloves in her shoulder bag, pried Sammy off, and maneuvered him like a jack back into the box. Settling the carrier under her arm, she edged out with practiced speed just in time.

Walking briskly to compensate for the encumbrance of the carrier, Crystal proceeded to four metal elevators covered with graffiti in the dim underground. The razorlike jaws of one were snapping shut. Next to it another, four times the size of a conventional elevator, was open. It contained one middle-aged woman. Top-heavy with a French-twist wig, she chanted to herself from a bedraggled paperbound book. Depressing but not dangerous, but Crystal had a dread of people addled like that—that they would attack with a knife to her throat, avenging their madness against her sanity. Nonchalantly, so as not to rile the woman, Crystal shifted in front of another elevator. Somewhat uncertainly, as their radars tried to pick up the reason Crystal rejected the open elevator, several other people nonetheless pushed in with the chanter. When the elevator banged shut, it left Crystal and Sammy alone.

Instinctively, Crystal put the cat down to free her hands and be less vulnerable. She positioned herself equidistant from each possible next set of doors to fling open.

"Too heavy for you?" said a masculine voice behind her. The man approaching had sat catercorner from Crystal in the subway car. A shiny hard hat had been dangling between his legs, giving rise to a comparison with a penis and its helmet in Crystal's twitching mind.

He was better-looking standing. A dark-green khaki shirt with the Army Corps of Engineers insignia hung as an outer jacket on a broad-shouldered, muscular torso. A wide, pewter-buckled belt rode on top of his tight jeans, which, in turn, were tucked into rugged cowboy boots. He spoke softly, as though they had been carrying on a conversation. The way his blue eyes penetrated, Crystal imagined that this was how it had been. *Aha,* she thought excitedly, *this stranger caught a seed from my milkpod.*

If the other subway riders had seen only a peaches-and-cream beauty with a behemoth cat, Corporal Cowboy saw a woman dripping with sexual invitation. "Don't deny you were eyeing me on the train," he said.

"I didn't even notice you," humphed Crystal without a blink. She swung her sheet of hair over one shoulder nervously, and they both watched as it spread in a silky mat of tendrils across her chest. Her breasts looked like fat bunnies nesting in soft grass. "Like hell, lady," said Corporal Cowboy. "You sent out the signals for a three-alarm fire. Look, I don't start my job for another three hours. How about my coming your way?"

His bonny blue eyes were pleading. She had him, because he needed her back, and bad.

"I'm married," Crystal protested shrilly.

"Nice! That's okay by me. Married chicks excite me." Looking around to be sure they were still alone, he gave Crystal a downstroke graze to her voluptuous breasts and trim little belly to bring his remark home.

In a flash she was careful Crystal no more. In the curious drugged state of her altered body chemistry, Crystal found Corporal Cowboy as handsome as a movie star. Every nerve, every pore, was rapacious for intercourse. Her breasts swelled as she arched her shivering back and tipped her breasts up in mute reply.

The man, Jason O'Neill, the owner of a small appliance repair outfit in Queens, favored your basic Army-Navy surplus store or cowboy look. In his business he could dress as he liked, and frankly, he liked to strut. Jason lifted Crystal's hand by the wrist and jerked it toward the bulge in his crotch. Crystal sneaked a glance at his hard-on and jumped back.

"You are crazy," she retorted with a catch in her voice.

"This is crazy, but you want it. My name is Jason. Where do we go from here?"

Jason made a mock curly-headed bow that said he was waiting for Crystal to make the next move—to tell him her name, for instance. But as the heat rose up in her again, all she emitted was a moan. "Oh-oh." A vestige of her willpower objected, and she swallowed what might have been a sob. Then she let go, swirling into the eddy of want. Anything to release this fire.

They walked Indian-style to Crystal and Fen's apartment and walked the three flights to the door, but sense drew Crystal abruptly back. The stranger must not come inside.

Crystal's comely face tightened with sudden wariness,

and Jason looked at her in the inadequate light from the old tulip fixture. A delectable chick. This could be a morning to remember. Jason was not going to let the woman play him for the fool now.

"I feel like you do, sis. No use your husband finding us in bed. I can make you feel real good right here." He stuck a finger up her, stretching the drum of her panties—no more. The chick's eyes, he thought, were wild as pinwheels. He had to know she and he had the same outcome on their minds.

Crystal goosed herself against the hip pocket of his jeans. Green light.

So when Corporal Cowboy flicked his eyebrows, he did this in question not at Crystal, but toward the two other doors on the landing. "They're not home," Crystal reassured him. "I mean, an invalid lives there, and the other couple work. Nobody comes in and out in the daytime but me."

By common consent he was going to roger her in front of her apartment. No telltale traces for Fen to discover. And fi-fo-fum, if by any unlikely mischance Fen were to enter the building, Crystal would hear him. The Corporal Cowboy would be on the lam before Fen climbed the first landing. Crystal bit her lip with impatience. That any intruder might cause this stranger to leave her before he plowed into her with that bursting cock seemed too cruel.

Jason was serious. *So,* thought Crystal, *am I. This fuck will keep me sane. It is a physical craving like an addict's for a fix. I am lucky the guy seems respectable.*

"You go ahead and tell me how you want it," Jason slurred, searching her eyes, close at hand but not making contact.

"I want it—" Crystal said in a strangulated voice. To which Jason closed her mouth in a bruising kiss.

"You got it."

Crystal watched Jason pull down her underpants and push them, balled up, into her handbag. She twisted her peasant wraparound skirt up behind her back and remained standing. A warm trickle flowed in anticipation, and she closed her legs in shame. But he spread her legs firmly with a nudge of his knee, and with a hand puckered the swollen flaps of her sex to bring on more. "You want a condom?"

Crystal nodded shyly.

Jason grinned. "We'll use mine. I have 'em made to order. Your brand might not be big enough for me."

Crystal waited with her eyelashes fluttering down. Her legs did a little scissor dance on the hinge of her twat.

Jason teased two fingers up inside her pubic area. He was looking into space. He believed she would go all the way now. Soon he could relax his act, and the fraud, really, that he saw her as a person.

Crystal braced herself against the wall and squatted slightly. Maybe the stranger's fingers were all he had the guts to use. They were up to his knuckles in her, and, damp as she was, she suctioned onto him. Meanwhile, she didn't want to look into his eyes. Blue, made loony by desire, their rapidness reflected her own. She wanted to unzip his pants and pull him popping inside her. *Cut the he-man buildup,* her glance told him. *Or I'll explode.*

The fingers came out. As if by reflex, they crooked into a departing pinch of one naked pink lip.

Jason took Crystal's hand off his belt (where she had been holding on for dear life) and chuckled. "I have to lift out of these pants real slow," he demurred.

Crystal saw what he meant as he lowered the zipper over his swollen cock and shimmied his pants down to his hips. Corporal Cowboy was hairier than Fen, and the thing was wrapped in a wiry blue-black mass—huge. He pressed her palms against the decrepit plaster of the hall. Holding them there, he moved up into her in a neat arch. He stayed firm as she came again and again, racked by waves of lust in which every satisfaction seemed to trigger more need. Crystal braced against Jason, putting a distance between them, and he was fascinated as her body both drew him in and kept him away. He watched her jutting breasts heave from her rib cage and got more excited. But when he ejaculated, it was almost with an apology for an anticlimax—by comparison with Crystal's seismic shudders.

"I see I don't have to worry about getting you hot," said Jason with the cheering boasting of a funny line.

Suddenly Crystal shielded her nakedness against his body. She had heard it first, but now he tensed, too. A mouse in the garbage chute, someone dropping a shoe in the apartment above—something. Fear plunged Crystal into abject sorrow, convinced her she was on the brink of being found out. It was not that she reproached herself for her act, which felt absolutely necessary. Rather, to be found out seemed an impossible death. She would melt into a pile of salt. One supercilious look from the bloodshot eyes of her prized resident doctor spouse and zap, she would be expelled forever from the socially elite milieu. Destroyed for merely being true to herself.

Detached for a moment by her melancholy, Crystal looked down at herself wonderingly. There was a woman a lot like her, the wrong half naked, in heat with a worker she had picked up in the subway a half hour before. Was she the same girl who had thought that making out in the backseat of a car was dirty and disgusting? And God, it had thrilled her. . . . Until she got hit with the undertow.

Because next she thought of her future beautiful life as a physician's wife. Happiness was a gorgeous hydrogen balloon that Crystal once held within her grasp. Now she saw it fly up and away. Crystal had been a "material girl" before Madonna's hit song. Now she would trade every dinette set for the next great fuck. She had become a vixen unrecognizable to herself, changed on the inside as the outside from, you know, a good gal to a bad one. Fear and grief assailed her. Down she stumped in a kind of willed faint on her doorstep.

The stranger turned to go but changed his mind. Her helplessness appealed to him. Pearly jism laced in her vaginal hair. It revved his eager pecker up. Jason's hand reached out to touch. How warm the babe was. He stroked Crystal's hair back from her forehead, noticing that she cleaved to him, not breathing. If she fainted unconscious, he could think of a couple of things to do with her still.

A noise—*wham!* Jason pulled Crystal to her feet. She responded like a rag doll, but came fully awake. The noise issued from (a safe) three stories below on the street yet instantly broke the mood. He realized he was hungry. He had to get to work. Sex, food, a job . . . "You okay? Your cat's got restless?"

The rush stopped in Crystal's ears. She heard the plaintive mew. "Oh, darling Sammy!" *Maybe I'm normal again,* she thought. *Maybe I should stop for a bassinet for the baby.* "Whatever-your-name-is, please go."

Crystal lifted Sammy out—her first baby always—and smothered him with a hug. Sammy nuzzled her back. Crystal tossed back several red bundles of hair and shuffled in her shoulder bag for the key. Poised to put the key in the lock, she smoothed her bright, flat hair from the sides of her face and gave a vague smile. "Thanks," she said, her eyes cast downward.

Jason's return smile was forced, uneasy. He saw the woman who still throbbed from him treating him like an intruder.

A woman shouldn't suck a man's gold then boot him out like a rat. Ungrateful bitch. But he wouldn't bruise the peach. She had been a juicy one. She had a natural clenching grip. And he would remember her, oversized cat and all. . . . I'll just put my pistol back in the holster and clear the hell out.

"Cluck, cluck." In a corner of his mouth, Jason made a sound like a cowboy to his horse. A grin spread across his thin, attractive face. It had been great doing it with her. Before he moved into a shadow and hitched up his jeans, he even ruffled Crystal's hair—an awkward attempt at friendly closure. With a glance back at her, he was gone. And when she heard him exit through the front door of the building, Crystal stepped into the apartment with Sammy and reassured herself aloud, "Fen is not here." Then, because she did not want Sammy to observe her with his huge, knowing eyes, she closed him out of the bedroom and lay down. The peace was blessed, but it did not last. Crystal was not much for fantasies, but with her sex still throbbing from Jason, she was able to reenact what had happened with him. She was rougher with herself than he had been, but no matter how she felt, she tore and scratched at her secret parts. She had past experience to tell her she would awake, after a dreamless sleep, pretty and fresh as a conch shell washed by the sand and the sea.

Hands-on Training

BY EVA MORRIS

I had a meeting on Monday, so I was all suited up in silk and professionalism. Afterward—I can't quite remember how or why—I ended up at Denim and Diamonds, a country-western bar right smack in the middle of New York City. Nothing happened until I left twenty minutes later, my extra-long legs leading me off the curb and into the street. "Ma'am, may I help you hail a cab?"

I turned around, and for the first time all night, my green eyes had something to focus on. Something good? How's absolute fucking perfection sound? A blond cowboy who was simply poured into his jeans, with shoulders that were wide and real strong-looking—and probably very valuable during the spring roundup. Authentic boots, too. "Why, yes, please." (I spoke with a gentle lilt.)

First rule: I know my prey when I see it, and I begin the seduction immediately. Lost time now is one more afternoon fuck we could have slipped in later, I always say.

Rule No. 2: I match my vocal delivery to his, then add a distinctly feminine touch. For example, this cowboy drawls, so I drawl, but not as much—and just a little softer and sweeter. People like to hear themselves. It works every time.

I was standing there thinking, *Here I am with a five-foot-ten stud a mere three feet from me. What should I do?* Then I remembered Rule No. 3 and acted quickly. A man seduced is a man impassioned, and a man impassioned is always a better fuck. So I acted somewhat unsure, fumbled out an invitation to go cowboy dancing sometime, gave him my number, and quickly slid into the taxi. (Rule No. 3: When I pick up a man, shyness on my part works wonders.)

"Eighty-ninth, Park and Madison," I said, once in the cab. Then I slid my skirt up to my waist and pushed my stockings down so that from the backs of my knees to the top of my ass I was completely naked and sticking to the leather. I was doing something I love to do. I love to subject myself to sensory overload if I can. My whole lower body was sticking to a seat that could have been dirty— God knows it was worn—but still the blond hair on my legs was raised, like the fur on a cat's back, and I threw my torso forward to arch my back, gently landing my red-haired pussy-plane down onto the smooth material of the black seat.

I'm wet now, and I grow wetter with each stoplight I pass on my way home. I drop my head back, my lips are parted—well, actually, every lip I own is parted now—and I wonder how long his fingers are.

There's a look in a man's eyes—or a woman's, too, for that matter—when they know how to finger-fuck well. It's a cocky, strong look, and usually they'll have a habit of putting the tip of their tongue into the corner of their mouth when they're even thinking about finger-fucking me.

Bent to face me, he has one big hand holding my far

thigh secure, and with the other he's slowly sweeping his fingers up and down the inside of the thigh nearest to him. (Slow, gentle, rhythmic moves will be the death of me someday, I'm sure.) His hands, besides being large, are smooth but still a little rough, especially around the knuckles. Sometimes his hand comes within inches of the tiger. She holds her breath instinctively, then growls quietly when the fingers manage to escape. All this teasing has made me slick and wet, and the leather seat of the taxi could be a puddle of olive oil on cheap kitchen linoleum.

Arched back? Yes, my back is arched. It opens my mouth, creating a path that continues unobstructed. Both of my mouths are open wide, and my body is unconsciously arranging itself so that the tunnels within welcome the visitors from outside. Like in *Aladdin,* when the sphinx suddenly rises from the sands, throws open its great, vicious mouth, and then rolls out the red carpet—it's hard to say no, right? That's my hungry cunt! Makin' it hard to say no!

Words are important. While men tend to be stimulated visually, women respond well to audible stimuli. I myself take kindly to strong, dark, and mysterious language—few words, monotonic delivery, and that ever present directing power. Like when he says in a straight and low voice, "We'll just keep this thigh here so I can fit my hand in here to feel your . . . mmm, how smooth your skin is. It makes my hand want to discover all of your body. . . . Don't wiggle around too much now, not when I'm having such a good time. . . . [Nuzzling my neck] Mmm, you smell so good, I smell your perfume, I smell you, hold still so I can follow this scent all the way down. . . . Well, now, I believe you've set out to tease me, putting that perfume down between your breasts and then covering them up so. Make me happy and undo some of them pretty clothes you're wearing. . . . Don't let me do it or they'll rip soon enough. Yes [sucks in breath slowly], oh, yes, sugary little girl, yes, I am gonna do it to you!"

With his lips at my neck, he raises himself up and over me—not by pushing, but by directing me down and back. I'm lying on the seat of the cab with him at my pussy, and the Alien could suddenly be at the wheel of the taxi without catching his attention 'cause it's all on me. The stabilizing hand has left my thigh and is now under the small of my back, lifting it a bit, and his fingertips are doing the sea-anemone dance right straight toward me. When they brush against my red hair, my eyes close and roll back in the sheer pleasure of it all. I want . . . I want . . . I want . . . anything. At this point I can't be picky. Fingers, a cock—even a small cock—the Club car-theft-prevention bar, a Coke bottle (well, maybe not, but nearly anything else). And I feel so wide open, I feel like the Eisenhower Tunnel, and a finger would be a dachshund running into it. . . . But I'm wrong. When his finger (the middle one . . . ohhh!) slides into me, and he twists it around and cocks it toward my abdomen, I feel truly overwhelmed.

Now, I've heard some men say that women dislike finger-fucking because it makes them feel like the man is simply testing the water, so to speak. But in all my twenty-five years, I have met only one woman who didn't like it. But, perversely, she loved faking that she did. I've always chalked it up to the wrong finger at the wrong time. To me, there is no wrong time for a good finger-fuck. Before, during, or after sex, finger-fuck me. In the morning wake me by fingering me. Stick your biggest finger up my pussy and leave it there as you drive down the Long Island Expressway. When I ride your face and you're sucking gently on my clit, slide a finger up me and see me buck my way into outer space. Tired? Not in the mood? It's okay, baby, just lend me your digits and let me do the rest. Anytime, anywhere—finger-fuck me.

When he begins to slowly "itch" me with the finger that is deep inside me, I start to go crazy. That's the spot, boy, that's the spot to aim for. Ten points every time you hit it. But he's a big scorer as he slips another into the mouth of "red cat." This is literally hot sex. I'm soaked with perspiration, so is he, and I've lifted my whole body off the seat. I am wriggling like a snake that just ate a live kangaroo—partly because I want to get closer, partly to try to get away, and partly because I am this close to coming.

Now, I don't throw those words or that action around lightly. An orgasm is a beautiful thing that requires a whole hell of a lot of time, energy, and excitement to build. But his fingers inside me are touching places that simply have never been touched. I feel like I'm a burlap bag and there's a frantic tomcat inside me. Then the clincher.

He says, in a perfectly strong, dark, and mysterious way, "Do you think that's all this cowboy knows how to do? How'd ya like it if I gave you what we sometimes have to give a birthing cow?"

After the first finger or two, I am squealing, like I'm sure that heifer did, too, somewhere on the ranch or wherever this wild man came from. The passion in his eyes and the marching finger men heralding the king are making me so fucking excited—I have never been this excited before. I've gone beyond having a string of orgasms. I'm passing Go without stopping; I do not collect $200. I'm just going around and around the board at killer speed.

Remember the dachshund in the Eisenhower Tunnel? Now he's a 747 taxiing into my tree house.

Taking advantage of my delirium, he's pushing his fingers s-l-o-w-l-y in and out of me, still on his knees, between my knees. He twists them to a slightly different position with every stroke, and I, not having any idea of what's coming next, am reduced to moaning, crying, screaming, and messing up my hair in a big way. My little hands are little fists, beating wildly against the leather seat on either side of me. Sometimes I hit the divider between the driver and us. But believe it or not, I'm too far gone to even wonder what the Middle-Easterner-who-doesn't-speak-English-yet driver is thinking about all this.

Maybe to stop me from beating the cab senseless, or perhaps just to torture me in a new way, he smoothly lifts my back up and turns me over, holding that infamous stabilizing hand on my right shoulder. When he's behind me, he slowly unzips his pants so I can hear it. I hear it, all right. I hear every tooth of the zipper being pried away from the others. I feel like a zipper separating down the center. Then, using his left hand, which he has a little less control over, he is really giving it to me now. Why the unzipped jeans? To confuse me? To hint that he'll be using another tool soon? Because his jeans are too tight? I don't know, and I never will know, but I do know that all this not knowing takes my concentration off his finger thrusts. And just as I realize that his left hand has slipped out of me and is rubbing back and forth at the same pace across my clitoris instead, while just his thumb stays behind to guard the castle, I come, long and hard. I can feel my wetness dripping out of me and onto the leather seat, scenting the air with my own musky perfume. The city flies by in a blur as I lose myself in the talented rope work this cowboy is doing on me.

He doesn't stop, but slows his pace for me. To say that I need a breather is a real big understatement. I need an ambulance. What I get is his fingers, in different configurations and quantity, while I sit on his lap. Yes, this little piggy squeals all the way home.

A videotape of this will probably be on sale at the Yellow Cab garage sometime tomorrow.

I don't care.

Career Track

BY CECILIA TAN

I discovered my love for trains a long time ago. This isn't some kind of historical nostalgia I'm talking about. I'm talking about one evening on the overnight train to Florida, the train on which you brought your car along with you, when I went to bed in my tiny berth and snuck my hand down under my nightie and entered the magic kingdom for the first time. Maybe it was something about that particular orgasm or maybe it was something about the train itself—the rhythm, the vibration—who knows? All I know is that every time I get on one, I get as horny as the devil himself.

Usually, this isn't so bad. I put my Walkman on and go to sleep and have the most amazing sex dreams you can imagine! In my dreams I've had every hunky celebrity you can name. But there was one trip where that trick just didn't work.

I was about to graduate from college, and I had my first big job interview in New York. I got to the Amtrak station bright and early, wearing my navy-blue interview suit.

The skirt was tight, it came to just above my knees, and I could barely walk in the thing. But it did look nice.

The train was crowded, and people were pushing their way for seats. I sidled down the aisle looking for an empty one. They all seemed to be filled, and I was beginning to feel despair that I'd be standing up for five hours, when I made eye contact with a nice-looking redheaded man. He returned my smile and hefted his large suitcase off the seat next to him. "Would you like to sit here?" he asked. Nice, deep voice, like a radio announcer. He looked to be about thirty, in good shape.

"Thank you," I said, and settled into the seat.

By the time I discovered that my Walkman batteries were dead, the train was already moving. A baby began to cry in the seat in front of me. I was clearly not going to get any sleep. Mr. Nice Guy was reading a business magazine. I reclined my chair a bit and watched him out of the corner of my eye. I was feeling the motion of the train as we picked up speed, the gentle rocking. He had very nice hands, I noticed, and through his suit he looked like he had a broad chest. I wondered what his nipples looked like. I was starting to get wet.

I clenched my legs tightly together and tried to look away, but my eyes kept straying over to his legs, trying to get a glimpse of the bulge at his crotch. I imagined he'd have red pubic hair and how his long, smooth tool would look poking out of it, red and hard.

I imagined that we were in an old-style train compartment on a steam-powered train, he a perfect society gentleman and I his proper lady. Once he had given the conductor a generous tip, the compartment door would be closed and the tiny shades drawn. And then, only pausing to hang his hat, he would ravish me. He would draw up my frilly skirts—of course, I would be wearing garters—and he would plunge his cock into me. No, he'd tease me with the head first until I thought I'd go mad, then very slowly he'd inch his way in until I grabbed him and rammed him inside. Ah . . .

"Are you all right, miss?"

I gave a little gasp as I opened my eyes. I hadn't realized I'd shut them, or that I'd moaned out loud. My face very red, I said, "Oh yes, I'm fine. Just, uh, drifting off to sleep." I tried to keep my smile on straight.

He smiled back. "Are you on your way to a job interview?"

"Yeah. Did the suit give it away?"

He nodded. "It's quite attractive on you. You have a very nice figure."

I blushed all the harder. "I guess it couldn't hurt my chances of getting hired." I just hoped the guy I was supposed to meet wasn't a crotchety old pervert or something. I hoped, actually, that he'd be a lot like Mr. Nice Guy, here. "Although I hope they look at my figure first."

"Oh, what line of work are you going into?" His eyes, I noticed, were a beautiful green.

"Banking and finance," I said. "I figure there'll always be money in that business!"

He laughed at my little joke. "That's the business I'm in, also."

"Oh, really? You'll have to tell me more about it when I get back from the rest room." I made a dash for the lavatory.

I wanted desperately to get off in the bathroom, but people were in line, and I was afraid Mr. Nice Guy would smell it. So I just splashed some water on my face and took a deep breath. In the tiny compartment, I could hear the sound of the wheels over the tracks even louder, and I pressed my hand over my crotch. Mmm, I love trains.

When I got back to the seat, he seemed to be sleeping, with his head against the window. I slid in next to him without disturbing him, and took the opportunity to look him over without fear of him seeing me. He was in good shape, didn't have to suck in his gut, and now I could stare at his crotch all I wanted.

I reclined my chair all the way back and wished the train car were empty. If it were, who'd notice if we fucked? He could roll right over on me. I closed my eyes and pictured it. I could prop my legs up on the chair in front of me and he could slide himself right in. I imagined his cock would be thick as well as long, stretching my insides as he pumped in and out of me. I started clenching my thigh muscles as I imagined him fucking me, as I pictured each stroke of his big meat. I took off my blazer, laid it across my lap, and folded my hands under it. Now I pressed on my mound every time I squeezed, and no one could see it. There was no way I could get my fingers under the waistband of the skirt, though, so after a while I became even more frustrated. I pretended it was him—he was teasing me, playing with me, he wouldn't let me come. I stifled another moan.

I felt a hand on my knee, another over my eyes. "Shhh," he whispered in my ear. I kept my eyes shut as the hand fell away, and felt his jacket being draped over me. And then the fingers, working their way up the inside of my thigh. I sneaked a glance at him. In one hand he held the magazine as if he were reading, while the arm closest to me disappeared under the blazer, as if he were holding my hand. But he wasn't. He pushed my skirt up my thighs. I shifted slightly so it would go all the way up, and he slid a finger right into the wetness of my panties. It was so creamy down there, I would probably have to change them before the interview. His finger made its way right between my slippery lips and into my hole. I gave a silent gasp as my cunt tried to suck him in deeper. He pulled away then and reached over the top of my panties, forcing them down over my mound. They held his hand tightly against my fur and even tighter against my clit.

He began to wiggle his finger with a very small back-and-forth motion—nothing that anyone could see, but it was everything to me. It was all I could do not to buck my hips and grind myself hard into his hand. I whimpered, then I began to come, my thighs shuddering and shaking as the orgasm spread all through my legs. I could hardly breathe as I tried to keep quiet. Finally, I sat still. He kept his hand where it was, right between my legs, pressed into my cunt.

"I always try to help a woman in need," he whispered.

I opened my eyes. "Come with me."

We had to wait in line for the lavatory. I don't think anyone saw us go in together, but by then I didn't care. We could always make up some story if we had to.

I worked his belt loose and let his slacks drop to the floor. He put down the toilet-seat cover and sat on it. I took off my sopping wet panties and hiked my skirt up all the way. Then, placing my hands on his shoulders, I perched one foot on either side of the toilet and lowered myself down.

He waved his cock, just as thick and long as I'd hoped! He rubbed the head in my pussy cream, tantalizing me as I tried to lower myself onto him. Then, just about when I was ready to scream, I needed him so much, he held it still and plunged into me as I came down. I was so wet, he slid right in up to his balls. In that position I felt impaled and so full of him, I clutched his head and neck and moaned as I ground my hips around. The train went around a curve and pressed me even harder into him.

He put both hands around my ass and lifted me slightly. I held on to his rock-hard shoulders as he pumped me up and down on his tool, its massive head rubbing me inside until I thought I was going to come again.

I did come again, and still he kept pumping me, my slick juice running down all over his balls and ass. I was getting so sensitive, I wasn't sure how much I could take, but after all he'd done for me, I owed it to him to get him off. I bobbed harder with my legs, listening to him moan over the sound of the train wheels.

I climbed off him then and hiked myself up onto the little sink, propping my feet on the walls. I spread my pussy lips with one hand and beckoned. He stood between my legs and put his cock in, ramming me against the mirror with each thrust. Now he could really push, getting faster and faster until I came again. That put him over the top, and he pulled out, squirting white come all over my suit.

When I stopped panting, he helped me off the sink and planted a kiss on the top of my head. "Thank you," I said. My suit was a mess. I ran a paper towel under the water and tried to wipe it clean. The skirt was also a mass of wrinkles.

"Don't worry about that," he said. He pulled his pants on and took a business card from his pocket. "How would you feel about working for me?"

I gave his bulge a squeeze. "You know, I don't think I'd mind at all."

A Hot Movie Date

BY SAMANTHA FLESKIN

I didn't realize when I called Ted that I wanted to see him again. I thought I just wanted to find out how he was, to catch up on what had happened in our lives since we had last seen each other. We had dated steadily for about five months during the previous year (the greatest five months of my life!) but had broken up because he was too moody. I had been glad to be free of him when I left, and it had never occurred to me that someday I might want to be with him again.

But the truth was, my life now seemed like it was going nowhere. My job was a drag, the men I met weren't right for me at all, and I was lonely and horny and frustrated. And deep down inside, I longed to hold Ted in my arms, to have him kiss me hotly and make me crazy with his touch, to have his tongue dipping into me, to feel his hard cock inside me, opening my cunt to the familiar sensations of spinning dream images that exploded out of my orgasm.

While we were on the phone, it seemed like Ted didn't

even want to see me at first. I guess after a year he was still mad about our breakup. He had pushed me too far with his dark moods and had left me untouched for far too long, and one night he came home to find me in bed fucking someone he thought was just my friend. Well, we weren't exactly fucking—I had been giving my "friend" some great head.

I don't think Ted minded so much that I was going down on someone else in our bed, but it seemed to really bother him that the someone else I was going down on was his sister. It wasn't as if Ted didn't know that I liked to suck pussy—I guess he just thought that my sucking his sister's pussy added injury to insult. Our breakup was, as they say, immediate.

So when we talked on the phone, I was cautious with his tender feelings. Little by little I softened him up, talking about this and that, until I had him laughing with me. Once we were having a good laugh, I knew I could drop a hint. It wasn't long before he'd picked me up and we were riding in his car on our way to dinner.

All through dinner I was squirming in my seat, getting so hot for Ted. We sat in a beautifully decorated Chinese restaurant, but it all looked like sex to me: The spring rolls looked just like cocks; the dim sum resembled my round, firm tits; the wontons in the soup reminded me of Ted's balls in my mouth; even the fortune cookies looked like little pussies, their lips demurely hiding the fortunes. By dessert my bush was soaked, dampening my panties with my own sweet-and-sour sauce.

Ted was still a bit standoffish with me, so we agreed to go to a movie after dinner. Pretty neutral, right? He named a few films, but I wasn't really listening. I just said yes to the third one because I didn't want to be *too* easy to please. (I

knew that I'd be *very* easy to please later!) We got our tick-
ets, I let him buy me a lot of ice cream and popcorn, and
then we took our seats.

The movie Ted picked wasn't very popular, and there
were only about a dozen people in the theater. We pretty
much had the place to ourselves, but I still chose to sit way
up in the back row. As soon as we sat down, I put the food
on the next seat and snuggled up close to him.

Ted wasn't very attentive to the movie, so I tried to
think of what to do. I considered taking off my wet and fragrant panties right there in front of him, but I didn't want
to seem too sluttish. So I got up and went to the ladies'
room.

I stepped into a stall, hung up my long coat, and took
off my skirt. Standing there in just my high heels, match-
ing black silk panties and bra, and my sweater, I imagined
what I would look like right then to some usher who might
have poked a hole in the wall to peep on the girls. This got
me excited, so I pulled off my panties and, putting one
foot up on the commode, started to touch myself gently
between my firm thighs.

I unhooked my lacy bra and pulled my sweater up over
my breasts, rubbing the curves, lingering over my hardening nipples. With the other hand, I stroked my thighs and
the fur of my pussy, gently parting the lips and tickling
them. Then I plunged two fingers into my dripping cunt,
feeling the sensations in my vagina radiate up and through
my belly. I moaned, the thrill making my nipples tingle
and my asshole tighten. I wanted Ted to fuck me so much
I could taste it!

I almost brought myself to orgasm in the ladies' room,
but I wanted to have Ted's fingers do it, his cock sending
those quivers of pleasure through me, so I pulled off my

sweater and put it and my skirt into my bag. I stepped back into my panties, hooked my bra back into place, put my long coat on, and went back to my seat.

Ted was engrossed in the movie, so I casually opened my coat, exposing the whole front of my body to the flickering light from the screen. As I crossed one leg over the other, I could smell the honey from my cunt and I was sure he could, too. After pulling my arms out of the coat sleeves, I gently took one of his hands and put it on the damp, fragrant spot on my panties. Ted was so shocked, I thought his eyes would pop right out of his head! He looked at me leaning back in my seat, legs crossed seductively, back arched, coat flung off, wearing just a bra and panties. I rubbed his hand up and down the silk covering my hot cleft, pulling his face to mine with my other hand.

We kissed deep and hard, tongues darting around each other like flashing sabers, hot breath mingling with our moans. Ted's hands were on me, moving up and down my body, sending goose bumps over my skin. Then he knelt in front of me and bent his head to my belly.

He tongued my navel, sending chills through me. His hands found the catch on my bra and, in a second, my firm tits bounced free. He slid his tongue all the way up my belly to one nipple, pushing my legs farther apart with his body. I slid my ass forward in the seat, trying to get closer to Ted, fumbling with the buttons of his shirt, rubbing my pussy against his chest. I hooked one foot behind his back, clinging to him. Ted sucked my tits one at a time and gently bit my nipples as I ran my fingers through his hair. Meanwhile, I was grinding my soaked mound against him, stimulating my clit.

I pulled Ted up to kiss me again, but he had other plans. While we kissed, he used both hands to lift the thin lace of my panties high up on my hip and, with a single jerk, separated the elastic of the waistband. Then he tore the other side the same way. Ted's impatience thrilled me, exciting me even more than I had been before. He took the front of my ruined panties in one hand and the back in the other and started pulling them back and forth across my pussy. My clit grew stiff from the friction of the panties dragging across it. I was desperate to have him inside me, and this tease was making me frantic.

Then he bent to my wet, expectant mound. Ted's tongue was almost as hard as his cock, probing the lips of my cunt, stroking its pink folds and the soft, curly hair. I breathed faster now, close to orgasm, trying not to make too much noise. I put one foot on the seat back in front of us, draping the other leg over his shoulder. Ted's tongue was like a hot little cock pushing into my cunt as I gasped in short breaths.

Somehow Ted's tongue went deeper into my pussy. This is something I have always liked, and I moaned with passion as he put his thumb onto my clit while he tongued my hole. The orgasm was profound, building within me, lifting me as if on a tall wave. Then the wave was gone, nothing was below me, and I fell into pleasure, passion, lust, into the depth of the exploding orgasm.

Ted unwrapped one of the ice-cream bars and gently stroked my pussy with it. After a few strokes, he pushed the ice cream into my vagina, the cold making my cunt muscles contract around it. This sensation—having cold applied to my pussy while it was so hot—thrilled me even more. Ted fucked me with the ice-cream bar, pumping the creamy shaft into my grasping cunt again and again.

Then he bent his mouth to my pussy again, licking the melted ice cream from my bush, the folds of my cunt's soft lips, the insides of my thighs, the curve of my ass. Now the tingle of the cold was gone and my cunt was heating up again.

The next thing I knew, Ted's mouth was on mine, and I could taste my own juices mixed with the ice cream on his lips. I thought I had lost consciousness, but I had just gone somewhere else for a few moments. We were kissing, and the pounding in my ears was growing fainter.

My hands found his belt, and they trembled as I unhooked it. Then I opened his pants and pulled the zipper down. I reached into his shorts and felt Ted's hard cock— old trusty. I stroked the length of it, pulling it from his pants, feeling the wetness at its head. With both hands I peeled Ted's pants down to his thighs, feeling the hard muscles of his butt.

I guided Ted's stiff cock to my waiting pussy, wrapping my legs around him. I teased him a little to get back at him for tearing my panties, rubbing the head of his thick cock into the melted ice cream in the folds of my cunt. I wanted to make him beg before letting his cock into my pussy. His mouth was next to my ear, and he breathed heavily, "Please, let me fuck you! Please, don't tease me, let me feel my cock all the way . . . in your cunt . . . with you all around me . . . please. Please!"

So I put his cock right into the mouth of my pussy and pulled him forward, using my cunt muscles to suck him into me. His cock filled me completely and I wept, thinking of lonely nights I'd spent longing for this feeling, this fullness, this thick, long cock filling the empty spot down there.

No amount of masturbation, even with a fat, hard dildo, can match the feeling of a man's cock—the right man's cock—inside me, stroking away, pumping into my cunt, making me realize why the human species has survived for millions of generations. *This* is the most natural thing in the world, this culmination of all our social interaction, this thing called making love, this messy act, this *fucking*.

Ted was saying stuff in my ear—stuff like "I love you" and "Oh, baby" and "Oh, God, you're wonderful." But I wasn't hearing him—at least I wasn't listening. I was just riding up that wave again, feeling his cock slamming into my cunt, feeling my vaginal muscles contract around his thick, hard shaft of flesh, feeling the little and large orgasms sweep over me as we fucked in the flickering light reflected from the movie screen. I dug my nails into him under his shirt, raking his back, trying to pull him farther into me, to pull his whole body into my cunt, trying to fill myself with his flesh.

Then Ted came. It was like a shower of hot sparks going off inside my pussy. I could feel his cock muscles contracting, spurting, shooting me full of come, the thick, hot jism seeping around him inside my cunt, his whole body tightening with the release of that stream of slick sperm.

I came again, spurred by Ted's pumping cock, his squirting jet of come. My nipples felt so hot I thought they'd melt right into his chest. My throat was dry from the rush of wind in and out of my lungs; even my toenails and fingernails tingled with the soft electricity of orgasm.

I was drifting with the receding waves when I became aware of the applause. I opened my eyes, thinking the movie was over, but the light and shadows from the screen still flickered. I lifted my head to look past Ted's sweating face, over his shoulder, to see several people in the theater standing up and applauding while they looked at us.

Ted stood up hastily, trying to cover my nakedness, but I wasn't bothered by their searching eyes. He remained sheepish, nervously pulling up his pants, straightening his clothes and gathering himself up.

But I stood up slowly, ran one finger up the deep cleft of my pussy, and put it to my mouth, looking directly into the eyes of each of the people who had been our private audience. Not much can faze a woman who's just had two great orgasms, feeling her man's hot jism seeping out her cunt lips and down her leg.

Then I threw my coat over my shoulders, picked up my bag, and lazily left the theater, the grinding motion of my hips and my thighs rubbing together, giving me chills of pleasure.

Ted caught up with me at the car and fumbled with his keys, trying to apologize or something. I just kissed him gently, then took him home and made him fuck me once more. (I never brought up his sister again.)

Porn Queen
for a Day

BY MARCY SHEINER

I left the last class of the semester and headed for my car. It was a hundred degrees in the shade, and the car had been sitting in the sun for two hours—I couldn't even touch the steering wheel. I decided that I'd worry about it later. For now I'd drop in on my lover Ron, who lived just a few blocks from campus.

Ron's a shrink who specializes in sex—that is, he helps people, mostly couples, figure out how to improve their sex life. He's so good at his work that he's become a hot ticket at seminars and conventions, where he's often asked to deliver speeches to students or doctors. In fact, Ron has been the inspiration for my returning to school to study the very same subject.

Ron had told me the night before that he'd hired Laurie, a mutual friend who was starting out as a photographer, to take professional photos of him that he could use when sending out promotional materials or—hopefully soon—on the jacket of his first book. When I arrived at his apartment, he told me that Laurie had just called and asked him to make their appointment a bit earlier—she'd be there in half an hour. He was frantically trying to choose a shirt, tie, and jacket to wear for the shoot.

In the stifling heat, Ron wore only a pair of khaki shorts and sandals. I sat on the bed, admiring his tanned muscles and hairy chest as he tried on various shirts and jackets. When he finally decided on a blue shirt, navy jacket, and maroon tie, he turned from the mirror and asked me what I thought.

Well, I thought he looked pretty funny in a cute, sexy way, with his formal upper attire over bare legs and sandals. I couldn't help but laugh.

"What?" he asked, confused and hurt. One of the things I love about Ron is his vulnerability—he doesn't hide his insecurities from me. But I felt terrible that he'd misinterpreted my laughter and immediately put my arms around him.

"I'm just laughing because you look so cute half in a suit and half naked."

Relieved, he joked, "Which part do you like better?"

"The naked part, of course."

Like magnets, our pelvises came together. I felt his member swell beneath his shorts.

"Do we have time for a quickie?" I whispered.

"I don't think so—Laurie said she'd be right over, and that was ten minutes ago." His cock grew bigger even as he tried to dissuade me.

Without wasting another second, I fell to my knees, unzipped his fly, and released it from its bondage. Ron gasped with pleasure as I took his swollen organ into my mouth and began slavering it with my long, wet tongue. I glanced sideways in the mirror and had to suppress another giggle at the sight: Ron in his suit and tie with his hard-on bulging from his shorts and filling my hungry mouth.

I closed my eyes and began sucking in earnest, hoping Ron would come before the photographer showed up. Indeed, within seconds his cock grew to its fullest size and throbbed expectantly in my mouth. The salty tang of pre-come teased my tongue. But just as I was inwardly gloating that this would be the shortest blowjob on record, the doorbell rang. Ron let out an anguished groan; I jumped to my feet. Red-faced, he stuffed his meat back into his shorts and answered the door.

Laurie, a petite brunette, wore only a pair of white Danskin shorts and a pink halter top, showing plenty of her smooth, dark skin. Her thick curls were massed atop her head, and despite the heat, she was full of energetic enthusiasm. I sat on the sidelines so as not to get in the way while she rearranged furniture and removed paintings to create a blank wall for a background.

When the scene was set, Ron sat on a stool in his incongruous outfit. His hard-on was still raging, and I could see it bulging against the fabric of his shorts. Laurie seemed oblivious—or she was too polite to mention it—as she snapped her camera, every so often instructing him to turn his head or change position. As she bent over her tripod, her shorts rode up to reveal a pair of juicy ass cheeks—apparently, she wore no panties. I was seized with a sudden urge to simply walk over, stick my hand up her shorts, and squeeze her flesh. (I must confess that I get such urges rather frequently and at the most inappropriate times, like toward strangers in places like the supermarket; I've learned how to restrain myself.)

When they finished the photos, Ron looked over at me. "Want to have a picture of us together?" he asked.

"What, me in my T-shirt and you all decked out?"

"Just for fun," Ron said.

"You might as well," said Laurie. "I'm all set up."

I went over and stood next to Ron. He put his arm around my waist, and Laurie snapped the camera. Feeling playful, I grabbed his tie and pulled it as if I was going to lead him around by it. Laurie laughed and snapped the camera again. "Keep going," she said. "This is great. I can use these pictures in the artsy section of my portfolio." Ron and I cavorted around awhile, which inevitably led to some more suggestive poses. After all, his cock still hadn't gone down—when I bumped against him, I could feel it, hard and insistent. "Just let yourselves go," Laurie encouraged. "I need to get some practice doing candid shots."

"Can we do anything we feel like?" I asked with a meaningful look.

She smiled knowingly. "Sure."

I resumed where we'd last left off, on my knees sucking his dick, only this time I had a camera recording all my moves. I had never been watched by anyone while sucking cock, and that in itself was enormously exciting. But what was even more exciting was the knowledge that I was being photographed, just as if I were a porno queen. I imagined that the pictures would end up in a magazine and be seen by millions of people. Guys would jerk off to the sight of my masterful cocksucking skills. Responding to my imagined audience, I stuck out my ass, thrust out my chest, and took that dick way down deep.

Ron was, of course, also excited by the scene, though not for quite the same reasons, as he later told me. He didn't think about the photos as much as he thought about Laurie—the fact that another woman was watching his cock being sucked drove him wild.

But Laurie didn't watch for very long. Just as I thought I'd go crazy without some attention to my aching cunt, she abandoned her camera and got down on the floor behind me. I kept right on sucking Ron's cock while Laurie slipped off my shorts and panties and positioned herself so she could eat me out. Her masterful tongue worked its way up and down my labia and over my clit. She stuck a finger or two inside me and slowly fucked me while she licked. Her mouth inspired mine, and I took Ron's cock, so deep I thought I'd choke—but I didn't.

Standing over us, watching Laurie eat my pussy while I sucked his cock, Ron began to moan and gyrate his hips, pumping his cock deeper and harder into my mouth. With a final thrust, his prick held steady as a fire hose, spurting hot liquid down my throat. I gulped it, at the same time pressing my cunt against Laurie's mouth until I, too, came.

After our orgasms subsided, Ron and I turned our attention to our little photographer. I removed her shorts and fulfilled my fantasy of grabbing those ass cheeks—in fact, I chewed and nibbled on them until they were covered with hickeys. While I feasted on her buns, Ron took care of her pussy, licking her the way she'd licked me, until she came, screaming and moaning, all over his face. All the while we were engaged in our mini-orgy, I kept hearing funny little clicks. I looked up and saw that Laurie had set the camera on some kind of automatic timer. Our mini-orgy had been documented for posterity. When we were all lying in a sweaty heap of blissed-out exhaustion, I asked Laurie what she intended to do with the photographs.

"Well," she confessed shyly, "if you don't mind, I'd like to keep them in my private collection. I promise not to show them to anyone else."

I balked momentarily, but when I thought about it, I

realized that Laurie was a trustworthy person. She wouldn't show the pictures around. She certainly couldn't print them anywhere without our permission—she'd be liable to a lawsuit. So after telling her we wanted our own set as well, Ron and I agreed to let her keep the film and the pictures for her own private use.

Sometimes I imagine Laurie looking through the photos and masturbating. Sometimes I imagine her boyfriend jerking off to them. For all I know, she's thrown them out by now. One thing I do know for sure—there are at least two people who still get off on my day as a porno queen. Ron and I get excited every time we look at those pictures and remember our hot day with Laurie. Though we both feel that any more threesomes would be too complicated for our relationship, we're glad we've got a visual record that continues to inspire our lovemaking.

The Man Across the Tracks

BY CORAL M. WATSON

I carried my small satchel onto the train at Gare du Nord—the 16:05 to Limoges from Paris. This was a business run I engaged in weekly for my job with an American porcelain company. It was always boring and frequently uncomfortable, since my seats were not premier class. I walked down the overused aisles, which smelled of Gauloises and dust, searching for an empty compartment—or at least one with another woman in it. Since I was still struggling with my horrid French and getting over a destructive relationship with a fellow expatriate, I wanted only to read my mystery novel, not discuss the weather or fend off a masher's advances.

Being half an hour early, I found an empty six-seater easily, pulled up the window shades, and settled in. The intense lights of the old iron station temporarily blinded me. It was some minutes before my eyes adjusted and I noticed another train waiting on the tracks immediately across from my platform. All its shades were open but for one compartment parallel to mine. The curtains were con-

structed to be adjustable from both the top and the bottom—this compartment had the top shade halfway down
and the bottom shade halfway up. I was unprepared to see
a young man's torso perfectly framed within those confines. He was of medium build, nicely muscular with ex-
cellent posture and . . . completely nude from the top of
his thighs to the middle of his chest!

My first inclination was to turn away and draw the
shades. What if he could see me? As a solitary female trav-
eler, I have been witness to men masturbating on trains all
over the world. Usually, they are repulsive, threatening
types who scare me into calling a conductor. I've always
thought it was a cliché, that thing about the seductive
rolling motion making people out-of-control horny on
trains, but for some reason, this time it was affecting me. I
was powerless to move, and we hadn't even left the station.

His right hand came into view and began to very softly,
slowly, stroke himself. I was riveted by the delicacy with
which, palm open, he gently petted his crotch, as if it were
a small, beloved animal. My last boyfriend had been very
selfish and always too rough, usually demanding sex before
I was ready. I hadn't made love in over two months and was
unaware that I was missing anything. Watching this penis
nobly straighten up, though, I imagined he was the sort of
man who would make absolutely certain I was primed; the
kind of man who would go down on a woman just because
he likes her taste and smell. With some embarrassment I
began to feel a tender moistness flow into my panties. I
undid my trouser button and relaxed the zipper, slipping
my right hand down into my pubic hair and manipulating
my full lips. I slouched down in my seat, still keeping the
faceless man in view. My hands strayed to my breasts,
where I distractedly unlatched my lacy brassiere to free

them. I wet my finger and tipped my nipples back and forth, fantasizing it was his mouth that made them erect. In this dream, I ran my fingers over his firm, masculine shoulders while he nibbled wickedly away until I could no longer stand any more and begged him to enter me.

Without thinking, I jumped up and adjusted my shades to match his. If I gave any thought to another passenger entering the compartment, it was swiftly banished as I got up on my knees, pushed my velvet trousers and panties down, and placed my torso saucily in the window. Immediately, his erection took on new vibrancy. *Ah, so he can see me,* I thought, beginning to rub my vulva tenderly.

Suddenly, he stopped touching himself. He turned his body in profile so I could more properly see the length and breadth of his excitement. His stomach was flat and firm, with just the lightest dusting of curly black hair. He put his hands on his hips, as if defying me to resist him. I adopted this same proud stance, deeply enjoying our sexual Simon Says. One-two, went his hands on his dick. One-two, went mine against my mound. We touched ourselves rhythmically, as if we had done this before, as if this were our favorite game, our favorite dance. He turned round to display his bum, and I leaned over and wiggled mine. Our views were limited somewhat by the cracks in the woven shades, but I could see perfectly the moment when he dropped his hands, opened them up, and beckoned to me, sliding them down the shaft of his beautiful cock and bending his index finger. "Come to me," the gesture said. "Come now."

I knew I was being incomparably foolish. This was dangerous business. This was frightening and heart pounding and I could feel a light sweat begin to mist under my breasts and armpits, but I pushed down my anxieties, grabbed up my bag, and left the train. I counted back the number of compartments from the opposite engine and climbed up the steps to where I estimated he was. My first guess was wrong. An old woman sat with a basket containing a small dog and looked at me blankly. The floor began to hum from the vibrations of the train's ignition, and my anxieties grew sharper.

I hesitated at the second door but knocked anyway. He opened it with a rakish grin, pulled me in, and began to kiss me before I could get a full look at him.

"Ah, mademoiselle. Très joli. Vous êtes très, très joli." Thinking back on it now, how was he so sure he had the right woman? Maybe his penis pushing against the leg of any female would have elicited a positive response. I had no choice but to be overwhelmed by its insistence, its confidence, and I grasped it hard enough to cause him to cry out. I could feel the veins, stiff, engorged with potent blood. Wriggling out of his embrace, I dropped to my knees to sink it deep into my mouth. He groaned and sighed and stroked my head tenderly, the way he had touched himself. I let my tongue feel the texture of his gallant tool. I spiraled it slowly up and down the thick shaft, enjoying the tiny imperfections of his skin.

I could have kept this up for hours, he tasted that good, but he clearly wanted something more and pulled abruptly out of my tight lips. My sweater vanished over my head. He sucked my nipples, hard as nail heads, and I let fall my slacks and kicked off my shoes. We fell back together against the well-worn corduroy of the seat. He made a move to kiss my pussy but I needed him, commanded him, to enter me now, hard, fast, before the trains could leave.

My back scraped rhythmically against the fabric, the

chafing beginning to hurt but making his thrusts that much more palpable. He pushed in rough. He pulled out fast. We banged into each other with a feverish thirst born out of our total anonymity. I struggled to reach out one hand and grasp his balls. We were both near climax when I remembered the window. He followed my upward glance and, in perfect understanding, we uncoupled momentarily and repositioned ourselves.

At first we faced outward and my breasts, pressed up against the chilly glass, were flattened and released, flattened and released, as he pounded me from behind. I reached back, took his rock-hard ass in my hands, and held him inside me, forbidding him to move. I wanted to see just how deep he could go. I could feel his cock twitching—his release was quite near. His hands dropped from my hips, tickled my clitoris, and I came with a scream that should have brought the porters running. Or was it just the departure whistle?

He began to hump me slowly again until my pussy stopped convulsing, then he turned us sideways to the window to give our performance a better frame. I smiled to think of who might be watching us now. Perhaps there was someone sitting in the very car that I had so recently left.

"Fuck me harder now. Goddamn it, just fuck me," I cried out to him, knowing he would understand this English. He pressed his hands tightly into the skin just above my womb and, with a deep, glorious moan, filled it superbly, richly, with his hot sperm.

He kissed the back of my neck, sniffing lightly behind my ears, and slipped out from between my shaking thighs.

I grew unaccountably shy now. He seemed to also, and we dressed quickly, away from the window. I gave a fast look at my wristwatch and a long glance at the now perfectly ordinary businessman in front of me. We shook hands. How bizarre! Then we kissed on both cheeks and I ran back to catch my train, acutely aware of the time and the warm rivulet flowing gently into my panties.

The Wedding

BY SPIKE FULTON

*T*here's something ghastly about weddings. The pews are filled with people who say things like, "Her third marriage and still wearing white!"

"You'd think virginity was a renewable resource." It is, isn't it?

My name's Kate. My friend Cindi is the unflappable one in white. She tells me "Three's the charm," and Carl looks promising. He's a nice guy—smart, strong, kind, and delivering an incredibly goofy smile from time to time. Cindi also reports he's lusty and funny in bed. So good luck to them. Me, I've never been married and have no intention of being so. I love sex. Marriage would eliminate so many possibilities.

Cindi invites me to these functions because I'm her friend, but also because she needs the loose female, the available arm, the dance partner, and the object of interest to otherwise disinterested males who get roped into the festivities. Hey, I'm game.

The reception's way out in the fields on her granddaddy's farm, which is one grand postcard of meadows and rolling, grassy hills surrounded by piney woods. The barn's had a once-over with streamers, flowers, and bunting, and food has been laid out from stall to stall. There's a dance floor made of smooth blond wood, and Cindi and Carl look great spinning around it. There doesn't seem to be a whole lot of men asking me to dance, so I wander outside and there they are, men and boys and girls, playng soccer in the field. Wish I hadn't worn this dress. "Come on," one of them yells as I lean over the fence. That' s Carl's college buddy, Rolf. Sure looks good—sunshine, sport, running around, scrambling, and laughing. Okay. I go to my car to get my sneakers—my canvas, rubber-toed basketball sneakers with the vegetable motif.

The next thing I know, I'm deep in a heated game of soccer that becomes a contact sport, once the kids have been called back by the parents for family pictures. It's just me and a few guys kicking up dust and laughing.

My bare legs are flashing under my skirt as I run from one side of the field to the other in the sunshine.

There's that guy Rolf again. He's muscular, blond, and stripped down to his rolled-up shirtsleeves and pleated trousers. We lock legs a couple of times, and he smiles pretty good. "Nice sneakers you got there," he says.

A couple of guys peel off to get beer, then Rolf kicks this booming ball way into the woods. "That's gone," one of the players says. "Call me when you get out of the poison ivy." He goes off, looping arms with a pretty woman in pink chiffon.

Rolf glances at me, then wanders off into the brush in search of the ball. Another one of the players gets thirsty and heads toward the barn, taking a couple of pals with him.

I'm still by the fence catching my breath, watching the woods for any sign of Rolf. His friend Kurt gives me a look, then sort of gestures to the wilds. We both wander off into the trees.

Nobody kicks a soccer ball that far, we're thinking as we stroll deeper into this stand of tall white pines and low brush interspersed with pokeweed and wildflowers. The sun comes through the branches in streams. Kurt and I split up, calling Rolf's name. A bird answers, and just as I'm rounding a stand of mountain laurel, I feel a man's arm around my waist. It feels good. I look up at Rolf, and he gives me that quizzical eyebrow, measuring if I'm in the mood. I'm in the mood. And before I can say yes, he's got his mouth on my mouth, my neck, then down to my breasts, and his hands are working their way under my skirt.

His tongue is darting down the front of my bodice, searching for my nipples. He unbuttons me and my breasts come free, and he buries his head in them. My fingers go to his hair. It's blond and curly and warm from the sun.

He sucks one nipple into his mouth, then the other, rolling each on his tongue until I'm sighing out loud. I bend down to kiss his hair when he parts my thighs with his right hand and touches my clitoris. I lean back, and he supports me with his other hand, then plunges his middle finger inside me. Up and down it goes. I'm getting wet, and I feel the exhilaration growing as he finger-fucks me and sucks my breasts.

My body's shaking so much, we ease down together on the bed of grass and leaves. He hikes my skirt up over my face and puts his tongue between my legs. He pushes my thighs apart, and his fingers are inside me again. He's licking me and using his fingers inside me. I'm rolling my own nipples between my fingertips when I hear the *brrrt* of his zipper, and he shimmies out of his pants. Then his penis is against my clit. It slides downward and in, opening the lips just a little bit with a thrust, not more than an inch. He's big and I'm not.

He hesitates a minute, then searches for my mouth. He finds my face beneath the cloth of my skirt and puts his tongue between my lips. His hands are on my breasts, squeezing them hard, and he thrusts again, deeper this time. I'm surprised by his size and his hard-on. My hips buck against his. He feels like a poker, and he's driving into me now. It hurts and it feels great.

He stops my words with his tongue, then pushes harder, gaining a few more inches and shoving his penis up into my belly. Then with a couple more thrusts, he hikes my hips with his hands and drives in to the hilt. I cry out in surprise, and again his tongue is in my mouth, silencing me with passion. This guy's a lion. His shirt is open, and now my face is against his chest. He's pumping, and I feel his penis getting larger as he's ready to come. I'm ready myself, with a death grip on his back, and I'm about to let go when I look up and see Kurt watching the whole proceeding. Whoa! I explode as Rolf slams into me one last time. My juices are pouring, and my body is shuddering under him. He's making some noise himself, that lion. Then Kurt's shadow makes him glance up.

Kurt and Rolf both look at me like they're asking permission.

"Sure, come on."

Rolf pulls away from me, and Kurt drops to his knees. His cock comes out stiff, and he starts fucking me right there on the ground. Rolf watches a moment, still dreamy in his sexual satisfaction. Then he plays with my breasts and kisses my neck. I've got his penis in my hand when he shifts around behind me so my head is between his thighs. In a moment I've got his cock in my mouth, coaxing it back to full strength. Kurt, meanwhile, is fucking me like there's no tomorrow, and with four hands working over my body, I'm in a frenzy. We're in heat, warm from the sun and getting warmer.

Kurt says, "Can we do this from behind?" He pulls out, lifts my hips, and turns me around. Up goes the skirt, so my ass is exposed to the sun and to his hands, and he enters me from behind with a grunt. Rolf, meanwhile, is getting bigger and bigger in my mouth, holding my head gently and rocking me back and forth on his shaft. Kurt's hands have now gotten control of my breasts. He squeezes while he pumps me harder and harder, and the action makes thwacking noises against my thighs. Every so often he drops his head onto the curve of my back and licks me. My eyes are shut as Kurt slams into me again and his jism squirts up inside me. He falls on my back, panting. Rolf lets go at the same time and shoots down my throat. He helps cushion my fall to the ground under Kurt's weight, and I'm buried under these sweating, handsome men. We've only had a moment to recover when we hear the iron dinner gong being rung at the barn.

We collect ourselves and the soccer ball and pick grass from one another's clothing as we head back for the festivities. Rolf says, "You know, I really do like those sneakers."

We reach the barn just as Cindi throws her bouquet. It makes an arcing kind of trajectory in my direction and everybody's roaring, including Rolf, but I sidestep the toss and let some other woman catch it. I don't want to be the next one married. I like to keep my options open.

Marie

BY ROBBI SOMMERS

*O*kay, yes, I admit it. I paid for sex—paid for the drinks, paid for the room, and then paid for the woman. One hundred seventy-five an hour. A personal ad led me to her. The words—simple and to the point—caught my attention and wouldn't let go. Escorts. Women for women. Discreet. I meant to turn the page, to continue my search for Ann Landers's column, but instead I found myself staring absently at the tiny black-bordered ad.

Hire a woman? I laughed at the absurdity. Hire a woman? What woman would! And yet I couldn't seem to pull my focus from those five unembellished words. What harm in calling the number, just to see, just to have a feel for how these things work? Not that I would ever consider, not that I would have an interest . . .

I expected a sleazy answering-machine message, a quick eavesdropping into the life and fantasies of someone else, and then I'd hang up. But before I knew what had hit me, I was caught in the middle of a sex-for-hire transaction. Someone had answered the line. Someone wanted to know when, where, and what, specifically, I wanted.

"I want her to wear a suit and tie." *I do?* My mind was racing. *I do?* The sudden drop in my belly was reminiscent of a roller-coaster ride. The slamming of my heart drowned out my feeble words. Requirements seemed to be spilling from me. What was I doing? Why couldn't I slow this exchange down? "And she should be taller than me, five foot six, five foot seven, with long, tied-back hair." Oh shit, I was out of control! I should have hung up. I should have tossed that portable phone across the room and moved directly to Ann Landers, but I didn't. I held fast to that receiver like a kid does a balloon on a windy day, and muttered my demands.

"Older," I said. "Classy," I insisted. After all, for three hundred fifty hard-earned dollars . . . Yes. Two hours. Yes. I'd have cash.

"The Fairmount?" she suggested.

"Yes. Perfect," I replied. How surprisingly easy this was! "In the lobby, Friday night at eight."

I placed the phone on the table. I stared at the black-edged ad. Friday night at eight? Had I actually consented? Did I really think I'd go to the Fairmount and take some woman up to a room and . . . and . . . ? And what?

The transaction whirled around me like a hurricane. Two hours. Three hundred fifty dollars. Oh my God.

I sat in the lobby of the Fairmount Hotel like a reluctant patient in a dentist's chair. How I had gotten there, I couldn't be sure. I'd merely buy her a drink, make small talk for a bit, and then get the hell out of there as soon as I could. Even so, four one-hundred-dollar bills were crammed in my coat pocket. Not that I would actually go through with this scheme. Not that I would end up in bed with a woman for hire—but who could have guessed that I'd even be in a hotel lobby, waiting for a $175-an-hour date?

My heart thumped recklessly. My slinky black dress hiked slightly up my thigh. Had I not painted my lips ruby red? Had I not trailed a wet line of perfume between my full breasts, across my sloped belly, and into the soft tangle of sex hair? Life being what it was, circumstances twisting as they do, it was always best to be prepared in the off chance that . . . In the off chance that what? The sudden urge to hurry out, climb into my car, and screech out of the garage overwhelmed me. What was I thinking?

Dressed in black garters and lace—what the hell was I thinking? I reached for my keys, rose from the chair, and—

"Excuse me?" The voice gushed through me like liquid heat. "I thought perhaps you were waiting for me?"

I stopped. I froze. The sound of rushing blood swished loud in my ears. *Turn around,* something inside insisted. *Turn around and smile.* In a long, slow movement that seemed to last an eternity, I pivoted. And there she stood. Five foot six? Five foot seven? It was difficult to be sure, what with the distraction of her kohl-lined eyes, what with the allure of her cherry-red lips.

"Are you Marie?" My voice cracked.

She nodded and extended her hand. A sparkle of fiery red glittered from a thin gold ring that decorated her index finger. If I took her hand in mine, then what? If I lightly ran my fingertip across that jeweled band, then what? My palms felt clammy. A harsh hollowness ballooned in my chest. Take her hand.

"Nice to meet you." Her hand was warm, soft, satiny. In the lobby of the Fairmount, her hand in mine, I stood immobilized. Now what the hell did I do? My gaze slid from her Egyptian-shadowed eyes and lingered on those volup-tuous lips.

"Do you have a room?" She squeezed my hand lightly and then slipped hers from mine.

I felt the sudden lack of her softness and wrestled with the urge to grab her hand roughly and hold it. After all, wasn't this my party? After all, didn't I call the shots? Yes, I had a room. Yes, I had four hundred dollars in my jacket. And yes, yes, yes, I could grasp her hand if that's what I wanted—or could I? The car was through the doors and in the garage. I could be out of here and safe in the blink of an eye. Did I have a room? And what? We go up there? We take off our clothes? How the hell had I gotten into this sit-uation?

Once again, she took my hand. I felt abruptly trans-ported out of my hesitations and into the steamy sensation of her touch. One moment we were in the lobby, the next we were sitting in my room sipping champagne. Had we had a conversation? How much time had already passed? Lost in a golden champagne haze, I concentrated on the sparkle of her diamond earrings.

"You're very attractive," she said. She rose from her chair and let her suit jacket drop to the floor. "When I came into the lobby, I hoped you were the one."

Slowly, deliberately, she unknotted her tie and pulled it from around her neck. Her silk shirt, secured with small pearl buttons, opened with ease. Beneath, she wore exquisite lace lingerie. Her black bra barely contained her tempting breasts, and the arc of her brown areolas spilled above the low demi-cups. I had an immediate hunger to see more. Were her nipples large and square? Small and pointy? Would their brick-red color contrast with her olive skin? Or were they pale? Or pink? Or a deep, deep plum?

I leaned forward. I was breathing hard and my mouth felt sucked dry. Would she unhook the bra? Would she show me what she had?

"Marie." Had I spoken, or was her name ricocheting inside my mind?

"Marie, Marie, Marie."

She ran her hands across the black lace. And yes, oh yes, she released the bra's silver hook. Thicker than I could have dreamed, larger than I could have hoped, her nipples stood out like fat cherry pits. I felt suddenly dizzy. A creamy aching throbbed between my legs.

Marie, Marie, Marie.

She plucked a nipple between her fingers and twisted and tugged. Twisted and tugged.

"Marie," I whispered. "Marie," I begged.

She unzipped her pants and they crumpled to the floor. Her bikini panties rose high on the delicious curve of her hips. She stepped out of her shoes and sat on the edge of the bed.

"Would you like to see all of me?"

She separated her legs and ran her finger along the lace border of the panties. A dark fringe of hair teased from beneath the lace. The panties stretched tight over the thick bulge of her lips, and I was certain her sex would be bulky and lush. And yes, yes, yes, I wanted, needed, had to see it all.

Her fingertip grazed the center point of her crotch. It was difficult to be certain, but the material seemed to be wet. If she pulled those panties aside, would her moisture glisten in the light? Should I move closer? Fall on my knees at her feet, rip those panties aside, and see for myself?

I imagined her clit pouch—a ruby in pillowy folds. If she'd move those panties aside and spread open her lips,

I could know for sure. The fragrance of sex hung heavy in the air. Entrancing musk blended with an intoxicating spicy edge into a primal, raw scent. All I could think of was her pussy. All I could consider was the color of that clit pearl buried like a treasure behind the lace veil of her panties.

Like a desperate baby, I crawled across the floor for the honey and sweets. Marie was laughing. The room was spinning. Marie, Marie, Marie. I yanked those panties aside, pulled that flimsy lace out of my way, and buried my face in her soft charms.

She was slippery heat. Submerged in dark desire, I found her tiny bead with my mouth and sucked, sucked, sucked. She was all over me. She reached down and cleaved her lips open. Ravenous to see more, I pulled back. Her clit sac dangled like a dark pink ornament. I licked it once, lapped it again. Marie, Marie, Marie. The lower lips parted like rose curtains. Wanting more, needing more, I grabbed them between my fingers and split them wide, exposing her swollen entrance.

Sex juice shimmered on the raised rim. I dipped my finger, stirred my finger, pierced my finger into the soft indentation. Marie was squirming; she was grinding her hips. I burrowed into the velvet pie.

Her clit strained forward. Her lips wrapped around the base of my finger and her pussy clamped hard.

I jammed my other hand under my dress and into my dampness. As I fucked her, I flicked my finger across my clit. I was hard. I was oversized. I was warm and oily. In and out, I pumped my finger into her. Back and forth, I whipped my finger across my clit. Again and again, over and over.

Engulfed in pinks and reds, surrounded in the hot perfume of lust, I spun in a vortex of pleasure. It was dark. It was light. I was swimming in slippery gels, floating on a sun-baked lake, swirling in a tropical storm. The slapping sounds as I pounded into her lifted me high in the air. Again and again, more and more. Marie, Marie, Marie.

Okay, yes, I admit it. I paid for sex—paid for the drinks, paid for the room, and then paid for the woman. Not that I would ever consider, not that I would have an interest . . . But the following week, when I called the escort service just to say thanks, a disconnect notice was all I got.

Rational curiosity, and nothing more, compelled me to hire the private investigator.

Marie. Marie. Marie. Where are you, Marie?

Swashbuckler

BY JOAN T. SHERWOOD

*T*onight she would be the daring swashbuckler. God protect anyone who got in her way. Elaine was horny, and the guys she knew from the office just weren't an option. Pickings weren't slim; they were anorexic. After taking a good look at herself and her surroundings, she decided that a change of style and a change of scenery might do the trick to get her out of this slump. After all, if you want something, go out and get it.

Wearing a long-lusted-after pair of black thigh-high pirate boots, she now stood, feeling self-congratulatory, surveying herself. She had gone through much trial and error to assemble a complete look to go with the boots. It was a metamorphosis from her old appearance, and with it came a change in attitude.

Minimize. You've been trying too hard, she told herself. Without the rollers and hairspray, her hair regained a softness she hadn't enjoyed since junior high. A more subtle makeup application let her real face show through. Classic black completed the look—stockings, miniskirt, and a

T-shirt that hung from her breasts, almost exposing her midriff, but not quite. She caressed her belly.

This new woman she had become had always been with her. The acquisition of the boots was merely a catalyst to release her spirit, like a magic potion drunk and then forgotten once its effect took hold.

Of course, there's adventurous, and then there's reckless. In an outfit like that, she needed a screening process. That's where Alec came in. Alec had a good memory and was a good judge of character. He was also one of Elaine's oldest and best friends, making him the perfect choice as casting director for her little seduction scenario. She'd known him since high school, when she, the shy, brainy nerd, had befriended him, the misunderstood, loner outcast.

The joint where he tended bar was a funky, cozy neighborhood pub. Its antique appointments had been well maintained, and the establishment had recently gained a chic status and was attracting a very diverse crowd. The perfect kind of spot, she thought, to find a nice conquest or two—something out of the ordinary.

When she stepped out of the cab in front of the Black Sheep Tavern, she felt a trickle of moisture run down one leg and stopped in mid-stride. *Oh, Jesus, am I starting my period?* she wondered in a quick panic. *No,* she reassured herself, the timing was wrong for blood. It was anticipation. Her confidence restored, she tugged her skirt down a little and strode into the bar like a sinister superhero. Her deeds tonight would benefit mankind, but her methods might skirt the law.

The little saloon was dark, narrow, and deep, booths on one side, a bar on the other. Exposed pipes painted flat black lent an air of industrial art to the low ceiling. She noticed Alec waving her over to a bar stool as he whisked away a reserved card. The card itself had garnered attention, but when Elaine slid onto the stool, leaned back against the bar, and crossed her legs with a flourish, she smirked to herself, thinking she had just passed the scent of sex to the primitive part of every male brain in the joint. Her legs were poised like leather-clad guardians sent to challenge any suitors who dared seek her favors. She'd let a little intimidation weed out some of the duds.

She heard Alec clear his throat behind her. He had placed a drink down on the bar with a fresh cocktail napkin. Now everything was set. The signal they had worked out earlier was simple. If someone who was a known jerk approached her, Alec would remove the napkin and replace it with another. It was up to Elaine to get rid of the guy.

Alec leaned over the bar to get an eyeful. "I think I'm glad to be back here where it's safe," he said with a grin. "You could kill a man looking like that."

"I'm not dressed to kill, baby," she said, smiling back at him. "Just a little maiming, and I'll be on my way." Alec just shook his head, then went about his business, keeping a watchful eye on customers.

Elaine swiveled around to face the room, legs crossed at the knee, one foot jutting out into the narrow walkway between the bar stools and the booths. All over the room, men were rising to their feet, turning to adjust their crotch or check their hair self-consciously in the mirrors.

They were all staring intently at Elaine. Her pussy surged with a sudden defiant sensation. She was a matador. She had waved her red cape in an arena full of bulls.

The first man to approach carried two empty glasses. Elaine could see a woman sitting alone in the direction from which he had come. *Very rude,* she thought. Behind her, Alec picked up her drink, switched napkins, and set it down again with a little bang. Still, the stud suited her as far as eye-candy went. She looked him directly in the eye.

Unfortunately, that prompted him to open his mouth. "Honey, it's a good thing these jeans aren't flammable, 'cause you might set my pants on fire."

He might as well have belched in her face. She wrinkled her nose in disgust. "You hurry back to that poor girl with those drinks. I'm sure she needs one." Elaine had no idea where that response had come from, but it felt good. She turned her back on the man.

She heard him mutter "Dyke" as he picked up the fresh drinks. Elaine was preparing a nut-withering retort in her mind when she noticed in the bar mirror that his girlfriend had viewed the whole scene and wasn't as clueless as her circumstance indicated.

Before he knew it, the boor was wearing his drink. His date, an attractive, athletic-looking woman, was fed up with him in a big way. "You squirrel-dicked pile of shit, I'm over this crap. Go fuck yourself," she yelled at him. Elaine admired the white-hot fury of the woman, who was now storming toward the rest room. She realized she was incredibly turned on, and a wave of wickedness overcame her. The man, his arms stretched wide, face dripping, called out "Kaaate!"—elongating the name into several syllables of complete incomprehension. Elaine caught his eye, winked maliciously, and followed his girlfriend into the bathroom.

Elaine burst into the rest room as forcefully as her predecessor had. There was a lock on the door, and she threw the bolt to ensure a little privacy.

Kate had red hair and, apparently, a healthy temper.

She wasn't weeping like some women might be. She looked like she was ready to rip the tampon machine off the wall and go shove it up a certain someone's ass. She reminded Elaine of Maureen O'Hara in *The Quiet Man*, pacing with rage. She wore a full, long skirt, a tailored white blouse, and sensible flat shoes.

The fury whirled around to find Elaine right in her face. Speechless, Elaine chose the strong but silent approach. She bolstered her courage, thinking, *You wanted something new, you've got it.*

She cupped one hand behind Kate's head and wrapped her free arm around the woman's waist, pulling their hips together with a jerk. She delivered the hottest kiss of her life, and Kate kissed back, their mouths open to each other and the combined energies of lust and fury pulsing between them.

Elaine was impatient, having been keyed up for weeks.

Her red-haired cohort overcame shock quickly, burning with the need her rage had ignited. She slid her hands up Elaine's inviting top, cupping her bare breasts, squeezing her nipples and twisting them in tandem.

Oh, yes, thought Elaine, *good move.* She reached down and grabbed the woman's ass, pulling her pelvis tightly to her own, and began to grind.

Kate broke the kiss, pushing Elaine away. Her eyes blazed as she stood, sizing up the stranger in black boots.

I might want to brace myself, Elaine thought, half expecting to be stretched out on the floor in a second, and not in a nice, painless way.

But Kate was ready for a little daring, too. She grabbed Elaine's shirt, yanked it up over her head, and cast it on the floor. Her eyes never left Elaine's.

Elaine followed the garment with her gaze and caught

a glimpse of an observer peering out of a stall door. She only hesitated a moment. She had felt adventurous before, but now, with an audience, she felt like showing off.

A glance at the buttons trailing up Kate's chest offered only one course of action. She grabbed the shirtwaist with both hands and tore outward. A rain of buttons skittered across the tile floor.

As Elaine unfastened the woman's bra, revealing creamy, firm breasts with pink nipples, Kate pulled herself up onto the roomy countertop of the sink and hiked her skirt up to her thighs.

Elaine set her lips to one tit, tracing the point of her tongue teasingly around the nipple and then zeroing in to suck it hard. Marvelously soft skin met her hands everywhere they traveled. Inside and out, sensory messages were flooding her brain, urging her to move on while at the same time lulling her to take all the time in the world.

Then she heard Kate's voice: "Fuck me."

Eager to oblige, she slid her hand up the woman's bare thigh toward the demanding heat of her cunt. Droplets of cream hung in the rust-colored fur.

Kate spread her legs wide for Elaine and deftly cleaved her swollen lips, moving upward to finger her clit. Elaine bowed to inhale the lush, heady fragrance, and, for the first time, tasted the slick wetness of another woman with her fingertips. She knew her own desires, and so she knew the other woman's need. Easily, she thrust two fingers deep inside and pulled forth from the woman a great gasp of pleasure.

Elaine eased in her ring finger to make the fit tight and began to churn her fingers in and out. Reaching in and up along the vaginal wall, she pulled and thrust, exploring the limits of Kate's pussy. She reeled with the knowledge of the sensations she was creating.

Kate's fingers dug into Elaine's shoulders. Her head was flung back, pressing against the mirror, her red hair doubled in brilliance by its reflection. Moans escaped in sync with Elaine's pumping rhythm. She released her grip and hooked her hands underneath her knees, lifting them high and wide.

Elaine was euphoric. Her own pussy was dripping hot juice down her thighs. An empathic burn deep inside her begged her to satisfy the want. In the heat of her passion, she interpreted her own thoughts as if they were Kate's. Obeying the impulse, she increased her pace as she watched the pleasure spread across Kate's face. Kate bucked and cried out loud, kicking. Elaine persisted, un-relenting until she felt the walls clamp down on her fingers like a vise.

Her movement restricted, Elaine stopped altogether. Her jaw dropped as she felt the distinctive, band-tightening muscle spasms of an enormous orgasm. She counted seven clenches before Kate ceased shouting and let her whole body slump in exhaustion. Elaine felt exhilarated. Her heart raced as she embraced the woman.

Kate sat up slowly, spread her lips in a mischievous grin, and said, "I feel much better now." They kissed again, much more sweetly this time, with a trace of fire lick-ing their lips.

Silently, reverently, they composed themselves. Elaine picked up her T-shirt from the floor and spied a pair of feet in the stall. She had completely forgotten their voyeur. She casually shook out the shirt as she would have if she had just removed it from the dryer. A small, pearl-colored button clicked across the tiles. Elaine smiled wryly as she pulled the shirt over her head.

Her consort had refastened her bra, arranged her skirt, and now seemed to be wondering about her button-less blouse, as if she had no idea how it had gotten that way. She looked up at Elaine, flashed a devil-may-care grin, and proceeded to tuck in the tails, leaving the front gaping open. Elaine smiled in approval.

Conversation stopped and heads turned when the two women emerged from the ladies' room. They walked casu-ally back to Elaine's spot at the bar. Alec leaned over be-side the taps. "Her, uh, friend ran out of here when the howling started, so I called a cab. It's waiting outside," he whispered, trying to conceal a smirk.

Elaine turned back to Kate and found her standing, hands on hips, facing the crowd as if she were prepared to stare each and every one of them down if it took her all night. She took Kate's hand and led her outside to the waiting cab.

Before she got in, Kate reached down into one of the deep pockets of her skirt and pulled out a business card. Handing it to Elaine, she said, "If you ever want to dump on one of my boyfriends again, call me." She winked, kissed Elaine on the cheek, and stepped into the taxi.

The room was abuzz when Elaine returned. A woman was mobbed by a small crowd in the far corner, next to the rest rooms.

Elaine realized she was incredibly thirsty, and although she felt she had made a pretty good start, her lust was really in high gear now—her night of conquest was far from over. She walked back to the bar.

She motioned for Alec to bring her a tall glass of any-thing and watched him with an appreciative eye for the first time. She took inventory of his hard flat pecs, his handsome features, his nicely rounded ass in loose-fitting jeans, and mostly of the bulge in his crotch that showed even through a bar apron. He had become so familiar to her that she had failed to notice what he'd grown into.

He walked over and handed her a whiskey with a water back. Never breaking eye contact, she slugged the shot and took a long drink from the water. She set down her glass and motioned for him to lean in so she could tell him something.

"Alec, come with me. There's something you need to fix in the ladies' room."

All Afternoon

BY LAURA WHITE

*D*o my back, Ellie?"

Valerie Feldbaum, buxom girlfriend of my twenty-year-old brother Kevin, hands over the Bain de Soleil. She has no idea what she's doing to me.

I look at her parents' house, then at the pool, then back at the house. "Your back?" He must not have told her about me.

"Yeah, come on."

The lotion has liquefied in the heat. I pour a pool into my palm and drizzle it between the two pieces of her bathing suit. I smear the oil around, trying to be brisk. Her skin is warm and smooth. I speed up near her bikini bottom. What if I give myself away?

Next I do her shoulder blades. "There." I rub my hands together, work the oil into the dry skin around my nails. Give a silent prayer of gratitude that I'm not a guy, that nothing shows.

After dropping out of my second graduate program in as many years, I'm going to visit old friends. My brother, who's living here with Valerie's family for the summer, was on the way.

When I rang the doorbell late last night, she answered. A head taller than me, broad. Wild black hair, olive skin; dramatic, but a crooked nose makes her not quite perfect.

"Kevin's asleep. Working early tomorrow. He said you wouldn't mind."

"I'll just crash here and hit the road in the morning."

"No!" Valerie put her hand on my arm. Short nails; I liked that. "Stick around for a while." She lowered her voice. "We have a pool."

At ten-thirty this morning I'm lying awake in the guest room when Valerie walks in and throws a bathing suit at me. "Put this on." She leans against the doorway, facing me. "Meet me out back. Hurry."

I pull off the T-shirt I slept in, step into the old Speedo. There's no mirror, but I guess I look all right. My small tits are cute, and my pallor is the trade-off for my hair—dark red.

When I get out to the pool, Valerie is stretched faceup on one of two chaise longues, bursting out of an anti-freeze-green bikini. On a low table next to her are a bowl of cut-up melon and a white plastic watch.

"Sit down."

That's when she asks me to do her back. I've just recovered when she asks me to do her legs.

"Just the tops," she says. "I already did my calves."

Okay. Either Kevin hasn't told her or she's decided to torture me.

"Ellie? What's wrong, is it empty? There's more lotion in the house."

"No, there's still some in here." I flatten the tube and coat my palms with the oil. I put one hand on each of her thighs, moving them up and down a little. Her bikini bottom is French-cut, high on the hips. With my fingertips, I outline one side, then the other. It takes everything I have not to go under the elastic.

"Thanks," she says. "That feels good."

"Sure." It comes out like a croak.

She rests her head on her arms, and I lean back in my chair. I oil my own legs, extra careful at the tender diagonal where leg meets hip. I nudge the elastic. Touching Valerie has made it sexy to touch myself. I take my time.

I lie back and watch her through my sunglasses. Who is she? What's the story with her and Kevin?

"You know what's weird?" Valerie says. "I had a feeling about you."

"'What?"

"Just from seeing a picture. Kevin didn't say a word. And it's not like you even have short hair or anything."

"What are you talking about?"

She turns to face me. "Ellie, you've been leering at me since you got here."

For a few seconds I forget to breathe. Then I jump up from the chaise and run the few steps to the edge of the pool. I dive in, expecting refreshing cold. Its like bathwater, but I swim anyway. Before I know it, I'm on my way back.

I do laps. Eventually, only because it's inevitable, I push my way out of the pool. I stand over Valerie. Water from the ends of my hair drips onto her ankles.

"You're fast." She's got a big smile on her face.

"Why didn't you tell me to knock it off?"

"Who says I minded?"

I fold my arms across my chest.

"Why do you think I'm wearing this bikini that hasn't fit me since I was fourteen?"

I stand speechless.

"It's amazing how much you look like Kevin."

"He looks like me. I looked this way first."

"Your eyes—I've never seen anyone else with his shade of green. They're beautiful."

I lie down in my chaise. Flattery goes a long way with me.

"Have you had a lot of girlfriends?"

"I've had my share." I shrug. "What about you? I mean—"

"One boyfriend in high school. Then Kevin. The summer before college, though, I worked at this camp. There was this girl, another counselor . . ."

"What happened?"

"We messed around. We'd get stoned and, you know, do stuff." She pushes her sunglasses up on her head, locks her gaze on me, like a dare. "I liked it."

"You want a medal? Lots of teenagers experiment."

"It wasn't experimenting. I've thought about it since then, thought about other girls." She looks off toward the pool again. Her voice gets quiet. "I've thought about you."

"Oh, yeah, Valerie?" I punch her name like an insult. "What have you thought about me?"

"How your mouth is like Kevin's. How maybe you kiss like Kevin."

"How does Kevin kiss?"

She turns back to me. "It's hard to describe. I'd better show you."

Then she's next to me, her hip pushing against my thigh. A thin gold chain snakes across her tan collarbone.

In the time it takes her to move in, I smell perfume, deodorant, shampoo, and, finally, lip gloss. Fruity.

She kisses me so hungrily it's hard to doubt her sincerity. Finally, she breaks for air, leans away, looks at me. The dream is over, I think. She's about to realize her mistake. But she groans and clamps her mouth back onto mine.

She straddles me, kneels. Her slick legs press against mine. With both hands, she yanks down the straps of my bathing suit to expose my chest. My arms are pinned to my sides, but if I move them I'll break the spell. She'll wake up.

She palms one breast, rubs the nipple with her thumb. She stretches out on top of me, attaches her mouth to the other nipple. She's heavy, but the weight feels good, even in this heat. She bites, lightly at first, then hard. Too hard.

"Watch it."

"Sorry."

I free my arms. She tries to pull my suit down the rest of the way. I could lift my ass to help her, but I don't. The yard isn't completely private, and suddenly I'm thinking about Kevin. But mostly I'm testing her. I have to know she wants it, wants me.

"Goddamn it, Ellie."

She stops struggling with my suit, gives me a look that says, *I'll show you.* She shoves her hand down the front, rough and sudden. Then, with torturous slowness, she strokes me. Two long fingers. Doesn't go in, just slides them up and down. For a long time.

"Please," I say.

"Please what?" She knows what I want, she's just making me say it.

"Go in."

"Like this?"

I'm swallowing her fingers. How many? She's pushing into me.

"Like this?" She pushes hard, deep jabs, the way I like.

I nod. I think, *Exactly like this.* Still, I give her my favorite line. "Don't be too gentle."

I lie back on the chaise. She's totally fucking me with her fingers. Relentless. I squeeze against her touch and look up. The tops of the trees are moving—there must be a breeze. She keeps at it, and I start to get that inevitable feeling. I close my eyes. It's just me, and I am just this pulsing, gripping center and a tiny corner of my brain that is pure gratitude. Then it happens. She keeps going and it happens again. *I love you,* that corner of my brain wants to say.

I'm afraid to open my eyes. I just lie there, like some cartoon oaf who shoots his wad and rolls over to sleep. Finally Valerie's hand is on my shoulder. "Hey," she says. "Ellie. What's up?"

"Kevin."

She takes her hand away. "Think he'd mind?"

"How should I know? You're his girlfriend." Again, that tone. "How long have you guys been together, anyway?"

"Since Christmas. Scoot over." She lies down beside me. We're face to face, everything else to everything else.

"How'd you meet?"

"Discussion section."

"You liked him right away?"

"I thought he was cute."

"He is cute." A flash of sibling pride, or loyalty, or guilt. "He's damned cute."

She strokes my side. The suit is still bunched around my waist. She pets me like a cat. Leans forward, licks my lips. Slowly, for a long time, like she's never heard of kissing. Then her tongue's inside and everything's starting up again.

I want her. I pop her tits out of the bikini top, easy enough. The bright fabric frames them. Her nipples are dark, the way I knew they'd be. They're in my mouth.

She pushes her bikini bottom off so hard it rolls into a coil. She flings it onto the grass. "Touch me."

I do, but only for a second before I kneel on the grass and go down there with my head, with my mouth. I'm about to move in when it occurs to me—Kevin's been here. Kevin comes here. Kevin's a regular at this particular spot.

"Are you on the pill?"

"No. Why? You gonna impregnate me?"

"What do you use? A diaphragm?"

"Condoms," she says. "Rubbers."

He doesn't come in her. Maybe once or twice, but I can pretend it's pure there. I don't have to contemplate traces of my brother's semen on my mouth. "When was the last time you fucked him?"

"This morning. He couldn't believe how horny I was. He was like, 'What's gotten into you?'"

"What'd you say?"

"I want your sister, but in the meantime I'll settle for you."

I smile and dig my nails into her ass.

"Liar."

"Ellie?"

"What?"

"Lick me."

"I think there's a word missing from that sentence."

"Lick me now."

When I taste her, desire hits me so hard I feel it in my

gut. Having her doesn't make me want her any less. I'm all hunger, all mouth. Her moans, even, sound far away.

How long have her fingers been in my hair? She's twisting, pulling, thrashing. Until her legs go rigid. Then she shudders. I stay where I am until she pulls me up toward her. My knees ache when I stand.

For a long time, we lie quietly, eat chunks of warm cantaloupe with our hands. My hair's almost dry. She combs it with her fingers. Once in a while, she kisses me.

"What time does he get home from work?"

"Around six."

"I'll leave at five."

"But—" She stops mid-sentence. Shows me big, sad eyes, big white teeth. Her hair's in a ponytail, stray pieces falling into her face. "Are you sure?"

I just look at her. Then I smile. "Think of it this way. We've got—" Her watch is facing away from me and I can't reach it without letting go of her. "We've got all afternoon."

Carmen Visits
the Ladies' Room

BY LINDA HOOPER

I had one of the peak weird experiences of my life last
week. Some friends and I went out to the Palomar for dinner. It's a Mexican restaurant and bar that tries to be
fancier than it is—they added blue corn tortillas long
ago—and it was full of straight cruising folk: yuppies and
chamber-of-commerce types. So naturally everyone got
kinda quiet when we walked in, and heads turned to look
at us—the usual. So at one point during dinner, I got up to
go to the bathroom.

I was in there just washing my hands when this woman
came out of the stall and said, "I just gotta ask you—can I
touch your hair?"

She was probably a Republican wife; she had the Republican hair, the red suit, the fluffy bow tie even, the perfume, the makeup, the perfectly polished not-too-long
fingernails. I thought, *This is an adventure,* so I said yes. She
started rubbing my head.

"Your hair is really purple, isn't it? What do your parents think? Do your parents know?" All the while she was rubbing her hand over and over the top of my head.

My hair had grown out a little then, so it was about a quarter inch on the sides and a good inch and a half on top. But she was pressing herself up against me. It was really wild. While she was rubbing my hair and asking me all these questions, she was putting her other hand on my shoulder, and even brushing my breasts. Then she was holding my waist and pulling herself against me, and her face was really, really close to mine; she was watching her hand flick back and forth through my hair.

This all happened very fast, of course. Then her friend came out of her stall, and I heard her shriek, "Carmen, what are you doing?" and then laugh hysterically. But then the friend came over and asked, "Can I touch your hair?"

Thinking, *This is really bizarre,* I said yes. And then they were both petting me at the same time, touching me in fairly intimate places—for strangers—like my waist, and squeezing my hand. They were touching each other, too, through their stiff Republican dress-up suits, putting their arms around each other, reaching around to brush each other's breasts from the side, and laughing into each other's face while they brushed my hair back and forth. Of course, I was laughing too, even though this was not my usual bathroom visit. And they were saying, "Can you imagine dyeing your hair like this?"

"Yes, I could, but Michael would shit," as if making Michael shit were something very fun.

"Forget your husband, what would your hairdresser think?"

"He'd never have me again." And they laughed hysterically again, like they'd made a double entendre never heard before.

Now, since they had brought up sex—their Republican fashion, anyway—I decided to push it, so I said, "Carmen, I really like your perfume. Can I smell it?" Before she answered, I put my face in her neck and started nuzzling her. My hair was touching her face (which I know felt good), and her friend was watching (and I knew it looked good), so I started kissing her and touching her breasts lightly through her Republican suit.

"You really, really smell good," I said, though, I must admit, I didn't really like the perfume that much. But since the smell was part of the whole scene, which I did like, very much, I guess I wasn't exactly lying.

I heard her friend laughing hysterically again. "Carmen, I think she likes you," she said in a sort of taunting way, but not threatening to me. Maybe they were lovers?

"And I like her, too," Carmen said decisively, and she pushed me back against the wall, just missing the towel dispenser, and kissed me hard on my mouth, shocking me with the chemical taste of her lipstick—which I love. I opened my mouth, and she put her tongue in. I grabbed her closer, pushing my hands in the small of her back so her cunt pulled into me, and I kissed her back.

"Oh, I gotta see this," the friend was saying somewhere close to my ear, and when I took one of my hands away from Carmen's ass to feel her breasts, well, imagine my surprise to find the friend's hand already up there, and Carmen's suit being unbuttoned.

Carmen and I kept kissing like teenagers, and since her tits were occupied, I decided to pull her skirt up, and I found this very small pair of panties surrounded by a garter belt that held up her stockings—and I found a very, very wet Republican pussy. In went my finger; she stopped kissing me.

"What are you doing?"

"You must know what I'm doing, because your pussy told me to do it."

"Oh my god, Carmen, what is she doing?" But the friend knew what I was doing, because she reached around, and her hand followed mine into Carmen's skirt. I think she stayed there awhile, doing something to Carmen's ass, but Carmen and I started kissing again. She moaned and fucked my mouth with her tongue as my finger went in and out of her.

I think around that point someone opened the door to the bathroom, but they left. I don't remember anyone actually coming in and flushing or anything, but I was busy—I could be wrong.

Carmen was fully, fully involved. Her friend lifted up her hair and was sucking on her neck and such, pulling down her clothes and licking her shoulders, anything she could get her tongue on. Carmen had her hands up my T-shirt by that time, and her friend followed her hands up there too, so they each had a nipple and a breast.

It's unusual to come while standing up. I know, I've tried it with many girls. It happens all the time in erotica, but that's why they call it fiction. Carmen started getting up to it, I could tell, and I wondered if she was going to be able to come like that. Her body was ready and wanted to, that's for sure. I could feel her clit getting very hard, and it was reaching for my finger. Carmen's body did that fast dance, and then the slow one that brings the orgasm, the boom, boom, boom. She pressed her clit into, and then away from, my finger each time, and then she did come.

Oh, oh, oh—like that, sobbing against me, and then she squirted, too, into the palm of my hand. I really liked that, but I didn't tell her. I thought it might bother her if she knew I noticed. Her friend loved Carmen's orgasm, and covered her with kisses, although they didn't kiss each other. Carmen kissed me at the end, but left me with a little less tongue with each passing second.

She was weak in the legs. I held her up, but then they started laughing again, and her friend and I helped Carmen get her clothes back together. "Are you going to tell them what took so long?" I asked her, giving her a final peck on the cheek.

"Do you think I should?" she asked her friend, not at all serious.

"Depends on how much you love your husband . . . or your husband's money!" And they laughed hysterically again, their red, red mouths wide open, like cheerleaders, and very close to each other.

Carmen needed to fix her lipstick. I tucked my shirt back in and told them both I probably needed to get back to my friends.

"You're really a great kid," Carmen said. "And I love your hair."

"Thanks," I said. I met the pair's eyes. "That was real fun."

"Oh, anytime," Carmen said, and they both laughed together again, giddily. I left them still laughing in the bathroom and went out to the dining room. I sat down with my friends and stuck my finger out into the center of the table.

"Guess what took me so long?"

Candy

BY RENEE L. OTT

I can hear the distant sounds of talking and laughter as I slowly walk toward the room. For a brief moment my courage fails me. My palms feel sweaty and my stomach flutters. Should I stay or should I go? Taking a deep breath, I walk in.

Looking around, I count at least seven tables. There he is, but where is she? She's got to be here, she's just got to. I really need her support, even though she has no knowledge of this yet. Finally, I spot the blond head I know and love so well. I make my way toward her, stopping to hug and "hi, how are ya?" with different friends.

A quick hug and smile for my best friend stills the questions in her eyes. Her hand caresses my arm and moves to rest gently on my hip. The mere touch of her fingers sends the butterflies in my stomach spinning toward my crotch. A short glance at her face mirrors the passion. Before she can open her mouth to ask, I slide into a vacant chair a few seats away.

The one thing I truly love about twelve-step groups is

the consistency. No matter where I go, or which program I'm in, they are basically the same. They start the same, talk about the same twelve steps, and end the same.

The familiar droning voices could be heard reading from each table. Mine was no different. Sighing quietly to myself, I fade out, lost in my own thoughts. Of her. Remembering the first time we were together.

We were going somewhere, a dance maybe. I was running late, as usual. She was running even later, as usual. As she was getting into the tub, I was stripping off my clothes, too hot in what I was wearing. I rummaged through her closet for something cooler.

I heard her calling, so I stuck my head out of the closet to yell, "I can't hear you!"

"Come check my heart out—I might get lucky tonight and I want it to be perfect," she said, again. I caught my breath as I walked into the bathroom. A perfectly heart-shaped bush thrust itself just above the water. I sat on the edge of the tub and leaned over to touch it. "It is beautiful," I whispered. I heard her sharp intake of breath as my fingers worked their way through her soft hair and into her wet pussy.

My eyes followed my fingers as they traveled across her stomach, over her hard nipples, and to her mouth. Her teeth caught my fingers. She sucked and licked them just as she has sucked and licked most of the cocks in her life. I raised my eyes to hers. Her eyes, usually blue, were a gorgeous deep shade of violet. I've learned over the years that her eyes change to that shade only when she's overly tired or incredibly turned on. No wonder they say that eyes are a reflection of the soul.

I silently held open a towel, and she got out of the tub. The towel was lost as we kissed for the first time. Slowly, she pushed me back onto the counter. Kissing each breast, she took off my panties and spread my legs. Her fingers found my hard clit as her mouth teased my breasts in turn. Harder and faster she rubbed. Her lips found mine as I came in her hand.

Her eyes begged for release as I slid off the counter and lowered her to the rug. My mouth couldn't wait to taste that delicious little heart. Teasing her, licking everywhere but the spot she wanted. Finally licking her clit, she came.

We still laugh about the best dance we never went to. Smiling, I'm drawn back into the present. I feel her eyes on my face. Can she read my mind? I hope not.

Reaching into my purse, I throw a dollar into the basket and a handful of candy onto the table. Selecting one for myself, I smile invitingly to the others at the table. Quick smiles of thanks are returned as some of the hands reach out to take one.

I can still feel my best friend's eyes upon me as I partially unwrap my candy-stick. I hold it by the unwrapped end and slowly dip it into my coffee. Stirring, I look around my table.

A good mix of people. More males than females—as almost always. Median age somewhere around twenty-five to thirty—the norm. Some fidgeting, some listening intently—also the norm.

The reading ends at my table and the sharing begins. I stop stirring my coffee and twirl the stick gently between my fingers. The wrapper crinkles as I lift the candy-stick to my mouth.

Closing my eyes, I savor the hot, sticky candy as it passes over my lips and onto my waiting tongue. The taste of peppermint is strong as my tongue tentatively probes the invader. Recognizing the shape of the long hard rod, I welcome it into my mouth.

In and out. Slowly the candy-stick glides across my tongue. My tongue pushes the hard rod to my lips. My fingers lightly push it back. In and out. My back arches as the full sensual in-and-out motion takes over my mind and body. My other hand gently rests on my inner thigh.

Opening my eyes, I look toward my best friend. Her half-parted lips and violet eyes are clear indications of what she's feeling. I visualize her wet pussy as my hand slides higher up my thigh. *What are you doing here?* she mouths at me. I smile and shake my head. Later. You'll understand later. I hope.

My tongue searches in vain as I release the rod from my warm lips and lower it once more into my coffee. Swirling it a few times, I raise the candy-stick to my lips. My tongue runs up and down the shaft, licking the bitter coffee from wrapper to tip. I slide it back into my waiting mouth. Again the in-and-out takes over.

I sense the eyes upon me. I meet their eyes with a challenge of my own. Looking over the room, I see him watching me. Finally his gaze moves from my mouth and my candy to meet my eyes. I lick the rod slowly, starting once more at the wrapper and deliberately flicking the tip lightly with my tongue. *Want some?* my body says to his. *You know I do* is his response.

A small shiver runs through me. A simple look from this man makes my palms sweaty and my nipples hard. My legs spread just a little wider. My hand longs to run down his back and across his smooth ass.

In and out. The candy-rod becomes his cock as I picture him naked before me. Long and slow, my tongue teases his cock. Licking the shaft and kissing the tip, I finally take it into my mouth. In and out. Ever so slowly. My fingers find their way across his belly, stopping to play with his belly button. He's an "inny." The fingers stop when they reach his hardened nipples. Gently my thumbs brush them before my fingers glide across his skin, to his hips and thighs.

In and out. My mouth licks and sucks his warm cock. My hands work their way down his thighs, finally coming to rest under his ass. My fingers can't resist playing in the soft warm crack, especially with the hole they find there. Obligingly, he rolls onto his side.

My mouth leaves his warm cock and my hand takes over. I lick and kiss his cock, his balls, every inch of his ass. I linger on his anus, drawing from the fact that each lick and probe sends him closer to orgasm. His cock is wet in my hand as my mouth makes its way up the shaft. In and out. I can feel his hand touching my hair, my shoulder, my hard nipple. He rolls it, pinches it as he comes in my mouth.

He moves slightly in his chair as he adjusts his jeans. I notice the bulge in his crotch before raising my eyes to his. I pull my gaze away and slowly lower the candy-stick to my coffee cup. It's my turn to share. I lean forward—letting my breasts rest lightly on the table. The males at the table, almost in unison, lean forward too, their primal instincts obviously hoping for a better look.

"My name is . . . and it's so stimulating to be here tonight. I've never come here before." I pause to look at my hand stroking my thigh and continue. "What this step means to me is powerlessness. My hands are tied." I demonstrate by putting both hands behind my back, arching my breasts even higher. And I am waiting! My hand moves of its own accord to my warm inner thigh. "My

Higher Power comes to me in ways that are too numerous and exhilarating to explain. I can feel His power when He is within me. He moves me to great heights and ecstasies. I am so glad I came tonight. Thanks for letting me share."

With that short, breathless statement I go on stirring my coffee. I hear the amazement and disbelief in my best friend's voice when she murmurs, "Thanks for sharing." Smiling brightly, I pop the candy-stick back in my mouth, ignoring the disgust on the women's faces and the lust on the men's.

Everyone shares and we get up to close. Out in the hallway, we form a circle, arms around each other. Hugs are shared and my best friend and I finally meet face to face. "What in the fuck are you doing?" she hisses in my ear, still smiling.

"I'll talk to you later," I whisper, also smiling.

"You got *that* right," I hear, as we move back to our table.

Smiling, I put on my coat, gather my purse, and finish my coffee. His table is getting up as I pop the candy back into my mouth. I feel his hand on my arm and his hard cock pressing against my leg. His hand finds its way up my arm, barely brushing the already hard nipple. I smile sweetly as my teeth bite down on the candy and grind it. The passion and longing are evident in his face as he is whisked away by his tablemates. I hear their closing prayer as I walk out the door.

Later that night, I'm lying in my bed. My fingers are playing with the clit they had longed to play with all night. As I gently rub my wet swollen pussy, the lips part. My fingers reach in as far as they can go. My legs spread wider as my fingers leave my wet pussy to play with my nipples. Wet with pussy juice, they arch in anticipation.

I'm hot and sticky with peppermint candy. I have discovered that candy-sticks might taste great, but make lousy dildos. The rod itself is much too thin to ever replace the cock I want, so it's time for my fingers to take over.

The phone rings. Smiling, I let my fingers caress my clit, my breasts, my thighs. I visualize his face above mine. His eyes, green like mine, search my face even as he kisses me.

Encircling my waist, his arm tightens as my body rises to meet his. His other hand leaves my breast and slides between us to rub my hard slit. My hands slide across his ass to his warm, furry cock. A slight pressure on his anus pushes his cock deeper inside me. His hand leaves my pussy, seeking and locating one of mine. He impressions my hand with his, my lips with his, and comes deep inside me.

Knowing this is him, this is the cock I want, my body responds with each ring. My fingers tease my clit, rubbing harder as I picture him on the other end of the line. The phone stops ringing and I come, wave after delicious wave pouring through me,

Still smiling, my sticky, satisfied body falls fast asleep.

Bi-Curious Female Seeking Same

BY SCARLETT FEVER

*B*i-Curious. That's what the ad had said. Bi-Curious Asian female, five foot five, twenty-four years old. Visions of Suzie Wong—long shiny blue-black hair and tight satin China-girl dresses—danced in my head. I'd been fantasizing about women for a while, occasionally skimming the columns of personal ads. Women Seeking Women. Whatever's Clever. Adventure Team. The titles made me nervous, but Bi-Curious had a sweet and sexy ring to it. It meant that she would be the same as me—twenty-four, curious, and a little scared.

Interested, but not experienced. I left a message on her voice mail, using my best come-hither voice, hoping I didn't sound silly, and went off to work.

Work is a club called the Wild Pussycat. I'm an exotic dancer. You're thinking I'd have access to all the tits and ass I could handle there, that I wouldn't have to check the ads out, but I didn't want anyone to know. Not till I knew for sure. There are a lot of girls there that go both ways, and a couple that only go with women, so I knew no one would think anything of it. It's just me, I guess. Even though I spend my nights stripping and strolling for strangers, I like to keep some part of me private. A girl's gotta have some mystery about her, and this stuff was all still a mystery to me. I love being with men—I wouldn't be working here if I didn't—but I had to know what was going on with the sisters.

Something shifted inside me after I made that call. It was apparent once I started dancing that something had changed. Usually, I just sway to the beat, do my routines, make some tips, flirt a little—but that night was different. After leaving the message for my Oriental princess, my mind started working overtime. I had visions, visitations, and all kinds of excitations. Every roll of my hips got me hotter. The fabric of my G-string rubbed against my swelling clit. I couldn't keep my hands off myself.

My nipples were hard, my skin tight and tingly. Everyone could see how wet I was getting whenever I spread my legs. Just thinking about what could happen between us was threatening to get me off. I didn't want to climax on-stage, with everybody looking. Luckily, the music for my set came to an end just when I thought I couldn't stand it anymore. If I couldn't be alone and finish myself off, I thought I'd explode. I left the stage and went directly to the dressing rooms in the back. I knew they'd be empty by now; almost all the girls were either grinding onstage or grinding on a customer. I closed the door behind me, threw myself down on the velvet couch in front of the mirror, and tried to catch my breath. It was shallow and rapid. I was panting like an animal. There were small beads of sweat around my hairline.

Stray blond hairs were matted to my flushed face. I stared into the brown velvet of my eyes and wondered if this is what my cat felt like when she was in heat—desperate for release.

"Where the hell did that come from?" Damn, I forgot to lock the door behind me. I looked up to see where the silky voice was coming from. It was Cherry—Wild Cherry, she called herself. The lanky twenty-seven-year-old red-haired Texan dropped down next to me on the couch. She'd just started working there a couple of weeks ago. We'd gone for breakfast after work once or twice when she was mad at her boyfriend, but we weren't really close. The lights around the mirror twinkled off the silver sequins of her costume.

"You've never danced like that before. You looked great, darlin'. Looked just like you were . . . well, hell's bells, Starr, you're still lookin' all worked up." Her drawl killed me. She moved closer, wiping the beads of sweat from my forehead with a soft white towel. Her face was just inches from mine. Her skin was flawless, even this close. The sequins on her bra brushed painfully across my swollen nipples. I didn't mind, but it made my frustration worse. I tried not to look into those big emerald eyes, tried to ignore that waterfall of soft red ringlets cascading past her shoulders, just brushing the tops of her tits.

I tried not to inhale her smell—it was somewhere between musk and cinnamon, and it was making me dizzy. Her bottom lip was the kind I think of whenever I hear someone talk about pouty lips, the kind you want to bite. I wanted to bite it. I wanted to taste her, to smell her, to touch her. No, I thought. No. Not at work. I looked away from her, into the only other place to look, the mirror. It didn't help. She kept toweling me off, and I watched.

"Tell mama what the matter is, sugar," she murmured. She pressed the soft towel slowly against the back of my neck, dipping it in cool water, pressing it against my back, down my spine, massaging my neck with her other hand. I began to suspect I was no longer in control.

"I'm . . . Cherry, I just . . . kinda . . . lost control out there, I guess. I don't usually get excited onstage. I guess my mind was elsewhere tonight." I wanted her to go. I wanted her to stay. I didn't think I could wait any longer. I needed to touch myself, I needed someone to touch me. Cherry didn't seem to be going anywhere. I decided to tell her the truth—honesty being the best policy and all that. I don't know what ever made me think that.

"Look, Cherry, I made this call tonight. I answered this personal ad." She just stared at me in the mirror, listening and rubbing my neck. She was behind me now, spoon fashion. I watched her hands on my shoulders and felt the heat of her long, muscular thighs next to mine. I was going to have to spell it out.

"It wasn't a guy's ad. It was a chick. I've never done that before. Been with a girl, I mean, or answered an ad, for that matter. I was curious. I guess the anticipation was more than I expected it to be." She nodded and kept rubbing my shoulders. I was still horny as hell, but a lot less freaked out about it.

"So, you haven't met this little honey yet?" she purred into my ear. I shook my head no and watched in the mirror as she slowly lowered her head and kissed me on the neck. Her hands had never stopped, and now they were moving down my back, where I couldn't see them anymore, but I could feel them.

"And this little dumplin'—has she ever been with a woman before?"

I shook my head as her hands snaked around and

cupped my breasts. My nipples were still hard, and getting harder.

"Well, you cain't have that, Starr. That's like two virgins rollin' around on the floor. Nobody knowin' what's going on or what goes where. It's my duty to help y'all out here. Jes' relax now, and when something feels good you jes' try and remember it for this little darlin'. Remember, pay attention, there'll be a quiz at the end."

Trouble was, everything was feeling good. I knew I'd have no trouble remembering any of it. I got to feel it and watch it all at the same time. I watched her long fingers trace their way around my breasts. Her dark red nails made their way to my nipples, gently tugging and pinching them. I arched my back and leaned into her, her huge Texan titties making a perfect cushion. I turned my head and kissed her mouth. There was no stopping now.

We both slid down on the couch, the lush red velvet caressing my back, while Cherry's soft mouth caressed my front, sucking hungrily on my nipples. I couldn't wait. I needed it now. My hand went down between my legs, rubbing myself, my swollen clit. She pushed my hand away. "No, Starr, sugar, that's not how you play this game. You cain't touch yourself. Only I can do that. And you're the only one here who can touch me." She took my hand and brought it up to her breast.

"Touch me, Starr, touch me all over." Her breasts were smooth and soft, both of them free now from the silver-sequined bra. She slid up to me. We were face to face, titty to titty, and pussy to pussy. We lay side by side, and her tits made my hands look delicate. They felt heavy, like ripe fruit. I wondered if that's what mine felt like to her, only smaller. But I was beyond speech at this point. I could only follow her instructions and my own instincts. My instincts said, *Taste her. She smells good. She feels good. Taste her.* I bent my head and filled my mouth with her hard pink nipple, rolled it around in my mouth, tickled it with my tongue, the way I like it when guys do it to me. Cherry stroked my hair, moaning and pulling me closer to her. Our legs entwined, each of us riding the other one's thigh. The friction was killing me. Our hands traveled all over, exploring each other's hidden caves and curves. I ran my hand down to the curve of her ass and marveled at the perfect roundness of it. Her long legs wound around me and drew me to her. Her fingers found their way into my G-string, which promptly came untied and found its way to the floor. Her tongue tasted sweet and filled my mouth. We covered each other in warm, wet, desperate kisses. I was hungry and she fed me. We fed off each other.

She slipped two fingers into my soaking wet pussy, pushed them all the way in, teasing my clit with her thumb. My whole body went icy cold, then hot. Then the floor fell out from under me. I started pumping my hips. The wave was coming, my breathing sped up, my hips hit third gear. "Ohhh. Not yet, little sister. Not yet. Slow down, Starr." Cherry slid herself down my body, sucking and licking and tickling every spot she passed until she got to my steaming pussy. She spread my legs apart, and ran her tongue from the bottom to the top of my pussy. She flicked my clit back and forth with her serpent tongue. She thrust her tongue deeper and deeper into me, one hand squeezing my ass, her fingers worming in and out of my pussy. It felt like there were three different people working on me. I felt the wave come rolling in again. This time there was no waiting. The cold spasm hit my body and I rode the wave in. I was all pins and needles, juices flowing, muscles pulsing.

Cherry's face was buried deep inside me, lapping up the nectar until the flow subsided.

Spent, I dropped deeper into the couch and let the gentle aftershocks rock me slowly. I looked down at one very pleased-with-herself Texas ranger.

"So, darlin' . . . find anything you like?" My Texas teacher grinned at me, her face shiny with my juices. I held my arms out to her and she crawled up into them. I kissed her and tasted the salt that was me on her lips. I slid my hand down between her waiting legs. It was warm. It was wet. It was my turn to show what I'd learned.

Needless to say, I went home with the taste of Wild Cherry on my tongue and an A-plus in Bi-Curious 101. And when my personal-ad honey calls, she gets to play teacher's pet!

Double My Pleasure on a Double-Decker

BY S. PITTSBERG

*A*lthough it was my third trip to London, I still got as giddy as a virgin tourist when I rode the double-decker buses. I had spent a lovely evening at a jazz club in Covent Garden and was waiting in Trafalgar Square for the infrequent night bus that would take me back to my hotel. There were other people at the bus stop also, mostly tourists speaking a plethora of European languages. When the number 29 bus finally arrived, only two of us got on it: me and a handsome Italian who quickly kissed his friends on both cheeks as he left them at the bus stop.

I headed straight up to the top level of the bus and found it empty. I made my way down the aisle and took a seat in the front row, where I had the best view of late-night London from my perch.

The ticket-taker came upstairs a few minutes later to collect my fare. She spoke with a lovely Caribbean accent and, as there weren't any other customers, she was very chatty when I handed her my money.

"Where are you from, with that broad American accent?" She smiled as she gave me my ticket.

"I'm from Boston—I'm over here for a month to use the British Library. I'm a researcher, and a very curious person. Come sit down here and tell me about your work!"

I watched her shake her head slightly and knew that she was thinking, Oh, these cheeky Americans! She grinned and answered, "Well, maybe a bit later, but right now I've got to go back downstairs."

When I twisted around to watch her make her way down the aisle, I noticed that the young Italian fellow was sitting a seat or two behind me. He caught my eye, smiled, and then moved up to the front row also, but on the other side of the aisle. I stared out the window, and soon realized that if I looked in the glass at a certain angle I could see the Italian clearly. I alternated between watching the view and watching him watching the view.

I got the idea, since we were all alone on the top deck of the bus and since he was so cute, to be a little naughty. I began to fantasize about making it with him, and started to open up the buttons of my blouse. I reached inside with one hand and began fingering my nipple, happy that I was not wearing a bra. I played with my other nipple and then began rotating the palm of my hand more firmly around my bosom. All this time I was staring straight out my window, but when I snuck a glance at his reflection, the Italian seemed to be happily ignorant of my show as he admired the London night scene.

I decided to up the ante, so I let my blouse slip down my shoulders and gently began raising my skirt. With one relentless hand still on my nipples, I slipped a couple of fingers of the other inside the elastic of what the English call my knickers. I had never done such a thing in my life—at least not in public. But being in another country where no one knew me gave me the courage to act out fantasies I would otherwise have kept well within the realm of imagination.

As I massaged my labia, I used my other hand to alternate between my tits, grabbing up as much flesh as possible and squeezing almost to the point of pain. The situation was making me very hot, but every time I glanced in the mirrorlike window toward my neighbor, he seemed not to be noticing. As I slouched a bit in my seat to gain better access to my pussy, I got a fuller view of the Italian. And then I saw that he had an erection straining against his jeans!

The idea that he was surreptitiously watching me with excitement caused me to get really wet. My fingers slid around my cunt with ease, and I could not resist pressing my clitoris rhythmically. Nor could I help turning my head and looking directly at him. The moment I did, he swung around to look in my eyes. He smiled like a knowing collaborator, and then leaned forward to look me up and down. When his eyes returned to mine, he was no longer smiling. His breathing had become as labored as my own.

I slipped a finger inside my vagina, and he seemed to know that I was climbing to a higher level of titillation. His own hand rubbed over the bulbous bulge in his crotch, fingers curling around the shaft. Suddenly, he unzipped his fly and pulled out his amazingly long, thin dick. Although he curled both hands around it, the head was still uncovered. The wet tip caught some light as we passed a street lamp and the sparkle reflected back to me like fireworks on the Fourth of July.

By this time I had three fingers inside myself and had moved my other hand down from my breast to my clit. I was like a glutton, both hands stuffed under my skirt, inside opposite ends of my panties. I turned in his direction and stretched my legs out on the seat toward him as I leaned against the sidewall. His eyes were glued to my crotch as he used both hands to pump on his long tool.

He propped one leg on the seat so that he was facing me, and pointed his long lengthy staff toward my breasts. Instinctively, I looked down to where his moist prick seemed to point. My tits felt like they were straining toward his dick, so I took my hand temporarily away from my clit in order to scoop my hungry breasts out of the confines of my silky blouse. Freed, they seemed to swell in the direction of his shiny cock head, the nipples hard and straining.

A subtle smile passed over his lips and he began moving his dick back and forth, as if he were massaging my tender nipples across the distance between our seats. My hand lingered for a moment on my fleshy breasts before returning to flick my clit in a rhythm that matched his.

I felt so lewd that I was out of control. I wondered what my colleagues at the British Library would think if they could see me like this instead of hunched over books. Surprising myself with my own kinkiness, I whipped off my undies and tossed them in his direction. He caught them, wrapped them around the head and the shaft of his dick, and began wanking at an astounding speed. I tried to match him by vibrating my finger on my clit and fucking myself with my fingers. Just as he came with an incomprehensible moaning tirade in Italian, soaking up his come in my panties, I felt my body overcome with the shudders of an orgasmic release.

"Honey," I heard someone say in a Jamaican accent, "that was a show to behold." The ticket-taker was standing over me in the aisle. "I think I'll take up your offer to join you now." She lowered to her knees, facing my cunt, and spread my legs. Before I even had time to feel embarrassed by her presence, she began nibbling up one side of my calf and then did the same to the other leg. She tickled my thighs and I found myself trembling on the verge of another orgasm, without her ever approaching my love button.

Then she pulled me toward her, buried her face in my crotch, and began to suck on my already overstimulated clit. My head was propped against the side window, and when I opened my eyes, I was amazed to see the Italian behind the ticket-taker. He had pulled his slacks down to his ankles and was slipping a condom over his lengthy tool. He lifted up the skirt of her uniform and knelt behind her. He seemed to be running the head of his prick back and forth along her slit. The beautiful woman moaned, and for a minute stopped her attentions to my cunt. I pumped up and down involuntarily, in frantic need for her to continue. From behind her, he pushed her head back down into my dripping pussy, then caught my eye and smiled conspiratorially.

Staring directly into my eyes, he entered her with one strong smooth movement. He began to fuck her, and each time he thrust, it knocked her teeth against my clit. The pleasure was like nothing I had ever experienced. I kept my eyes on him, and somehow I felt like he was fucking me. His movements were so clearly transmitted through her mouth to my cunt. I had never kept my eyes open before, but I was transfixed. The ticket-taker had stopped licking me and, between her moans and grunts, was knocking against me with her chin. The way her chin banged my clit before sliding into my hole was causing me an unbelievable sensation.

Meanwhile, she reached up for my exposed breasts. She grabbed one in each strong hand, and every time he rammed into her for full penetration, she clutched my tits roughly as if they were a sensuous anchor. I felt like my whole body was experiencing his thrusts.

Aware of my heightened arousal, he increased his speed, plowing her from the rear so that she was jarring my crotch with greater speed and power. I nodded to him, *Yes, yes, yes,* and he grabbed her hips and began a violent pounding. Communicated to my pussy, it quickly brought me to the edge, and I cried out with orgasmic joy. As I did, he closed his eyes and I knew he was coming. He fell on her back, pumping as he came, and reached around to massage her clitoris. As he stroked her love organ, she made some staccato moans—muffled under my skirt—and then collapsed in between my legs.

There was silence for a few moments, then the Italian stood up, pulled up his pants, and, in a gentlemanly gesture, helped the bus lady to her feet. He smoothed down her skirt in an affectionate way, and she held on to him as she tried to steady her shaking body. She looked at him, probably for the first time, and then kissed him on the cheek. She leaned over to me and kissed me on the lips, deeply, her probing tongue electric in my mouth. "Boston," she said, smiling, "you can ride my bus anytime!"

After she made her wobbly way down the aisle, the Italian turned to me. "I believe these belong to you?" He held up my sticky knickers and we both laughed.

"I get off in a couple of stops," he told me. "Would you do me the honor of accompanying me?"

I looked toward the back of the ticket-taker as she descended to the first floor of the bus. "No," I answered. "Since I missed my stop long ago, I think I'll go on to the end of the line."

The Baby-Sitter

BY MARTHA MILLER

*D*an had been fucking the baby-sitter all winter. Cory was suspicious the first time she met the blond-haired, blue-eyed graduate student from Kansas. Dan told Cory that Heather needed to supplement her income while she wrote her thesis, and that she loved children. Cory noticed that their nine-year-old, Jamey, didn't get along with Heather any better than he got along with his father. When Dan wouldn't offer an explanation for the time away from home and his lack of interest in their sex life, Cory made excuses for him. She decided he was depressed about his fortieth birthday, the new head of the English department, and Cory's recent five-pound weight gain. Then, on a Tuesday night in April, Cory returned early from a faculty wives' dinner. When she entered the living room, she discovered Dan on his knees in front of her favorite chair, his face buried between the baby-sitter's thighs.

Cory cleared her throat, "Um—excuse me?"

Heather looked at her and smiled weakly. Dan obviously hadn't heard. Heather tried to gently push his head away. Dan moaned and attacked his feast more vigorously. Heather lay her head back on the chair and shrugged, as if to say, *What can I do about it?*

"Dan!" Cory's voice had a strange high pitch. He didn't budge. Finally she sighed and asked Heather, "Where's Jamey?"

"He went to Michael's to play Nintendo," Heather answered in a slightly shaky voice. "I told him to be home by nine."

"Did you say something, sweet pea?" Dan finally raised his head and looked at Heather.

Heather pointed at Cory.

Dan's chin and cheeks were glistening in the light from the TV. "Home early?"

"I—I had a headache," Cory started to explain.

"Heather, maybe I should take you home," Dan said.

"I'll take her home," Cory interrupted.

Only then did Heather pull her legs together and stand. She brushed her skirt into place and gathered her things. The long drive back to the campus was tense, and thankfully silent. When they reached the sorority house, Heather turned to Cory and said, "Listen, no charge tonight, okay?"

Cory felt a weight on her chest. Her breathing was slow, labored. "How long has this been going on?"

Heather looked at the ground. "It started last January, I guess. I'm sorry. It's over now, honest."

During the drive home, with the headache buzzing between her ears, Cory weighed her options. A divorce right now was out of the question. She could go home to her mother for a few days, but then she'd have to listen to her I-told-you-so's. There were the payments on the bedroom furniture and the roof on the garage. She thought about Jamey. What would a separation do to him? This wasn't

Dan's first infidelity. Actually, he'd been cheating on his first wife when he started dating Cory. Back then, she had been the enthralled student. . . .

That night, Dan begged her forgiveness. She cried. He held her, stroked her hair, then slowly and gently made love to her. His erection was huge. He was more excited than she'd seen him for a long time. Her headache dulled while the rest of her body responded intensely. As she came for the third time, she closed her eyes and saw Dan, on his knees in front of her favorite chair, eating the baby-sitter. It pushed her over the edge, then and in the months that followed, in a way none of her other fantasies could.

Cory used all her resources to find a new sitter. She placed an ad in the newspaper, checked agencies, put notes on Laundromat bulletin boards, and asked her friends.

Finally, Marsha Endeley said, "I know a student you might like better."

"Another student?" Cory sighed.

Marsha nodded. "She's nothing like Heather."

"What's her name?"

Lisa Monette was five foot ten, weighed close to two hundred pounds, had a Mohawk haircut and wore six earrings in each ear. She owned a motorcycle, though it was broken-down most of the time. Her eyes were black, and her skin was dark. Dan smiled cordially when he met her, then he looked at Cory with a frown, and she knew she'd made the right choice.

Jamey loved Lisa. She owned her own joystick. Over the course of the summer she taught Jamey to catch a pop fly, and to bat without closing his eyes. Eventually, she started showing up at his Little League games, at Jamey's invitation.

Cory was uncomfortable about it at first, but she pushed the feeling away. Every time Jamey was at bat, Lisa hollered and clapped. "Get 'em, Jamey. Knock it out of the park!"

One afternoon, Jamey connected with a ball that was high and outside. He hit it deep into center field. Lisa jumped up from her seat, yelling, "Go, Jamey, go!" Someone behind Cory took up the chant when he rounded first base and headed for second. Cory stood and hollered, "Go! Go!" Cory noticed that thanks to Lisa's lead, the entire small bunch of disinterested moms were on their feet, yelling. Jamey ran across the dusty home plate and headed toward the crowd. Cory opened her arms with pride, but he ran to Lisa.

"That's my boy!" Lisa hugged him. "What a hit!"

"Good job, Jamey," Cory said.

"Oh, Mom." Jamey embraced Cory suddenly. "I did it, Mom."

Cory ran her fingers through Jamey's damp, sweaty hair. Later that afternoon at the Dairy Queen, Jamey would ask for a Mohawk haircut. And to her own surprise, Cory seriously considered it before she said no.

It was the self-esteem seminar that finally rocked the boat. Several of the faculty wives signed up for the all-day Saturday workshop. Most of the husbands were at a meeting in Chicago and would be away all weekend.

"All day? I have a thousand things to do." Cory hesitated when Marsha brought it up.

"Do something for yourself for a change!"

"I don't know, Jamey has a game. . . ."

"Let the baby-sitter take him. Come on."

It did turn out to be a nice Saturday, away from everything. After a long lecture, the women sat in a circle and talked about what they would change if they had higher self-esteem. That was when the woman next to Cory said softly, "If I felt better about myself, I would divorce my husband. He's been screwing around for years." The woman started to cry. Cory scooted closer and put her arm around her shoulders. She thought about the night she walked in on Dan eating the baby-sitter. She blinked back her own tears.

After the session, Cory refused a dinner invitation from Marsha, and slowly drove home.

Lisa's motorcycle was standing in the driveway. The house was quiet when Cory entered. "Anybody home?" Cory called.

"In here."

Lisa was reading in Cory's favorite chair. The image flashed. Heather. Her legs spread. "Where's Jamey?" she asked.

"His grandma came and got him for a movie and dinner," Lisa answered. "They left about five o'clock. I just hung around to make sure you wouldn't worry about him."

"God, that was two hours ago. You could have left a note."

"Aw, it's all right. I'm as comfortable here as my place." Lisa smiled.

Cory's shoulders slumped.

"You look like hell, if you don't mind my saying so."

Cory's knees gave and she sat down hard on the couch. She could feel the tears starting.

Lisa came across the room and knelt beside her. "You don't look *that* bad, come on. I'm sorry."

"It's not you," Cory stammered. Lisa slid onto the couch beside her. Cory started talking. It all came out. The seminar. The woman beside her. Heather. Dan between her legs. Cory's favorite chair.

"That sucks," Lisa said softly. "Why, if I had a woman like you, I'd never look at another."

"You mean if you were a man and had a woman like me," Cory corrected her.

"No, I don't."

Cory realized that Lisa was stroking her arm. Goose bumps rose beneath her touch. "I've never cheated on Dan," Cory said softly.

Lisa whispered, "Maybe you should." Her lips were close to Cory's ear. Cory could feel Lisa's hot breath tickle her neck.

Cory leaned back, and Lisa was on her—unbuttoning her blouse and kissing her neck. Cory moaned, surrendering. Somewhere in the back of her mind she wondered who would do what and how. But her cunt was tingling. Her nipples were hard. Lisa pulled her blouse off and with one hand reached behind and unhooked her bra. Her breasts fell loose. Lisa gently clamped her mouth over one, then the other erect nipple.

"We shouldn't do it here," Cory protested.

"Why not?" Lisa slid her hand under Cory's skirt and squeezed the damp crotch of her panties.

Cory reached to help pull her panties down over her hips. She pulled one foot out and with the other kicked her underwear across the room. They landed draped across an expensive lampshade.

Lisa's hand worked slowly, sliding two fingers inside her. Cory rocked her hips, gently fucking. Each time she came down on the hand, Lisa's thumb pressed against her clit. Just as Cory thought she might come, Lisa pulled her hand away.

Cory whimpered.

Lisa replaced her fingers with her mouth.

Cory could feel the hot moist tongue wash her swollen vulva. She raised her knees, reached down, and pulled her wet lips open as far as she could.

Lisa slid two fingers back inside and fucked and sucked her slowly.

"I'm going to come!"

"Don't."

"I've got to!" Cory tried to distract herself. She thought about the housework. She thought about Jamey. She thought about the home run, the crowd cheering. A white-hot flash, like a jolt of electricity, went through her. Tingling spread through her body to the tips of her fingers and toes. Her pussy started to convulse. "Oh—oh!" she cried, pulling Lisa's head to her. She ran her fingers through the stiff Mohawk and rubbed her cunt in the woman's face as she experienced the most intense orgasm of her life. At last, gently and reluctantly, she pushed Lisa away,

"Well." Lisa smiled broadly up at Cory from between her legs. "If you've got to, you've got to."

Cory laughed. She was breathing hard. Her body felt weak, like she couldn't move. Lisa was laughing softly, too. Then they were both quiet.

It seemed like hours had passed when Lisa said, "Right there in that chair, huh?"

"Yes," Cory said softly.

"He was on his knees?"

Cory looked at her. She hadn't sat in her favorite chair for months. She'd considered throwing it away. The whole family seemed to avoid it. From somewhere far away she heard her own voice saying, "Take off your pants and get over there in that chair."

Let It Rain

BY BLAKE C. AARENS

*I*t is a wet and sloppy San Francisco day. The rain comes in gushing downpours, followed by stillness and silence as the clouds part like the legs of a ready lover, and the hot ball of the sun blazes through. I sit in an aisle seat, on the bus, my dripping umbrella next to me. I wear dark shades; I want to be left alone.

That is, until *he* gets on.

Tall enough that the top of his head grazes the ceiling of the bus. The weight of the pack on his back pulls at his shoulders. He balances a stack of books against the front of his body. His big hands cup the bottom volume; his elbows lock to keep them in line. His glasses slip down his nose.

In my haste to make room for him, I forget the wet and slide into the inner seat. Instantly I am soaked through—jacket, skirt, panties even.

He lowers himself into the vacated seat, lowers the books to the tops of his pressed-together feet. His knees gape open to straddle the stacks of books. With one hand to balance the stack, he shrugs out of the backpack, with apologetic glances at me for all the accidental bumps against my breasts. Finally, he wrestles himself free. Setting the pack on top of the books, he sighs and sits back. Even relaxed, the muscles of his arms and chest strain the fabric of his rain-streaked button-down shirt. Brawn and bookishness—just my type.

"Student?" I ask as I notice a line of pale skin on the third finger of his left hand.

A quicksilver grin flashes across his face. He shakes his head no. "I got kinda carried away with my library card."

I smile. "No TV?"

He answers a quick "She took it," a little whine in his voice like that of an angry boy.

I place my hand on his leg. The tremble in his body tells me how hungry he is. I decide to feed this man.

"What are you reading?" I ask. I pull his left leg toward me, widening the gap between his knees. He lets me. I check out the stack of books. Robert Heinlein, D. H. Lawrence, Anaïs Nin, Anne Rice.

"You like to read out loud." It isn't a question.

He gulps. Nods.

"Wanna read to me?" My voice is little more than a whisper, and he ducks his head down and leans in to catch my words. In that posture he reaches for the first book on top of the stack, slides it out from under the backpack. *The Moon Is a Harsh Mistress.* He opens to the first page, and I place my hand over the words.

"Not here."

"Oh. Okay." He speaks like a man in a dream.

The ride to his apartment is bumpy and quick, a minor detail to be disposed of in order to get on to the more important business at hand. He unlocks the door and then steps aside to usher me in. It is a studio apartment with hardwood floors, ten-foot ceilings, and an entire wall of windows. One of them is thrown wide open to the rain; I can smell how wet it is outside. The clouds are still dumping. It takes effort to turn away from the fury of the storm, from the scent of it. A sturdy ladder leads up to a sleeping nook. The bed looks like a huge nest.

"Uh—what should I read?" He is standing behind me. I don't turn around, just feel him there, his irregular breath warm on my neck.

"Pick two," I say, "and follow me."

I hear him swallow hard as I head for that huge, inviting bed. I wait until he is again standing behind me before climbing the ladder. I want to give him the chance to look up my skirt as I climb. He does me one better; he climbs faster than I do and ducks his head under my skirt and nuzzles the cheeks of my ass. I can feel the stubble on his face through the thin fabric of my damp panties. I leap onto the bed. He climbs up after me, two books spreading wide the fingers of his left hand. *Lady Chatterley's Lover* and *Interview with the Vampire*.

I take the Anne Rice book from him and start flipping the pages.

"Are you gonna tell me your name?"

I shake my head over the top of the book and don't look at him.

"So this is gonna be one time only?"

"Depends on how well you read." I hand him the open book and lie back on the cushions.

He reads to me of the vampire Louis stalking the night and coming upon a woman sweating over a cook-fire. The rumble of his voice shakes something loose between my legs. The sweating woman mistakes the vampire for a partygoer and directs him upstairs. He goes for her neck instead.

I groan and squirm on the bed; he stops reading.

"Liked that, did you?" he asks.

In answer to his question, I fan my skirt over my thighs as if trying to cool myself off.

"Let it get hot," he says.

"It already is."

He spreads the book facedown on the bed and cups his hand over my crotch. "Warm, but not hot yet."

"How hot does it need to be?" I ask.

He looks toward the windows. I can see his pulse in his throat, his Adam's apple twitching with each swallow. "It's awfully cold out there," he says. He's not talking about the weather.

"Come back." He only partially obeys, turning to face me again, but the look in his eyes is far away.

"Take your shirt off."

That brings him back to me. He sits back on his haunches, looks down at the mattress, chews on his lower lip. That reflexive swallow again.

"Slowly," I instruct him.

He nods. Says, "Yes."

The blunt, padded tips of his fingers are too big, and he fumbles with the tiny white buttons down his front. It takes forever for him to expose the coarse hair on his chest and the tight, puckered little nipples. His pecs are molded, his arms a series of swollen clumps of muscle leading to the big hands. He follows my line of sight and stretches his hands flat, palms up.

"What?" he says.

"Gimme those hands."

He crawls forward on the bed. "What do you want me to do with them?"

"My panties are wet."

His grin is crooked. "I hope so."

"No, no. I sat in water on the bus. They're soaked. Will you help me out of them?"

He says, "Okay," but doesn't move toward me.

"Want me to?" I reach under my skirt and lift my ass off the bed.

He puts one of those big hands on my belly to stop me. He looks at my crotch, at my tits, at my mouth. When he reaches my eyes, he looks back down. "It's been a while," he says.

"And you're hungry."

His inhalation is a sharp catching of breath. His body twitches again. I can see his erection. It's straining straight up and making his zipper bulge out. He grabs at it and squeezes. Hard. He clenches his teeth and exhales through his nose.

I raise my ass off the bed again, and flip my skirt up on my belly. I wait for it, for the first touch of those hands on my bare skin. When it comes, it's terribly gentle. My pussy clenches. He rolls my panties down my legs with such deliberateness. I lower my bottom; raise my feet. He pulls the damp fabric the rest of the way off, grasps my ankles, and spreads my legs as far apart as they will go.

His face is inches from my pussy. He inhales deeply and closes his eyes. Now it's his turn to groan and squirm.

Suddenly, he lets my feet go. He rips his pants off. He's not wearing underwear. His cock points up at the ceiling between us, at the roof that's being beaten by the rain.

He stretches his body over mine, reaches over my

head. It takes him a long time to find whatever it is he's looking for. I rub my face in his chest hair.

When he sits back, he's already ripping the wrapper of the condom with his teeth. I raise up on my elbows and watch him put it on. Watch him hold the head of his cock with the fingers of his left hand and roll the rubber down with his right. He kneels like that for a moment, pinching the head and letting it pulse back against his fingertips.

He grips my ankles in his big hands again, arches his back, and guides his cock into me with just the action of his hips. I know this man is gonna rock me. I reach behind my head for something to grab hold of. Something to anchor me so I can move against him.

I feel my pussy start to spread open, start to suck him inside. He moves just a little—that beginning ache and spread and throb. He looks down at the juncture of our bodies, amazed at his own control.

"Can I?" he asks, his voice tight and high like his cock.

"I think you'd better," I say.

And he does. Pushing hard into me, filling my pussy, pinning me to the bed, and bouncing me up off it when he pulls out. Almost all the way. Long strokes. Hard. To the depths of me, and back. Keeping up a relentless rhythm in time to the pouring rain.

"Bring your legs together," I say.

When he does, the angle shifts, and the mound of his pelvis bumps against my clit. A tickle and a tease. My own orgasm starts to build, but it's not enough.

"I wanna roll over."

"Yeah." He stops moving in me then. Pulls back. Lets my ankles go. I spin around on his cock, without dislodging him, until I'm on all fours. He grabs hold of my hips, and with the leverage he finds there begins to thrust and thrust and thrust. I reach up to touch myself, to touch both of us. My pussy lips are all slick and swollen. I raise up so he's fucking up into me. I cup his balls in my left hand, squeeze my clit between two fingers of my right.

He is grunting now, and the push between us expels the air from my lungs. A shudder of pleasure passes through my body, from the soles of my feet to the crown of my head. He pulls out of me, quick. My pussy is bereft. I lower myself, trying to find him again. He slides between my pussy lips, against me, not inside. The head of his cock finding the hard knot of my clit again and again. I press my hand against him to keep him in the right place.

"I am so close. I'm gonna come so hard."

"Tell me when it starts," he whispers in my ear.

The wail that is the voice of my orgasm erupts from me. I couldn't stop it if I wanted to. And I don't want to.

He pushes back into me, spreading open my clenching muscles, and I go over the edge. He wraps his arms tight about my waist, buries his head in the crook of my neck, and comes. I can feel the pulse of his cock, the shock of pleasure as he moves his hands up to cup my breasts and pinch my nipples hard.

Slowly our breathing synchronizes. He lowers me to the bed and stretches his body out on top of me. He kisses the sweat at the nape of my neck and tells me what a sweet pussy I have.

Watching Back

BY GABRIELLE IDLET

I have never liked pretty boys. My neighbor Jack is no exception. He has that polished, varsity look, like life has stroked him smoothly, evened out his edges. Worse still, he has woken me many times hosting late-night parties for gangs of college jocks. Someone inevitably pisses on my mailbox or falls asleep along a row of my freshly planted bulbs. I wake to roars of laughter and fragments of conversation about women's bodies. "Tits," I heard them scream last month. "Tits, show us your tits!" And I looked out my window in time to see a frail woman being passed over the heads of the partygoers in Jack's backyard. Although she wriggled and winced with anxiety, she pulled off her shirt to reveal a black push-up bra. "Not your bra, baby, your tits," someone called, but the woman drew the line there, and was allowed down after much begging and squirming in the air.

My straight girlfriends frequently remark how handsome Jack is when they see him shooting baskets against his garage. I challenge them on it, describing what I've

130

seen of his ugly lifestyle. It never seems to matter, though. People drift into fantasy watching beauty from a distance.

Despite my disgust, Jack interests me. Perhaps this is only because his bedroom window faces mine, just a bit higher on the hill. Jack closes his blinds most of the time. I never close mine. I took my curtains down at first because I hate to feel closed in. I enjoy the night sky, the moon; I like to wake up to the sun on weekends. I've since realized there is a second benefit to stripping my window: I can give Jack an education. That is, like the public-school system, I can offer it to him for free, and he can do with it what he chooses.

Martha will be visiting from New York. She's a friend from college, a tall woman with short blond hair who works as a botanist and carries herself like James Dean. Martha and I always make love when she comes to town, then catch up on old times and mock jealously at each other's more serious romances. Ultimately, she's a friend, not a lover. But I've never been able to keep my hands off her.

The night Martha arrives, I spot Jack early on. He glances out at us, then ducks behind the molding to switch off his light. He seems to feel invisible with his room darkened. But the light from my nightstand falls across him, and I can see his expression as he sits down on his mattress to watch.

Martha drops her leather jacket on the chair near the bathroom, then corners me against the closed closet door. I haven't had sex with anyone in going on eight months, and so I press against her with more greed than usual. I yank the hem of her T-shirt out of the rear of her jeans, run my nails up her back, then unclasp her bra in the same gesture I use backward on myself undressing at night. Only now the familiar motion is charged: The faster I pull her bra off, the faster I'll have one of her pale, full breasts in my mouth. She lets me push her away just far enough to pull everything off her upper body. I see Jack leaning closer to the windowpane.

Martha begins to break a fine sweat, as she does when she gets excited. I ask her, "How was your flight?" as I bend to kiss her navel. She gasps and her pelvis leaps toward me involuntarily, then she straightens and pulls open the buttons of her jeans. No underwear—just that gorgeous thatch of sandy-brown hair, straight as the hair on her head, in a dense V. It travels in a line up her belly, even sprouts loose strands around her nipples and in the crease of her chest.

I tug her jeans down to her knees and blow on her shining slit just long enough to make her lurch again. I want her unbearably wet a few minutes from now. But my body can't tolerate skipping over her breasts. I stand up, still fully clothed, and turn her around by the shoulders so that she's pressed against the wall and on full display. I don't want to interrupt Martha's passion by pointing Jack out, but she and I have had public sex a number of times— in cars, in parks at night, once on the roof of her dorm, and many times before windows. She has described how aroused she can get thinking someone might see her. Anyway, she's naked now, fully lit, and aware at least that she is facing a wide, blank windowpane, about to have her breasts sucked by a thirsty friend.

I lean into her, take the white skin of her right breast between my lips gently, surrounding but not quite touching the areola. She moans quietly, and I feel her legs strain to open against the jeans that hold her fast at the knees. I like the idea that she wants slightly more freedom than she can have just yet, as her pussy gets wetter and hotter.

I open my mouth wide and suck as much of her breast as I can. Then I let a little slip back out so I can focus on her tiny peach-toned nipple, by now hard as a pearl. I squeeze her other tit, flicking its nipple gently with my fingertip, while I suck and lick this one. In a minute she's rocking against me and reaching for her cunt with a clumsy, wild hand. A pulse starts in my crotch as Martha begins to jack herself off, thrumming her clit with her thumb while jamming three or four long fingers at a time into her hole. When her breath catches and she lets out a rough groan, I decide it's time to take things into my own hands.

Martha is big and broad, and though I'm stockier than she, I enjoy the leading role sometimes when we fuck. Frequently, she pushes me away and takes over, but this time I think she's enjoying my intensity. My hunger comes not only from an absence of sex. Knowing that Jack is watching—and that at this point he must have a rock-hard cock—makes me wetter still.

I pull Martha onto my bed, which is angled—truly by accident—so that Jack can see us completely. The lamplight falls across Martha's belly and hips, and sparkles on her wet mound. I pull her jeans all the way off now, remove her shoes and socks, then push her legs apart with my knees, so that I sway above her. I kiss her briefly, lick her tongue with my own. "There was turbulence," she says.

"What?"

"You asked how my flight was. There was turbulence." She laughs to herself. I close my eyes, take a breath, run my tongue from the bottom of her throat down the center of her body all the way into her cunt. She sighs loudly. I readjust so that I will be able to eat her for a while without straining my back. I can see Jack this way, off to the right. I suck in air. He has his pants down and is stroking his penis slowly, watching us with dazed eyes. He spits into his free hand, then smooths the wetness over his cock, repeating the move several times so that the thing begins to shine. Perhaps we look like his late-night cable porn, I imagine, or some dirty movie he'd watch with the guys from the team. I like being clothed for this show. Even my audience is stripping.

I stick my tongue deep into Martha's hole. She releases a breathy "Aaah." I pull it out, then push it in again, pressing especially hard against the top of the opening, which always gets her squirming. She assures me she has a G spot, and that that's where it is, though I haven't found a parallel place on my own body. I take her word for it. I lick her awhile there, with considerable force, glancing occasionally at Jack across the way. He's milking himself a bit faster now. His face holds the faintest suggestion of a grimace, as if he were trying to take a troublesome crap.

I decide time is running out, and I want him to see Martha come before he climaxes. So I move up to her clit, gently tonguing it before clamping down with my lips to spread her inner labia apart. She groans louder now. I place some fingers inside her, just to keep her warm and filled, then set to work licking her clit as rhythmically as I can. I manage to stretch the hood of her clitoris wide with my own mouth, so that my tongue's path rubs against the buried center there, where she is most sensitive.

Her genitals have swollen huge, her bulbous clit fluttering each time my tongue brushes against it. She is moaning loud enough that Jack must be able to hear her. I peek his way and see that he's pumping his dick furiously, biting his lower lip, watching us—almost glaring at us.

Martha's voice begins to crack, like a grinding machine. She is getting close. Still licking hard, I look up her trembling torso to her face, which is twisted with the pain of yearning, not too different from Jack's. I get wet for her in a hot gush, and find myself tunneling my fingers in and out of her pussy so that my roughest skin works against that G spot. She calls out, with a hoarse sort of howl, and her vagina squeezes against my fingers like a clenching fist. I lick her with all the strength that my tiring jaw has held in reserve, flicking the tip of my tongue over that pulled-taut clitoris in sharp, vibrating strokes. She howls again. I purse my lips and suck her clit now as hard as I can, pulling the small length of it all the way into my mouth over and over. Her cunt contracts faster, until it's a steady, pulsing shudder.

"Fuck me now, just fuck me," she whispers hoarsely, pushing my face away. I sit back a bit and shove my fingers in and out of her slippery opening. She's gone, breathing hard, eyes closed, letting out loose short breaths like a woman giving birth.

Now I look at Jack. This time, I stare directly at him. And I smile a wide smile. He is on the verge. When our gazes meet, his eyes bulge, horrified. He scowls and shakes his head as if to urge me to look away. But I've caught him too close to coming for him to stop now. His cock is slick with precome and he keeps working it with a blurred hand. He has his other forearm twisted under a buttock. He must be screwing himself in the ass with a finger—or maybe, I speculate, a secret dildo.

His face twists like a rag, then collapses with a silent roar as he shoots against the windowpane. His head snaps back, he shoots again, then falls out of view onto the bed. I look down at Martha, who's drifted into semiconscious-ness, with me slowly fucking her to sleep. Jet lag, I guess. I look back to my neighbor. Jack has disappeared. *My God,*

I think, *did I embarrass him? I mean, did I truly mortify him, this nice college boy? I bet he's in the john throwing up because some dyke saw him come.*

He doesn't return to his bedroom tonight, from what I can see. I turn off my light before undressing, then nudge Martha over and climb in beside her. As I drift into the vague state between day and dream, I picture Jack in some future circle jerk with a group of buddies, watching naked women on TV. Jack gets up wordlessly to change the channel, because he is plagued by an irrational fear that the women on the screen might actually be watching back.

Virtue Is
Its Own Reward

BY TSAURAH LITZKY

*D*id you ever do it before, Owen?" I asked him as I climbed on top.

"Oh, yeah, many times," he said, but I did not believe him; the down on his face was as soft as a flower and his body hair was so spare, just a feathery plume or two on his chest and no genital hair at all. But his rosy mouth excited me, and his limp pink cock was thick, longer than my hand, and promised much pleasure if only I could get it to stand to attention. He shimmied beneath me like a nervous fish as I stroked his cock up and down with my wet slit. Last night he told me I had lovely eyes, but he pronounced it "luuve-lee," having just come up from Louisiana to work in his brother's Cajun seafood restaurant; and lovely in my panties was what I thought he would be, but now in my bed he was hesitant, tremulous, scared, a young cock who didn't know what to do with me. I should have known better, but how I love my foolish pleasure.

All the time he had sat at the bar and sipped his Guinness his eyes had played with my big, D-cup tits, but now with them hanging just above him he was too shy to touch them. I put my hands beneath their heaviness, hefted them, made them shake and dance a jig. I lowered a big, brown nipple to his face and brushed it back and forth across his rosebud lips as I kept slowly stroking his cock up and down with my wet slit. He started to thrash and moan. "Oh, mother," he said, "oh, mother," which was not what I wanted to hear, but I was so hungry for it I would have fucked him if he called me Michael or Gregory. I lowered my head, covered my teeth with my lips so as not to bite, and sucked him hard. He smelled like talcum and bread, and the more I sucked, the more the juices simmered between my legs. After a while the sap rose in him, his prick began to quiver and twist. I took a condom from the box beside the bed and peeled it out, but when I turned to sheathe him, hop astride, and ride to paradise, I saw his mouth was slack, his eyes were shut, his head lolled back— he was asleep.

No fool like an old fool, I thought, as I climbed off, went to the refrigerator, and selected a fat carrot from the stock I always keep there. I washed it and cased it in the Ramses X-tra sensitive, X-tra thin I had opened for Owen, put a generous dollop of K-Y on the tip, went into the toilet, and, seated on the throne, made myself come three times and then one more time as a prayer for a better-luck next fuck. When I got into bed, I poked Owen several times in a nasty fashion, but he did not move, his snoring echoing through the room. I lay down beside him and tried to remember the names of all the lovers I had taken that I had picked up in bars. I remembered thirteen and then drifted off to sleep.

I was awakened by a flurry of soft kisses around my neck and on my shoulders. It was still dark outside. I

turned to Owen, returned his kisses, and we cuddled together wrapped in the lap of night. Reaching down, I
found him hard. I got another Ramses from the box, slid
it on, kissed the latexed tip, rubbing it between my lips but
not taking it farther into my mouth. I teased him with my
tongue until he cried out, "Oh, oh, oh," and this time he
did not call me mother. I turned over on my back and,
seizing hold of him, pulled him on top of me, parting my
legs to let him slide in. On the first attempt he got my pee-
hole and I had to take him in hand to lead him home; he
thrust wildly three or four times and then came as fast as
an exploding rocket, leaving me forlorn on the launching
pad. Whatever virtue there might be in initiating a young,
inexperienced man, it seemed that virtue would have to be
its own reward, for I certainly was not getting any other satisfaction from young Owen.

In the morning I made coffee. I set a steaming cup before him as he sat at my kitchen table. "I was your first,
wasn't I?" I asked. I poured myself a cup of coffee and sat
down naked across from him, spreading my legs so he
could get a good look at my thick bush and the pert, pink
lips within. He blushed, averted his eyes, and denied that
he had been cherry. "Owen," I said, "you are not being
truthful, and I know you'll always remember me in a special way." He did not comment on that, just started talking
about his brother James's restaurant. I couldn't wait for
him to finish his coffee and leave, which he did sooner
than I expected because on the second sip he found a
cockroach floating in it belly up and I didn't offer to pour
him another cup. As soon as he was out the door, I turned
the shower on. I wanted to scour his ineffectual little
chicken kisses off my skin, and in the shower I started to

write a song about a cock as hard as a rock that would fuck me through millennia.

Then I drank three cups of Café Bustelo, black with four sugars, and got to work on my novel about a poet who works as a barmaid in a bar where they sell guns and cocaine, which they do not sell at Monty's, where I work (although Monty can get you a diamond or a VCR, and if you are short on money he'll lend you some at 15 percent a week). Monty has four daughters, and told me if a guy gets too fresh to always let him know. He calls me Bazooka Tits, and I don't mind—he watches over me, pays me on time. He tells the customers, "Bazooka's a writer, and one of these days she's gonna leave us when she wins the Nobel Prize."

When I go to work that night, Carlos, the bouncer, gives me what on his face passes for a grin, which means he opens his mouth and salivates. He says, "Well, how was he?" I lie and say great, then go into the bathroom and change into my work costume of black jeans, black leotard, and the padded push-up bra that makes my big tits look like watermelons. I rub some peach body oil into my cleavage and, checking myself in the mirror, think Camille Paglia is right—if you've got it, use it.

I am now ready for work, and soon I am dancing up and down behind the bar, pouring Absolut straight up and J. W. Black to secretaries with Joan Collins hairdos, red-tape brokers, water-cooler jokers, and femme fatales who work for the phone company. Monty believes in pouring with the glad hand, business is good, and soon they are lined up three deep and Monty has to step behind the bar to help me.

I am happy to be going home alone this night. I shower, dry myself with my favorite pink towel, then spread the towel on the bed, lie down on it, and coat my-self all over with cocoa butter. I love to oil my breasts until my nipples thicken and grow hard; then I get out my hash pipe, fill it, light it, and a few puffs later I want to go to Africa, I want to ride a camel across the desert, I want to be penetrated by a Berber chieftain with my back pressed into the hot sand. . . . I go to the refrigerator and get another carrot. It does not disappoint me.

I have the next three days off, and work on my book without making much headway; mostly I fart around and ask myself why I am in this world. When I go back to work, Carlos tells me someone has been looking for me. Who, I want to know. Carlos says, "I never saw him before." What does he look like? I ask. "Looks like a model in a maga-zine," says Carlos. This doesn't sound like anyone I know. I change in the john, and then Monty cashes me in.

"You look good, Bazooka," he says, "rested." Cocoa butter and carrots, I think, and say thank you.

My first customers are two Bass ales in flannel shirts, and then a couple comes in. I turn to go to the cash regis-ter and notice I am being watched by a man at the end of the bar. I wash a few glasses and observe the fine bones of his face, the broad shoulders beneath an expensive-looking leather jacket. The big hands he has placed on the bar are manicured, well kept, no wedding ring, but then the ring could be in his pocket. His blue eyes sparkle, and he is smiling right at me; there's something familiar about him, yet I can't place him. I remember what Carlos said about the guy who looks like a model, and I think this must be the one. As I walk down the bar toward him, his eyes are on my cleavage, and I lean forward to give him a better view. He orders a Guinness, and as I draw it from the tap I do this little trick of moving the glass under the spigot to form a shamrock on the foam. When I set the glass in front of him, he says, "You've put a shamrock on my Guinness."

"Maybe this is your lucky day," I say.

"Maybe," he says and smiles wider. He reaches inside his jacket and extracts a wallet made out of some strange leather I've never seen before. "What kind of leather is that?" I say.

"Stingray," he says. I think of it as some kind of exotic shark, and sleek and sure of himself as a shark is what he is as he pulls out a twenty and pushes it across the bar.

"Keep the change, girl," he says. I tell him I haven't earned such a generous tip, and that I don't want what I don't earn.

"Owen said you were a smart one," he says, and then I know why he looks familiar to me: He's Owen ten years older and ten times as tough, Owen's big brother James, come to check me out.

I give him half a smile and then take the bill. While I'm ringing it into the register, I suck in my belly and open my mouth to make hollows under my cheeks like Katharine Hepburn. Then I bring him back his change and turn without looking at him as I move down the bar, serving drinks, joking with customers, emptying ashtrays that are already empty. Maybe he fancies himself a shark and wants to chew me up, and I just might let him.

As I set down his fourth Guinness, he says, "I want to thank you properly for what you did for my little brother."

"No thanks necessary," I reply. I wonder what Owen has told him, that he fucked me five times, that he had me down on all fours begging like a dog?

Then the big brother says, "Well, then, I'd like to thank you for being so beautiful," which is when I ask him what he has in mind.

"Come back to my place after your shift and I'll cook for you."

"Will you put Guinness in the sauce?" I ask him.

"I put Guinness in all my sauces," he answers.

Later, in the taxi, he was saucy all right—he put his tongue into my mouth when he kissed me, and taking my hand, he placed it below his belt. The swelling was as thick as a Campbell's soup can and I hoped it wasn't a trick, like some sort of inflatable prosthesis. He put his hand inside the waistband of my leggings and reached south until his fingers found my other mouth and fed me some sugar. The cabby was driving with one hand and the other was playing in his lap as he watched us through the rearview mirror.

"Say you want it, tell me how much you want it," James said as we were riding up in the elevator. He had one hand on the back of my neck, and with the other he had taken one of mine and held it cupped over that big bulge beneath his belt.

"Tell me how much you want it," he repeated, but I wanted to make him work for it, at least a little, so I said nothing.

Still holding me by the neck, he walked me out of the elevator and down the hall. He unlocked the door one-handed and pushed it open to reveal a room with white walls, black-leather-and-steel furniture, and a large, thick white rug. He pushed me down on a big leather chair, and only then did he take his hand off my neck. He pulled off my shoes and my leggings and spread my legs; his tongue was hot and rough as he licked my slit, and all the while he was holding my legs apart at the knees so I couldn't move. He found my clit and began to suck on it like a baby sucking on a tit, but just as I was about to come he stopped and stood up, leaving me wild and crazy for it. He unzipped and pulled out his cock—he had a lot to be proud of—and he stood over me, pointing it at the moist pelt between my legs.

"How do you like my big sword?" he asked. "Say you want it." But I bit my lip and said nothing.

He started to touch me with it, pulling it like a hot blade across my face, pushing it between my breasts, tapping it against my belly; then he knelt between my legs and sucked my clit so hard I came twice in a minute.

"Tell me you want it, tell me you want it," he said again, and I told him I was dying for it. Then he got up from between my legs, his cheeks wet with my cunt juice.

"Good," he said, "good," as he ripped off my sweater and bra with one swift motion. My big tits fell out, and he took one in each hand, pulling them, milking them. He led me by the nipples into the bedroom and pushed me facedown on the bed. I felt a ripple beneath me; I was not surprised to find he had a water bed.

"Spread your ass for me," he said, "spread it," and I did not try to swim away. Oh no, I put my hands on my cheeks and did what he asked. He must have liked what he saw there because he bent his head and started to rim my asshole with his tongue. He traced a circle round and round until I was squealing, yielding, and then he grabbed me by the hair and pulled my head back so I could watch him as he pulled on a giant love-glove. Then he pushed my head facedown again, reached around, grabbed me tight by the nipples, and rammed into my ready asshole fast and hard just like I like it, and all the while I was coming I was thinking how virtue is its own reward.

Saturnalia
in Cyberspace

By Mary Mercedes

*F*rom the beginning, ours is a love affair that defies
sanity. Caressed by the angels. French-kissed by Beelzebub
himself. We met on the Internet. Separated by three states,
we collide at 70 MHz right inside our computers. "I found
you on the very first night I signed up on CompuServe,"
he tells me later. I'm a sultry, hyperkinetic gadfly in mental stilettos, slinking and sliding through the sticky electronic interstices. My mouse slithers past the crudest of
cretins and zigzags around the most boorish of brutes. It's
all so exquisitely malleable. I simply mold the electronic
clay of cyberspace with a few strokes of my keyboard. Weary
of the rigid routines and heavy obligations of my life, I
look to cyberspace as an ideal pressure valve. Soon I am a
shameless renegade, with a following. A typing dervish
stuck in overdrive. A cyberdiva radiating erotic cyber-
shocks in my wake.

"Until you, I only used this computer for my business. . . ."

Later:

He shows me his factory, his office, his desk, his PC, where he writes hundreds of e-mail notes to me. The words tumble out when his blistering tongue in my ear finally rests.

"Until you . . ."

He bends me over his leather desk chair, lifts up my denim skirt, and fucks me from behind while his calm, neatly coiffured wife smiles sweetly at us from the crystal-framed photographs on the credenza beside us.

Like a possessed, rutting Mephistophelian savage, he takes me. In front of his monitor. On his desk. Again on the floor littered with spilled files and an overturned box of cold computer disks that leave square, pink impressions on my breasts and backside.

We drench the Persian carpet.

We break an antique cabriole armchair.

In between his hissing and moaning, his delirious pumping . . . the words never stop with this man, and I love him for it.

But this is much later. After the phone sex, the endless fabricated business layovers, and clandestine meetings in my town. After our long escape tryst in Jamaica. Before his wife finds out.

The background to our wildfire:

I am the target of fan mail, hate mail, and lots of just plain male mail. Uninvited, genderless strangers I.S.O. [in search of] a cheap thrill. Wannabe adulterers who always supply their phone numbers and detailed maps to their home streets in Shelby, Nebraska. Over-testosteroned teenagers bursting with chronic ball pain and zipper stress (in all forty-eight contiguous states and Canada).

A journey into my e-mail box is a trek into a minefield of schizoid musing.

"More obscene propositions?" I inquire with a giggle. "Oh no, please pleeaase! Not another guy with twelve tumescent inches of steel genitalia who wants to know (in 3-D detail) if I'm wearing panties?"

Ignoring almost all of these freaks, I rarely write back to anyone. Then Richard shows up. In the midst of a miserable February blizzard, he finds me.

Both of us are in second marriages. Both infected with midlife madness. Impeccably well-mannered, my Ivy League paramour is the frustrated, erudite CEO of a high-tech company in the Northeast crumbling under the crunch of a downsizing defense industry. He loves Beck's dark beer and the passionate pursuit of intensely sensual sex and ribald laughter. So do I. He loves trashy, provocative lingerie, and I love to model it. I adore articulate, intellectual men, and he is quietly loquacious.

Yin and yang. Perfect fusion.

Whispered, loaded words flick from our cold keyboards late into the winter nights. I beckon to him with sexy innuendos. He flirts back with fevered devotion. The electricity between us sparks and sizzles. His constant e-mail notes glow blue on my monitor, becoming far more than a light that I seek in the night. His words illuminate my life with sparks of the erotic and the impossible.

How could I not invite him into my life? More than witty and charming, he is fucking radioactive, easily the most irresistible man I have ever (not) met.

I fall asleep at the keyboard, night after night. Aching to hear his voice but not daring to admit it. I begin to wonder about the flesh-and-blood man behind the words on the screen.

My gut says, "Listen! This man is totally honorable and guileless."

My common sense says, "He's married . . . and so are you."

"That's all right," I say. "He's just a harmless, long-distance flirtation."

But the wicked Sibyl who always sits on my shoulder knows better. "Beware," she says. "This man is dangerous to your health. He's already more than a tingling heat in your head. More than a throbbing itch in your pussy. . . ."

She is right. I know it. But I am lost already.

I try to reason with Richard. "Do you know," I say, "that ending this now would be so simple?"

"Yeah, but do you think either one of us could ever vanish back into the ether now?"

"It's as simple as ignoring the other's e-mail. . . ."

"Yeah," he says, "and isn't that exactly why we are so open with each other?"

Together, we choreograph a long-distance mental striptease. Febrile daydreams and schemes. Evocative eruptions. Richard is always there, cooing his endearing good mornings. Flirting at lunch. Writing long and languorous heartfelt revelations at day's end. He shares his quiet thoughts, his laughter, his angst. I begin to know him in ways that I had never imagined knowing any man. From the inside out.

Our hearts link together with laser-focused emotions, yet I have never heard his actual voice. I am madly in love with an invisible man, yet I know his every lust and dream.

Smitten by a cybernetic warlock . . . finally, I give him permission to call me, VOX, the voice you can actually hear, and things get even worse. What is left of my mind now becomes his.

"I have to see you," he begs. "What harm can come of it?"

Heart-stopping pictures fly back and forth from our fax machines; then via FedEx. I sicken with anxiety and can't even look. "What if," I say to myself, "he's a peewee dud, a lecherous dog, nothing but a fraudulent dipshit?" The Sibyl, with a smirk: "Ah, but what if he's not?"

Richard is perfect. A cosmic cut above attractive, with dark soulful eyes, a delectable mustache, and a toothy grin that could shame any ten-year-old. And he loves my looks.

"Oh, your long hair, your gorgeous lips, your dancer's legs . . ."

After the pictures I roam about like a blinded celibate in a fog of perpetual heat. Pining. I'm always pining for him. I walk into the furniture, dreaming of the mustache in those pictures being all over me.

"God help me, you're over six feet tall and have dimples too."

"Yeah," he laughs, "I have dimples."

He doesn't understand that his dimples are more than ample compensation for the "thinning" hair he mentioned nervously earlier on.

I am straddling his lap sucking on those dimples, laughing, sucking up both his dimples, inhaling his scent, devouring his mouth, sliding my tongue into his ear, then down his neck to his nearly hairless chest. His wife's orange tabby cat in the picture is watching us both intently. Watching me trace the Caribbean Sea, the salty sea, with my ravenous dripping tongue on Richard's hard belly, watching me sliding farther down, down between his legs, going south and starving to get there, heading toward South America, heading, the compass is pointing south, head, I want to eat him flying over St. Vincent and Trinidad, the gulf, engorge him, heading south down to the cape, the Cape of So Roque, his cape, his cock, dear

God, his sweet delicious honeyed hard cock, and I'm starving. Huge yellow panther eyes, big black pupils open wide, staring, taking it all in. Richard's long pianist's fingers finally unbuttoning my blouse, sensual fingers finally off the damned keyboard, undressing me, peeling my bra down, stripping my breasts bare. Cat tail twitches, ears perk, Richard's beautiful mustached mouth opens wide, slurping, smacking, slavering, wet with lust, swallowing up my throbbing nipples. Sucking his dimples . . . I run through the red light and am almost killed.

A good friend asks, "What in the hell is wrong with you? Are you pregnant?"

"Dear, you're going through early menopause," a relative insists. "It runs on your father's side."

Three times a day, my own Cyrano de Bergerac comes to me. Not on a stealthy, snorting steed but on fiber-optic cyberwings. His office phone bills soar to six and seven hundred dollars a month. Then he begins to call from home. After his wife goes to bed.

"What are you wearing tonight, sweetheart?"

Richard is stretched out on the sofa behind the computer in his study.

"A simple blue silk kimono," I say, "and big, hard, carnation-pink nipples."

We drench our clothes night after night, making feral phantom love after our unhappy mates go to bed alone (accusing us of being reclusive, sullen, and uncommunicative).

At least once a day I force him to come again. In handkerchiefs, wastebaskets, boxes of Kleenex. In towels or empty cardboard coffee cups. Even his pants, his hands, or right on the carpet if we're in a hurry. I can't stop. I try.

An impartial observer, a Freudian fly on the wall, could

easily reach all the wrong conclusions about our mental health. This is worse than any conventional addiction. We are closer to divine madness.

He is so much man that just listening to him lower his voice two octaves is better than being licked and fucked by any dozen other men. I talk him into increasingly longer, wilder climaxes. My voice, baby-soft or talking blue-streak dirty, galvanizes his every erotic cell. My body changes. My nipples harden into a permanent burning state of erection, and are impossible to hide under my clothes.

"This is so bizarre," I fret. "How can this feel so shattering?"

"Like being blasted into outer space without a spacecraft?"

"Yet I feel more intensely focused than I've ever felt."

Perhaps we are both sick. But I have already learned most of his physical hot spots and mental triggers without ever touching him. We're as synchronized as two finely tuned piano wires that vibrate across the miles, and together we soar higher than either of us ever imagined possible. The horrible truth is no longer "What if the bubble bursts when we meet?" but "What if it doesn't?" Both of us go home each night with less and less to say to our spouses. My sleep is crippled by haunting erotic dreams of Richard. I can't even eat anymore. He's a dybbuk in the night, stealing my health and then my very soul away.

Weekends are times of anguished separation. Stuck at home with our partners, we languish in silence for each other. Two days are forever. Long holidays are bitterly punishing. Richard sneaks into his den, boots up his computer, and quickly e-mails me: "going in to the office to call you at 6 or 7 p.m. please be there."

He tells his wife, "I have a lot of extra work to finish up."

She gripes. She's caustic and angry and starts a fight. He gets into his car anyway, and drives through the rain. Back into the city to open up the empty, silent office. Back to me.

"Darling, I can't miss you this much. It's insane, impossible."

"Yes, impossible." I sigh at how he makes me as liquid as glycerin, soft and feminine as a mink. "So damned impossible."

"It's worse than being seventeen again."

"It's better. . . ."

We laugh. We're connected, wired, alive again.

I stare at myself in the mirror and describe, in practical, minute detail, what I am wearing and precisely how and where he is going to take me. His breathing changes dramatically. I know that he can see me now in his mind. Trembling, I'm instantly wet. Dizzy as a junkie on the edge. Perched to glide in his lust.

I'm trussed and tied up into an absurdly expensive, leather-laced corset, mail-ordered from Amsterdam. My hair, piled high into a loose Victorian twist, spills down my back with a single twist of a pearly comb. The corset is unforgiving. My waist is mercilessly cinched so small that I can hardly breathe. Each shallow, measured breath makes my breasts (already squeezed upward and beginning to swell) heave up and down. The slight pain spirals my senses upward onto a higher plane, intensifying every erotic sensation. I'm too hyperalive in this outfit to feel anything but elemental lust. Tonight I'm his willing witch, his personal whore, the love of his life.

"You're watching me sashay across the room toward

you. I drop to my knees and kneel in front of you. Richard, you're staring down into my exaggerated cleavage. You love it, and want to sink your cock right in the middle, don't you? Not yet, darling. First, I just have to sink my red lips into your belly. I'm slowwwly peeling down your pants and oh, sweetheart—your skin's so warm, my hands are cool on your skin. Where are your hands, baby?"

I am whispering now.

"Open your pants, babee . . . there. Now, put your hand on your cock. Yes, yes. Tell me. Tell me what it looks like. Oh yessss, I'm soaked, babee, yes, my cunt is aching for you. Squeeze my tits, babeee, oh yeeez, just . . . like that . . ."

I yelp loudly. "Oh god, I'm dying, u-n-l-a-c-e me nowwww!"

We are laughing hysterically. But in ten minutes I know that we will both be flat on the floor. Moaning, gushing oceans, hearing only each other's crazed climaxing.

Silently, we decide there is no longer an if, only a when. This can't go on. We both know that he will eventually fill me to overflowing. With his promise and his cock. With his lewd and heated cooing in my ear. With his surging sea of frothy silver semen.

There is something ethereal, almost poetic, about cyberspace. A bullet-straight trip that begins on a dryly logical, high-tech superhighway can lead one into the most exotic and erotic places. In cyberspace, I'm forever twenty-nine and my boobs are monumental. Make a wish. The anonymity is intoxicating.

Cream

BY CAROL QUEEN

*D*ark, smoky bar. Ceiling a little lower, I think, than is legal. And a pair of gorgeous women peeling deliberately out of their clothes, thrilled for once to have an audience of their own to dance for, not the usual males trying to mask their hopeless lust with boredom. A packed house of women yell the dancers on, once in a while even reaching out to them with a proffered dollar bill. Foxy as these girls are, it's hard for me to stay in the here and now.

The little stripper reminds me of Maria—Maria, who stole my heart away on my very first day at Club Lust. This girl has dark hair that tumbles in loose curls down her back, like Maria's, and flawless tits, body worked out and tight, but not at all like some of the too-skinny chicks who work the clubs. (Sometimes I can't even enjoy the show for worrying about anorexia or heroin.) Her face even resembles Maria's. But she's Maria in miniature, a foot shorter, must be a size 4. Maria was an amazon, a perfect woman made larger than life.

On my first day at Club Lust, Maria hiked her wasabi-colored spandex dress up over her ass and slowly spun round the brass pole, flashing flushed-pink pussy at all the men—and at me. God, I thought, I'm gonna like this job.

Tonight her tiny look-alike swivels her hips and hikes her tight skirt up just that way. She's dancing to "Cream," maybe the sexiest of sexy Prince songs. Maria loved that song. We even danced together to it once. What a dance.

"Cream," Prince purrs through the club's bass-heavy sound system, "Get on top. . . ."

Fred had called to give me some business. He knew all about my job at Club Lust because he was my accountant. In fact he was the one to point out to me that my legitimate business write-offs included wigs, rubber dresses, lingerie—and condoms, if I got into any mischief on the side.

"My birthday's coming up," he'd said on the phone, "and you know I always throw a big party. Well, this one's my fortieth, and I want something special, a girl-girl show—and I thought you might know someone you'd like to work with. Hey, it's only fair I should give you a shot at earning back some of the money you pay me for doing your taxes."

That Fred—what a sweet guy. "Do I ever know someone!" I said. "A long, tall drink of water, Fred. I'll get right back to you." I hung up and called Maria.

"It's a special show," I told her. "I mean, it's his birthday, and he is my accountant. But he's also like this big dyke trapped in a man's body. All his friends are lesbians. I don't think I've ever known him to socialize with men. All the guests at this party will be women. If you want to do this gig with me, we have to do it right. They'll all be able to spot fake lesbo action. They want the genuine article."

Maria said she didn't think we'd have a bit of trouble delivering the real thing.

"Great," Fred said when I called him back. "A hundred and fifty bucks each, okay, and be here at nine on Saturday. I want it to be a surprise, so come dressed like you're guests."

Maria and I pulled up at his hilltop home just before nine o'clock, dressed in pressed designer jeans and silk shirts, which is what I figured most of Fred's lesbian friends would be wearing. Whenever I ran into Fred and his pals at a club, the women were well-groomed professionals. I supposed all the dyke accountants in town would be there, probably a lawyer or two or three, and who knows who else. Not really the kind of women Maria or I socialized with, usually, but we could certainly dress the part.

Sure enough, Fred gave us the thumbs-up when he answered the door. "We'll do the show in about half an hour," he whispered. "Everybody ought to be here by then. Just go ahead and mingle. Leslie made a huge bowl of pasta primavera, help yourselves."

Of the thirty women who were at the party, only Leslie—Fred's roommate—was in on it. At twenty past, she led us into her room so we could get ready. "Do you want any special music?" she asked, and I handed her that new Prince CD.

That was the first time I heard "Cream"—following Maria out of the bedroom when Leslie came to get us, watching that same green dress Maria wore at work begin to hike itself up toward her ass cheeks.

Her walk was slinky, a slow stride that cocked her hips from side to side as she moved, and the movement itself—not her hands—brought the skintight dress up her thighs. By the time we had moved to the center of Fred's living room the bottom curve of her butt showed, and I reached out for it just like I'd always wanted to do. Oh, what a creamy, luscious ass. Day after day I watched Maria drive men to rock-hard distraction with that ass, and now my palms cupped it like she was mine, all mine.

I used to have a hard time finding women to have sex with, especially casual sex. I knew lots of women had that problem, but that didn't make me happy about it. Then I started doing all-girl shows at Club Lust. We were practically all bisexual there, and not just for the money. Even strippers who would never date other women outside the club thought the all-girl action shows were a big perk.

As I pushed my hands under Maria's clinging dress I reflected for a second on the splendid irony of it: Thirty pairs of lesbian eyes watched me while I explored Maria's magnificent ass. I would probably never be in a position to run my hands over any of their asses; for one thing, as a bisexual woman, I often didn't feel all that welcome in lesbian circles. And maybe if Fred weren't paying us a hundred and fifty bucks each to get to know each other better, Maria and I would have never had sex. I certainly wouldn't have been so bold as to grab her ass right away.

Nor to run my fingers up over the tight spandex to her breasts, just a little too large for my hands. Maria's hands were on me, too, touching, stroking. Out of the corner of my eye I could see Fred, looking pleased, so far. I was certainly pleased. Nothing feels like a tight body under tight spandex.

Nor can I think of anything that compares with the feeling of being stared at by myriad eyes as I start to get turned on—it made me aware of everything: my nipples going hard under her clever fingers, my own short skirt riding up my ass. Plus I had a surprise under that skirt, and now Maria began to rub against me so she could feel it.

My hands tangled themselves up in that long, silky brown hair. Long, tall Maria brought her mouth down to mine—she had to bend over to kiss me, just like a man would, and I had to tilt my head up. Prince's voice cast a spell over me, and I pulled her down to the floor. She knelt over me, skirt all the way up over her magnificent ass now, her legs spread wide, straddling me. "Cream," Prince sang, "get on top." You would have thought Maria was starring in the video.

Very deliberately, in the exaggerated way of sex performers, she rubbed her pussy on my strapped-on cock. Now we did the dance lying down, and it surprised me how quiet our audience was. At Club Lust this kind of action would have drawn hoots and cries of appreciation. These women sat silently, regarding us with as much fascination, I think, as a crowd of men would have displayed, but still as church mice.

Still, I had the best view in the place. I lay on my back, pumping my hips up slowly, trying to keep it sensuous. Hold off on the lewd body movements until the crowd warms up, I thought—if it ever does. I could look right up Maria's body, see her up on her knees straddling me— "you're wicked cute and baby you know it," Prince sang to her, and I could almost hear the way she would sassily concur: "Uh-huh."

Undulating on top of me, she stroked me into real heat, running her hands up my belly and over my breasts and inching my skirt up and up. Finally she revealed the strapped-on dildo. One brave woman yelled "Woo-hoo!" when she saw it. Too bad there weren't a few more cowgirls like her in the room.

I had a small tube of lubricant tucked in my clingy red top. Maria removed it, then worked the spandex up over my head. She could really get at my breasts now, and did, while I arched back and began to breathe hard. Then she slicked the dildo with lube and resumed rubbing her pussy against it, writhing now and, I could feel, almost catching her cunt on it.

When she finally did rise up higher and position herself on it, her ass and pussy in full view of Fred and all his friends, she winked at me before starting the slow slide on my cock. The weight of her body settling onto it rubbed its base against my clit. And she threw her head back and began to fuck me.

"Mmmmm, Cream, get on top. . . ." Maria, fuck me good, honey. Make these power-suit girls wet between their legs while they try to figure out whether it's okay to howl. She had my tits in her hands and pumped herself on me so slowly I started to feel dizzy. She let it go on for another song, and by the end of it I was bucking like a little pony, fucking the slick silicone cock up into her while she, with big, slow humping motions, thrust down onto it. By the end of the second song she was arching her torso over with each thrust down so that her hair fell over her face. With each upstroke she flipped it back.

As the third song began, she lifted off me, kneeling to one side so her ass was pointing right at the silent, staring crowd. As she unbuckled my harness, she rotated that perfect butt in little circles, a move that, when she did it at Club Lust, sometimes made men moan out loud. Here the silence only deepened—which I realized meant that all the women watching us, and Fred too, were holding their breath simultaneously. Maria tossed the harness and dildo aside and then pulled me up, where—standing, though a little weak-kneed—I felt her fingers push my skirt all the way up, leaving my pussy unobstructed. I spread my legs for her, rested my hands on her shoulders for balance, and her tongue crept up to my clit and circled it relentlessly. Just before the song's last chorus I came. (It's still a challenge to come standing up, but I've learned to do it; at Club Lust the staging of the show didn't always allow time to lie down. What was I supposed to do, miss the orgasm?) They never did hoot and holler, the dykes, not until our performance was over. With the last bars of the song we bowed, holding hands, and then slinked out just the way we came in, returning to Leslie's bedroom—hearing shouts and applause follow us the whole way.

The little stripper can't even take her G-string off tonight, because we're in a public club. But she strips down to that, and she and her dance partner caress each other, playfully tap each other's pretty butt, and kiss—careful to look sexy without getting the lipstick all smeared. Got to love those sex-industry femmes! Finally their song ends and they part, leaving the stage one after the other. All the way off they're still looking for tips and copped feels. It's amazing how eager we are for other women to do things that might get the men in the clubs a slap in the face. But stripping for women feels nothing like stripping for men. You see the difference in their eyes, which gaze on us with such wonder—whoever puts on a show just for women? No wonder they don't know how to take it.

It's been almost four years since we danced to "Cream." Now shows for women aren't quite so rare—but still, this club tonight is a temple where the little beauty, this miniature Maria, dances with her sweet blond friend to prove we deserve to watch someone hot, someone who's intent on making us gasp, making us howl. And we do.

"I love that CD," Maria had said as she tugged her dress, sweaty from the dance, over her chestnut hair. It wasn't very personal, but her sparkling eyes said a lot more.

"I love you, Maria," I said, meaning her dress, her dance, her flawless ass, her creamy skin and long dark hair, her flaming spirit.

We kissed Fred and ran out into the night.

Private Lessons

BY JoAnn Bren Guernsey

I rush into the dance studio, certain I'm hopelessly late, but my instructor has waited. It's after ten, and everyone else has left for the night.

"So very sorry," I tell him breathlessly. "Flat tire . . . damn rusty lug nuts . . . such a mess. . . ." I gesture with dirt-streaked hands to my torn dress and stockings and give up explaining further.

No tears, I warn myself, but I can't believe the bedraggled state I'm in. Especially after all my careful preparation for tonight's ballroom-dance lesson—my sixth and last with Tyler. My new dress (a skin-hugging knit, so short it barely covers my ass) and the sheer black panty hose fresh out of their package are equally ruined.

Tyler is leaning against the desk, smiling and shaking his head in sympathy. I notice, not for the first time, how this man's body suggests music and movement even when he's standing perfectly still. "Go ahead and take the washroom key," he says. "I'll wait."

"We can reschedule the lesson if you want," I say.

"No. It'll be nice having the studio all to ourselves, and you'll feel better after washing up. Take off those stockings if you like."

"Well, I'd like to, but I can't." I feel myself blush, and figure that's about all he needs to guess that I'm wearing nothing but the panty hose underneath my tight dress.

After washing my hands I check out the damage in the bathroom mirror. My hair and makeup are easily repairable, and even the dress can probably be salvaged. The main problem is a dime-size hole in the fabric, right in the center of my stomach. Oh well. Practicing the erect dance posture I've learned from Tyler, I watch in the mirror as my skin flashes coyly through that hole.

When I rejoin my instructor, he starts up the music. A nice mellow waltz. It seems as if he has somehow filled the studio with warm, heavy, fragrant air—the kind of air on which it seems possible to float. His strong lead makes me better than I am, and he nods his approval each time I pick up his nonverbal cues—now this direction, now that turn, now this variation. My body has learned his, and he has trained mine well.

The music switches to a foxtrot. A bouncy forties arrangement of "Let Yourself Go" inspires me, and I do really let myself go. All this motion makes me sweat lightly and releases moist whiffs of my perfume. I feel the cool air through the hole in my dress as though someone is blowing on my belly. I like it.

The studio has floor-to-ceiling mirrors on three sides and a full wall of glass facing the street. In the mirror I catch glimpses of Tyler and me, and decide we are, in fact, a rather striking couple. Both long and leggy, similarly built. His darkness complements my blond hair and pale skin. We are practicing all that he's taught me and moving quickly beyond, both avoiding the painful fact that I can't afford to take any more lessons. I concentrate instead on how solid his shoulder feels under my left hand and how his grasp of my right hand seems almost to swallow it whole.

By the time the music pulls us into a deliciously dramatic tango, I notice that we've attracted an audience. Outside the window a few pedestrians have clustered to watch. I know how difficult it is to resist looking in at dancers in this brightly lit studio, especially late at night. It was this sight that drew me into the studio in the first place. Now it is me gliding around the floor in the arms of this smooth, elegant partner. But the mirrors and windows have turned me into a show-off, and the result is a major misstep on my part. Tyler and I collide—my stomach against his belt buckle, my forehead against his nose. "Okay, enough gazing around," he tells me in his mock-stern instructor voice. "Time to focus." He leaves me for a moment to dim the lights, and our mirror image is no longer clear. But our audience outside the window is not deterred.

Now Tyler pulls me into a slow, sensuous rumba. Oh my—the dance of love. I feel his large hand on my back. It seems to be burning through the fabric, and with the continued sensations from the hole in front I'm beginning to feel as if fabric is being eased away from my body in pieces. Moisture is gathering between my legs, and I let myself wonder if Tyler's lessons sometimes give him an erection. Or if he ever dances naked.

He lets go of me for a moment, shifting his hands downward to ride on my hips. "Like this," he says, guiding me to undulate with the music. I've been struggling for weeks to loosen up and move my hips properly, but now, finally, Tyler's lower body lures mine into natural, seductive Latin motion. Looking directly into his dark eyes, I notice that he is changing somewhat. Softening. The teacher-pupil barrier seems to have dissolved. My heartbeat quickens, and the space between my legs becomes more warm, more wet, with each step, each movement.

This is beginning to frighten me a little, and I lower my gaze. He seems to understand, and twirls me around into shadow position—his chest is against my back and our feet are moving in unison. With his left hand flat on my stomach, I fight the urge to move it up . . . or down. And I feel an unmistakable stirring behind me in his trousers.

Then he finds it—the hole in my dress. At first his fingertip just brushes across my skin by accident, then it zeroes in. He slowly inserts his finger until the tear stretches and becomes completely filled with Tyler. The skin on my stomach becomes electrified. I realize that my erratic breathing and pulse are no secret to him, not with his finger probing and tracing the center line of my stomach. Up to my breastbone, down to the shallow pucker of my navel.

Now I want all those people outside to go away. To leave us alone. My temporary urge to flash has given way to a longing for intimacy with this man. I know he is feeling the same longing by the way he's breathing into my hair and beginning to move his hand in a decidedly non-dance manner. His touch grazes my left nipple, then pauses to let my breast fill and warm his hand.

"Wait a moment," he whispers, then goes to turn off the lights. Only the neon sign on the window remains lit, and it leaves us in near-darkness, tinged with gold. Most of the people outside leave. Only one man remains on the sidewalk. I'm dancing alone for the moment, touching my own body, engrossed in the sinewy action of my stomach and abdominal muscles.

Even though I can't see the observer's face, I feel his

eyes fixed on me and am surprised by the extra dash of arousal this adds.

Tyler brings a chair when he returns, and sits down behind me to watch my solo. Without turning around I straddle and hover over his lap, and as my ass moves against him, I can feel him getting harder. The man continues to watch from outside, and even when Tyler pulls up my skirt, I resist turning away from the window to face my partner. While one of Tyler's hands cups my breast again, the other slides between my legs. One finger begins to burrow, as if seeking a hole in my panty hose like the one in my dress. Since it isn't there, he makes one, breaking through the mesh to dip into the silky moisture inside.

The music has changed completely, but we are creating our own rhythm now. My backside is still moving against him as his one hand continues to explore my chest and the other widens the tear he's made in my panty hose. Soon one of his fingers is all the way into me and pushing to see if deeper is possible. The rest of his fingers are also busy, thoroughly exploring each nerve ending and fold. I begin to wonder how many fingers he has and if they ever get tired. At the same time, I don't care.

I'm on the brink of coming, but want to remain there for as long as possible, so I shift my attention back to the man outside. Maybe I'll feel self-conscious and distracted by this watchful silhouette; maybe I'll feel sorry for him. Instead I recognize how he has joined us, in a way, and this only pushes my body further into its free-fall. I grasp Tyler's hands and the rest of his solid, attentive presence with my whole body and reach a long, heart-battering climax . . . wave after wave after wave . . . until there is no strength or pull left anywhere in me and I crumble to the floor.

From there, between Tyler's knees, my fingers begin their urgent search for him. He's hugely erect and seems to be having trouble breathing, but he abruptly pushes my hands away and stands up.

"What—?"

He gestures toward the street. Our friend is still there, still darkly motionless. And I realize that Tyler has managed, in spite of his arousal, to remember where we are. And who he is—a professional dance instructor. And I am supposed to be his student, but that's over now.

"Of course. I'm sorry." I get up off the floor, straighten out my dress, and turn to leave. Thank goodness it's dark, because I don't want him to see my flushed face and tears.

Tyler clears his throat a few times, and I can sense how hard he is trying to regain his composure.

"Good-bye," I say. "Thank you."

"But you aren't going home now," my instructor informs me. "Not when your dancing has progressed this far. I believe you're ready to move on to the next level."

"But—"

"I have a small studio in my house where I've been hoping to give free, very private lessons to someone . . . in exchange, of course, for learning some things myself. I think I've found the perfect teacher."

The music is over. The air in the studio is cooling. But every molecule in my body is dancing now. Before we leave he takes a moment to remove what's left of my black stockings. When we get out to the parking lot, we notice our audience of one has vanished. After hesitating only a moment, Tyler walks over to the window to leave the soft wet panty hose like a puddle on the sidewalk where the man had stood . . . just in case he returns.

The Hot Line

BY JOLIE GRAHAM

I was looking at what passed for personal ads in Minor Midwest City, U.S.A. They all sounded depressingly alike, as usual. Whether this cookie-cutter phenomenon in the personals was because all the single men in town really were pretty much alike, or whether it was thanks to cribbing one another's ads, I wasn't sure. I had moved here only three months earlier and was still assessing the dating scene.

My new job was good, the pay and benefits were great, the cost of living was heavenly. But none of that was anything I could literally get off on. And things I could get off on were nonexistent here. With the exception of the Calvin Klein billboard on the interstate, no naked or even half-naked people of either sex were to be seen. Fortunately I had not thrown out my stash of dirty mags when I moved. Even more fortunately, I had Linden's number memorized.

"Hello, you've reached Hot, Handsome, Horny Hunks, a Woman's Hot Line. Phone charges at a rate of three dollars per minute will be billed to you," the pleasant male voice began. "If you wish to leave voice mail for one of our hot, handsome hunks and you already know his code, please press the code now. Our schedule this week—" I had Linden's number—boy, did I have his number—but I wanted to know what time he was working tonight. "Sean, 2 to 5 P.M.; Chad, 5 to 8 P.M.; John, 8 to 11 P.M.; Eric, 11 P.M. to 2 A.M.; Linden, 2 to 5 A.M. Our weekend schedule—" Beep, beep, beep, beep.

"Linden, this is Suzanna. Tonight, 2:45. Hot and hungry—'The Poet.'"

The advantage of the advance call is that I can advise him of the mood I'm in and he can prepare accordingly. He knows my fantasies so well that we've got it down to a few key words. "Beach house" involves a lot of fucking in the sand and surf. "Downtown" is a dance-club pickup scenario that he creatively expanded from dance-floor groping preliminaries and dark-corner sex to screwing in bathrooms, alleys, and once—when he got carried away— eating me out while I was perched on the club's bar. "Candlelight and oil" features a bath or hot tub and a massage, including, of course, fantastic fantasy sex. Sometimes I just give him a mood. He knows what I like.

Once when I said "sensuous" he described things to me in such a way that I came in less than a minute. Of course I was already a bit worked up when I called. It saves on the phone bill, but even if it didn't, how could I not be just dripping wet knowing that in the middle of the night this total stranger would be whispering all kinds of sexy, obscene things in my ear. Not like an obscene phone caller—these are things I want to hear. He knows the fantasies I will never voice to a lover. They're private, they are mine: secret pleasures I have no desire to share with anyone. But I can tell Linden and still maintain a sense of privacy as well as intimacy. He's the man of my daydreams. I can have the most dangerous, dirty sex imaginable with a stranger who can be, as the scene requires, kind or cold—and very often surprising.

"The Poet," as I call it, is one of his surprises. I had said "hot, lyrical sex" that first particular night. What I got, like tonight, was . . . "Hello, Linden."

"Suzanna, I've missed you so much. It's been months since I've licked you, months since I've sunk my fingers into your snatch. I've got the fire in the fireplace lit. It'll burn all night if you want it to."

"I love you, Linden."

"I love you too, Suzanna," he said softly. "You look so beautiful lying there on your stomach on that soft plush sheepskin, firelight licking your black panties. You are a portrait of desire. But not a still life, oh no," he breathed.

I was lying in total darkness on my bed, the speaker phone on the nightstand beside me. He could surely hear the desire in my breathing.

"Peel your panties over your ass. What a peach you are! Oh, I just want to bite into you. Raise your ass to my lips, feel my teeth and lips on your smooth cheeks. I run my tongue along the cleft until I come to the deep, tight spot where the peach was plucked from the tree. Did you remember to push smooth green silk leaves up your ass?" he asked.

I hadn't this time but just the suggestion of it made my heart beat faster.

"Winter is so cruel," he continued. "In summer you will have sprouted slender peach leaves, fragrant just like the luscious fruit."

I fingered my asshole, breathing heavily as I remembered last summer's erotic adventures with fresh fruit and leaves. "I'm pulling these impostor leaves out of your ass; they don't belong in such a lush, ripe fruit. I rub my thumb over the hole and press in."

Lying with my face to my pillow, my ass thrust upward, the hands molesting me were no longer my own.

"I want to peach you." His voice pressed into me like a hard object. "Oooh, so juicy, my thumb is slick. Peach oil is the best lubricant, don't you think? What a heavenly scent, like nectar. Oh, now the juice is starting to flow as I push my other fingers into your slit. Open that fruit wider, cleave you, reach in for that kernel."

My body tightened relentlessly with every sentence. I was scarcely breathing. "Ummm, Suzanna, my peach! Let me suck all those juices. I'm holding your ass up to my mouth, juice running down my chin, my fingers circling the kernel in the cleft, my tongue pushing into the peach-oiled hole. I'm eating you. I've pulped you with my tongue, pulped you with my fingers, now I'm going to pulp your flesh into sweet, honey-melting juice with my cock."

"Oh," I gasped. "Peach me! Pulp my pussy . . . ooohhh . . ."

The Poet doesn't always go for peaches, but he has never missed the mark. But then perhaps my desire is a large enough target that it would be difficult to miss.

A couple of weeks later, dateless still, I called again. Linden's been moved up to the eleven o'clock slot. It's "Candlelight and oil" this time.

"Hi! How are you doing?"

"Okay, I guess. A little stressed. I thought by now the new job would be less new. So far my acquaintances don't seem to have real friendship potential."

"Time for some TLC, courtesy of me. I've got a dozen candles lit. Would you like a nice hot bath before or after the massage?"

"Let's start with the bath. I've finally gotten a speaker phone run into the bathroom."

"A nice hot tub of water."

"Rose-scented bubble bath," I said as I stepped into the already prepared tub. He talked to me like a lover while I bathed. For some reason, tonight it just wasn't working very well.

"What's wrong?"

How can he tell something's wrong? Can he really hear the tiredness in my voice through the hiss of the phone? I confessed I was really too tired to stroke myself off after all. "That's the disadvantage of this phone fantasy—sometimes I really do need an actual massage. I can't work myself into a lather—pardon the pun—" I interjected, splashing loudly out of the tub, "until I'm relaxed enough to be aroused enough to release some tension."

"Yeah, I understand. Listen, you're in Plainsville, right?" I had, in a moment of real candor, told him where I'd moved.

"Yesss," I answered slowly.

"That's, what, two or three hours from St. Paul? I've got a friend in St. Paul who is a certified, licensed masseur."

"Isn't it against the rules for you to give out names, numbers, referrals?"

"Yes, but that's really just designed to prevent sexual solicitations of any sort. This is legit. Besides, if you don't tell, and I don't tell, and my supervisor is in bed sound asleep and not monitoring the call—Are you out there, Diane? Speak now or forever hold your peace—who's to know?" He gave me his masseur friend's name and number, wished me sweet dreams and good night.

I called in sick and slept late. I ended up working overtime as the next weekend approached, and felt even less inclined to drive two-and-a-half hours for a back rub than I had when Linden gave me the referral. But I did call a friend in Minneapolis to ask her to check the reference out for me. The next time I called Linden I got off so easily to the "Downtown" scenario that he asked afterward if I'd gotten a massage as he'd suggested. "No," I said with a laugh, still dizzy from the sex. "I'm not working overtime now."

Thinking about it later, drifting off to sleep with my hand between my legs and Linden's voice in my head, I halfway decided that I deserved a treat, a weekend in St. Paul. I called and made an appointment for a massage, and a reservation at a decent hotel. It had been so long since I'd experienced an actual oiled full-body massage that it was no wonder the fantasy was drifting away. *Next time I talk to Linden,* I thought, *I'll be able to feel his hands more vividly.* And there will always be a next time. That's the beauty of phone sex. It's real human contact, but no messy misunderstandings, no changing my life for another person, no insecurities because I've gained weight and more than a few gray hairs have shown up. If someday Linden isn't there for me, well, there will always be someone—which is more than I could say before I started calling.

I was sitting in the waiting room of Holistic Health & Aromatherapy in St. Paul as I was having these wonderful thoughts of sexual freedom. Then my name was called, and I realized I would now have to shed inhibitions and clothes, stretch out on a table, and be touched all over (almost!) by a complete stranger, with his hands rather than his voice. I undressed and waited for Steve, the masseur. As

I stretched out on the table and closed my eyes I began an imaginary dialogue with Linden, listening to his voice in my head, talking about warming up the massage oil and what kind of massage did I want, hard or soft? I could just hear the gentle teasing in his voice as he pressed his hands against my body. . . .

The masseur came in about that time, a tactile aid to my fantasy. I smiled, treasuring my secret carnal thoughts. "Would you like your massage hard or soft?" I heard Linden ask. "You know, peach massage oil is the best lubricant."

I very nearly came at the sound of his voice. I didn't open my eyes. I was so frozen with shock that I almost didn't speak. He was standing beside the table. I had heard the sound of cloth; he was clothed even if I wasn't.

"Medium," I managed to say, clearing my throat. "I may be too tense for a hard massage just now," I said.

The shock was wearing off and ebbing away into a different and very familiar sort of tension as he began with my back. My mind was racing—did he know it was me, Suzanna, the phone-sex woman? I had fallen asleep many nights fantasizing about meeting him, actually being with him. Now I suddenly craved distance. What my body craved was a different matter altogether. My body wanted contact. I opened my eyes. His cock was somewhere in those loose white drawstring pants, and somewhere below eye level. I think I would have pulled that drawstring, but his massage technique had turned my tight muscles into lank, docile lengths.

I floated, aware only of his hands and the wet sound of my pussy as I was gently rolled over onto my back. I was looking right up at him, staring right into the eyes of my dream date. His eyes were brown. He had crow's-feet. The stud who had split me in two, made me come so hard it hurt, was a middle-aged man, balding, nice build. He worked on my arms in silence. Then, just as he finished my left arm, he leaned over and nipped the flesh inside the elbow with his lips. He knew. He had to know who I was. Liquid trickled from my pussy to my anus. My cheeks were getting wet. I shifted my legs, trying to relieve the sensation of trickling liquid. He had draped a towel discreetly over my mons, but it couldn't hide the sound and scent of a wet pussy.

Linden's hands rubbed my belly all the way down to the fur. Next he moved to the foot of the table and massaged my feet. Then my legs, then my thighs. Up, up, not quite into my snatch. Back to the stomach. Up to the breasts. I noticed how deeply I was breathing. His breathing matched mine. Neither of us said a word. He pinched my nipples, twisted them very, very slowly. I was gasping. My legs were spread, dangling off either side of the table from the knees down. I didn't remember spreading them. As Linden massaged my breasts, I moved instinctively on the table. Images of that voice, those hands, and all the ways I had been penetrated by them, were flashing through my head. He grasped both my nipples with his fingertips and tugged them straight up. I cried out. He slid his hand into my bush and massaged my clit for about thirty seconds. That was all it took. I came so fast and so intensely that I felt buzzed, drunk, hallucinatory. When I finally came down, my body shook with chills and aftershocks. Linden wrapped me in towels, soft and plush, straight from the warming rack, then leaned over, covering me with his torso. The silence was strange.

This was Linden, right? The man who talks dirty,

evenings, Tuesday through Thursday. I had stopped shaking by this time. My whole body felt just unbelievable.

"Sweet dreams," Linden said, his eyes dancing with mischief and delight as he turned to go.

"Tuesday, midnight. 'Beach house,' " I said huskily.

He grinned and nodded.

On the House

BY SUSAN SCOTTO

*H*e was always coming by. He'd stop by the coffee-house at least once a day, sometimes more, when Jen was working. He'd flirt with me too, and I could feel his eyes checking me out as I steamed the milk for his latte. On days when I was wearing a loose top I'd make sure to dip down and pick a napkin up off the floor, just to give him a glimpse. He'd pretend not to notice, but I could tell that he looked.

When business was slow the three of us would sit and talk, mostly about music. He didn't always agree with what I had to say, and often, when he was making a point, he'd lay his hand on my arm, to ensure he had my full attention.

Jen, though, was his favorite. She had this long, curly red hair, its wildness restrained in a ponytail most of the time, just the way her wildness was hidden beneath her flannel shirts and jeans. But he knew it was there. He sensed it somehow. Which is why he bought coffee more when Jen was working than when I was.

Jen liked him. We both did. He wasn't tall, and he was muscular, but not obviously so. The overall impression you got from him was of a beautifully proportioned young man with a strikingly attractive face. About my and Jen's age, we guessed. Sandy blond hair, dark blue eyes, almost chiseled features. Lips that would rise just a bit on one side when you said something funny.

Lots of times I wished he was the one on the other side of the counter, so I could watch him make me a latte or lean over to get the milk from the fridge. You see, as beautiful as he was to look at head-on, the back view was even better. Sometimes when he was walking out I'd just stare at the way his T-shirt hugged his back and waist, the way his ass filled out his faded jeans. God, when I saw him in those jeans, all I could think of was how great it would be to do him. I could reach around and feel that ass as it moved up and down with the rhythm of his fucking.

Jen knew how hot I was for him. One day after he'd left she picked up a napkin.

"Need this?" she asked, motioning toward my crotch.

"I'm so wet I could take the Coit Tower," I whispered.

"Think he's the Coit Tower?" Jen asked.

"You find out," I suggested. "He wants you."

Jen shrugged. "Yeah. He's even asked me out. But I said no. He just doesn't do it for me."

"Unbelievable," I told her. "Honey, all I have to do is think about him and . . ." I shut my eyes and took a deep breath. If I could have slipped my hand up under my skirt, I'd have come in an instant. But two customers had just walked in.

"Well, I'm telling you right now," I said quietly as I waited for our patrons to order, "if you're not going to fuck him, I will. He walks around looking like that, he deserves to be—hard."

All evening I waited for him to come back in. Jen was working, so it was pretty much a sure bet he'd return before long. Sure enough, around nine he showed up—in the jeans. Jen was clearing tables, so I got to take his order: large cup of coffee, for here. Still facing him, I reached down under the counter for a cup, and as I did so, the thin strap of my sundress slid off my shoulder. I bent forward just a bit, knowing the front of the dress would gap open enough for him to see. I pretended not to notice what had happened, but he saw. It was just a moment, but a moment was enough.

When he raised his eyes, his gaze met mine. He knew I'd caught him looking. I smiled and slowly adjusted the strap of my dress. He smiled back. Then he said, under his breath, "Wow."

I wasn't sure whether he meant me to hear it, but I smiled again and handed him the cup of coffee. He took a seat at a table near the counter, where he, Jen, and I could talk when there was a break in the flow of customers. A couple of times I sat down with him. I'd drape my arm over the back of my chair so my shoulder strap would slide down my arm. I'd push it back up, of course, but every time it slipped, he watched.

At ten I was off for the night. Jen had to stay till midnight and close up.

"You walking home tonight?" she asked.

I nodded. "It's so nice out." I turned to him. "Walk me home? I live just up the street."

He thought for a moment, then stood up. "Okay."

He walked out first. When I reached behind the counter for my purse, Jen winked and gave me a thumbs-up.

Outside we strolled along slowly, enjoying the breezy summer night. The bottlebrush trees waved jauntily at us, and as we turned off Walnut Street, I caught the scent of jasmine from the yard next to mine. I wanted to wrap myself around him and discover his natural scent, the one he kept hidden beneath his cologne.

All this time we were chatting about something, I guess, although I wasn't paying much attention. When we reached my house I brought him around back. There was a huge raspberry hedge around the backyard. It was private and quiet. And dark. Usually I went in the front, but tonight I had a reason for using the back door. Finally I got the door open and flipped on the porch light. He was about to follow me in, but I said, "Wait out here. I've got something I want to show you."

He gave me a puzzled look. Then he shrugged and stuck his hands into the pockets of his jeans.

"Okay. Whatever you say."

I smiled, gave him a quick kiss. Leaving the back door half-open, I went through the kitchen into the living room and on into my bedroom, which looked out on the backyard, where he still stood, waiting. The shades weren't drawn.

I turned on my bedside lamp. It wasn't bright, but the light coming on in the otherwise darkened house would be sure to attract his attention. At least I hoped it would.

I put on some music, and then, without looking toward the yard, I began to undress next to the bed. I wasn't facing the yard, or even looking in that direction, but if he was looking, he'd get a good three-quarter view. Slowly, I pulled my dress up, past my hips, to my waist, and then up and over my shoulders. I was left in just my black silk thong. But I didn't take it off just yet. I reached inside, sliding my right hand down the front. I could feel the heat spreading from my cunt. Then I touched the ring that pierced the fold of skin just above my clit and pressed it down. It was like an electric shock. I opened my mouth and took a deep breath. Steady. I didn't want to come right away. And yet the thought that he was standing out there watching me was almost too much to bear. Slowly, thinking of what his reaction must be right now, I slipped my thong down. I slid my forefinger up between my lips for a moment and let the black silk fall to the floor. I resisted the urge to look out the window and focused instead on my clit. Resting one foot on my bed, I began pressing my finger onto the bead of the ring which rested just on the tip of my clit. Every movement of the ring sent sparks through me. I rotated my finger slowly, finding the spot where it felt best. With my free hand I began to squeeze my nipples, first gently, then more roughly.

I was moaning now, rocking back and forth. I could see my reflection in the black windowpane. I knew he was out there in the warm darkness beyond. I knew he was watching me in the rectangle of light. I knew he was hard from seeing me. I stopped and started, eager to prolong the show for him. Then I couldn't bear it anymore. Twisting my nipple between thumb and forefinger, I rocked and rocked, my other hand rubbing my clit as it slid in the wetness from my cunt. I closed my eyes and leaned my head back as I came, a hot shiver spreading from my nipples down to my clit. My eyes still closed, I held the bedpost with one hand to steady myself. After a minute I walked slowly to the window and, pressing my hands against it, peered outside. Where was he? I couldn't see him. Maybe he'd left and hadn't seen anything. I closed my eyes again, leaning foward just enough so I could feel the cool glass against my nipples.

And then I heard him. He'd come in through the back door I'd left open. He was finding his way here in the dark. I didn't turn around, just waited for him. A moment later, I heard his footsteps in my room, then right behind me. His hand fell lightly on my shoulder. He leaned down and began kissing my neck and shoulders, then my cheek. I reached behind and pulled him to me. He was sweating, and I could feel his erection pressing against my ass through his jeans.

As I turned around, he opened his mouth to speak, but I shook my head and put my finger to his lips. I ran my hands over his chest, somehow amazed that he was still fully clothed. Silently, I pulled his T-shirt out of his jeans and up over his head. Then, tracing the line of sandy hair downward from his chest with my finger, I slid my hand inside his jeans, wrapping my hand around his hard-on for a minute before unsnapping his jeans.

Once he stood naked before me I knelt down and began sucking his cock, excited by its hardness. I reached around and held his ass, both to keep my balance and to pull him deeper into my mouth. He began thrusting, gently at first, then harder when he realized I wanted him to, and I could feel the muscles in his ass contract with every push. The hair of his bush brushed my nose every time I pulled him toward me and smelled liked sweat and soap. I was taking him all in my mouth now, pulling him forward, swallowing him whole.

He began to moan and grasped me tightly by the shoulders, asking me not to stop. His cock was starting to taste like come, but he wasn't getting off that easy. I took my mouth from his cock and held it so I could lick his balls, running the flat of my tongue along them the whole way, from just in front of his asshole to the shaft, sucking them, taking their velvety roundness into my mouth, first one, then the other, then both. Then I rose slowly to my feet, running my hands over his body, kneading his muscles. God, he was even more beautiful beneath his clothes than I'd expected.

He was breathing hard. So was I. His knees were shaking. He put his arms around me and pulled me against him, so that my clit hood ring pressed against his balls. Kissing me, he seemed to be trying to devour me, the way I'd devoured his dick.

He wanted to move me over to the bed, but I shook my head.

"No," I said, barely able to breathe. "Against the wall."

I put my arms around his neck and pulled myself up. His biceps bulged as he supported me from beneath with his hands. I brought one hand down and guided him into my cunt. Instantly he started to thrust, and I began sliding up and down, my back against the cool wall, my arms and legs and chest covered with his sweat.

I clamped his waist tightly with my legs and bit his earlobes, his neck, his shoulders. I found his mouth and put my tongue in it as far as it would go. Then, moving away from the wall, he turned and laid me down on the bed. With every thrust I was pushed farther up the bed, but I clung to him, fighting, fucking back just as hard to meet him.

I reached down and grabbed his ass with my hand, relishing its muscular smoothness. I'd wanted this since the day I first saw him. I pulled him deeper into me.

Rising up on his elbows, he began sucking and biting my nipples.

"Harder, damn you, harder!" I whispered. As he sucked and nipped, I rocked against him, moving his cock in and out of me, until I came, digging my nails into his shoulders so sharply that he cried out.

The next day he came into the coffeehouse and laid his newspaper on his usual table.

Jen was standing behind him, clearing away some empty dishes. He hadn't even glanced at her when he came in.

"Large latte, for here," he said, coming up to the counter.

"Put your money away," I told him. "This morning it's on the house."

Thirty

BY KIM ADDONIZIO

*J*ust put on your sexiest clothes," Diana told me on the phone that evening, "and wait. Don't go anywhere. I have a surprise for you."

I was depressed, getting divorced, and as of today I was thirty. I wasn't in the mood for a surprise birthday present, but Diana was my best friend, and I figured I couldn't gracefully get out of whatever it was she'd dreamed up for me. I hoped she wouldn't want to go dancing; it had been a stressful day at the office, and I wanted to relax. Really, I just wanted to take a bath, curl up with a good book, and forget the fact that I hadn't had sex for four months, two weeks, and three days—ever since my marriage fell apart. But Diana had been insistent, so I took a long shower, got into my black lace panties, and slipped on the tiny red silk dress that had been languishing in my closet for weeks, ever since I'd bought it on a whim. I added black fishnets and red spiked heels so high I could barely walk in them; if Diana did want to go dancing, I thought, I'd have a good excuse to say no.

I felt better after I was dressed, my makeup in place. I checked out the woman in the mirror, her long blond hair, her dark red lips, and her shapely legs, and sighed. "What a waste," I said aloud. I turned sideways and admired my slim belly, the roundness of my ass and my tits. "You're thirty," I told myself, "not dead. Thirty." It didn't sound so bad. Maybe there was hope. My mother was sixty-three, and she had a boyfriend. Maybe I'd even meet someone tonight. The thought of having a man in my bed again made me wet. I imagined a smooth, sculpted chest against my tits, hard thighs, warm hands cupping my ass. I tried to imagine a face, but all I saw was the round, grinning mug of the obnoxious lawyer I worked for, and I definitely did not want him anywhere near my cream-colored satin sheets.

I prowled my apartment restlessly, waiting for Diana, feeling more and more horny. I lay down on the couch, settled myself against the big pillows, and slipped a finger into my underwear to touch my pulsing clit.

The phone rang.

"Damn," I said. I just couldn't ignore a ringing phone. It's one thing that drove my husband crazy. We would be in the middle of dinner, or an argument, and I'd have to answer instead of letting the machine pick it up. It's like a compulsion. The only time he didn't mind, actually, was when we were having sex; then he got a kick out of me trying to talk while he was licking my pussy or my nipples, or sliding his cock in and out of me.

Here I was thinking about my ex, and getting depressed again. Maybe he was calling now, I thought, to wish me a happy birthday, to say he'd realized that getting a divorce was a bad idea. He had never called, but I always hoped it would be him, always rushed to answer, somehow expecting his voice.

Diana was on the phone. "Ready?" she asked.

"I guess," I said. "I mean, I'm all dressed. What time will you be here?"

Diana laughed. "I'm right out front," she said, "on the car phone. Go to the front door."

I crossed the living room and opened my door. "Happy birthday, pal," Diana said on the phone. Then she hung up, and I watched her car disappear down the street, and looked in disbelief at the man standing there holding out a red rose.

"Michael," I said. Michael was Diana's boyfriend, and I had secretly lusted after him for the entire year the two of them had been together. I liked his impish, little-boy smile, the light in his blue eyes, the way he had held me when we danced, the one and only time we danced. How often had I slipped my fingers into my pussy at night, fantasizing that they were Michael's, writhed alone on my sheets until I came, and then felt guilty about wanting my best friend's boyfriend.

"What are you doing?" I asked. I got it, but I didn't get it. Diana must have forgotten something. She'd be back in a minute, and the three of us would go out as we had often done, to a restaurant somewhere, and I'd wonder whether to tell her that for a silly moment I'd thought she was actually giving me her boyfriend as a birthday present.

"Surprise!" Michael said. "Can I come in, or are you going to give me back?" He was wearing black jeans and cowboy boots, a white T-shirt and a black leather jacket. A red ribbon with a big bow was tied around his left wrist where he usually wore a thin gold chain. He handed me the rose, and I backed into my living room with him following me.

"Let's sit down," Michael said. He took off his jacket and tossed it onto a chair, then strolled over to my couch. He leaned back, flung his arms out along the back of the couch, crossed his legs, and grinned at me. "Come and join me," he said.

"Right," I said. I went over and sat down next to him, but at the very edge of the couch. I smelled his cologne and wanted to drown in it, to sink back and let the waves of heat washing over me pull me all the way under. I wanted to claw at his T-shirt like a wild animal and fasten my mouth onto one of his nipples and throw my arms around his neck and drag him deep into my pussy, wrap my legs around him and squeeze his ribs tight and not ever let him go. Instead, I sat primly on the edge of the couch, my legs together, and tried not to breathe.

"Uh—" I stammered.

"It's okay. Just relax," Michael said, and I felt the palm of his hand, hot as an iron, against the back of my neck. As he started rubbing my right shoulder, I took a long shaky breath, and the rose fell from my hand and lay there, red on the white wall-to-wall.

"Good," Michael said. "You're the birthday girl. Just enjoy it. You don't have to do anything. I'm here to give you pleasure. You're beautiful," he said.

"I'm thirty," I moaned, my head falling forward.

"So what," Michael said.

"You're a man. You're twenty-four. You just don't get it," I mumbled. It was harder and harder to talk. Both his hands were on my shoulders now, squeezing, his thumbs pressing in, the little knots of stress dissolving. The tension I'd built up from hunching in front of a computer screen

all day was traveling outward, humming through my
nerves, leaping into the room like sparks. Michael's hands
moved down my back. I opened my legs and slumped all
the way forward, hanging my head, feeling the blood rush
into my brain. His fingers were at the base of my spine
now, moving to massage my ass in deep, delicious circles. I
went completely limp.

"I know how you like it," Michael whispered. "I'm
going to do everything you like."

"I can't believe Diana tells you that stuff." A thrill of ex-
citement and shame ran through me, making me shudder.
Oh God, I thought, *I can't believe he knows all the things I told
Diana.*

"You'd better sit up before you pass out," Michael said.
He got a firm grip on my hair and pulled me back toward
him. I found myself lying in his arms, my legs sprawled
apart, my dress up, exposing my bare thighs above my
stockings, and my panties. I turned my face toward him,
and we began kissing, his hot tongue filling my mouth,
going down my throat, running along the edges of my
teeth. I kept my eyes open, looking into his. I was afraid
that if I closed them I'd see Diana, or my ex, watching us
disapprovingly. I wanted to pinch myself, to make sure I
hadn't made up me and Michael, passionately kissing, his
hands roaming over my ass as I maneuvered into his lap
and pressed my soaking pussy into the hardness of his
crotch. Diana had told me a few things about Michael, too:
that he loved the taste of pussy and would lick her practically forever; that he shaved the hair around his balls, and
liked to rub them in her face, over her eyes and nose and
down to her mouth so she could lick and suck on them.
The thought of Michael's balls in my face and the feel of
his cock as I ground myself into the fly of his jeans was too

much. I started coming, holding on to him as I squirmed and whimpered, the juices flowing out of me, soaking my already dripping panties, dampening my thighs, hot from friction.

"This is just the warm-up, baby," Michael said, as he slid me off him and onto the floor. I was still coming; he pushed the sole of one cowboy boot against my pussy, and I pressed against it, trying to finish my orgasm. He sat back and told me to take his boots off. I yanked off one, then the other. He stood up and stepped out of his jeans and shiny black briefs. Then he was pulling the crotch of my panties to one side, rolling on top of me to fill me with his big warm cock, intensifying my spasms of pleasure, making me cry out with each deep thrust. Somewhere in the back of my brain I realized we had ended up on top of the rose he'd brought, but I hardly felt the thorns pricking my body as he pounded into me, fast and hard the way I liked it. I thrashed around like a hooked fish, trying to open myself wider and wider, and with the next orgasm I let it all go and screamed.

"Good girl," Michael said. "That's a good little bitch. You've wanted it for so long, haven't you? You wanted to be bad, you wanted to have your friend's lover for yourself. I remember how we danced that night, how you pushed your hot body into mine. I know what a slut you really are, under that nice-girl facade." He kept talking, saying things that made me ashamed and excited, things I'd told Diana I wished a man would someday say to me. Diana. What a wonderful friend. I loved Diana. I started moaning her name as Michael withdrew his cock and put his tongue in its place, poking it in and out of me, moving up to encircle my clit, back deep into my hole, then my clit again, gently biting it and sucking it, tugging until I was begging him to fuck me again and fill me up so I could come on his hot cock. There was a knock on the door and Michael sat up. "Close your eyes and don't move," he said.

I lay there, on the verge of coming all over myself, wondering what was going to happen next.

"Keep your eyes closed," Michael said. In a moment I knew. I felt a woman's hands on my face. Her soft lips covered mine. Her fingers dipped between my legs and then she put them in my mouth, and through the smell of my pussy I inhaled Diana's perfume.

"Happy birthday, sweetheart," she said. "You did want both of us, didn't you?"

"Yes," I moaned, as they stood me up and led me to the bedroom. They gently pushed me onto the bed, and I lay there and waited for the next pleasure. I could no longer think. I was reduced to pure sensation: the coolness of the satin sheets, the sticky ooze between my legs. I heard the high buzzing of a vibrator, Diana's laughter, felt rose petals falling softly on my breasts and belly. I heard the phone ring on the nightstand, and my arm shot out to pick it up, but then I let my hand fall, palm up, back onto the bed. The machine clicked on, my voice said I wasn't there.

"Ready?" Michael said.

Ready, I thought. I'm free. I'm thirty. It's going to be a great year.

Hot Sauce

BY BONNIE BOXER

*T*he first time I encountered Rosa at the corner bodega it was as if my pussy had been hit by lightning. I'd just stopped in for some hot sauce, and there she was, selecting ingredients for some sort of secret recipe of her own—molasses, thick and syrupy; pieces of hot, gnarled ginger; and cloves of garlic, the world's most suggestive aroma. Her jet-black hair hung in a shining braid all the way down her back; her brow was furrowed with concentration. She was wearing a faded denim jacket and very tight, very new blue jeans. Her nail polish was a dark, metallic blue; even her lipstick was blue.

This was clearly a woman who didn't mind attracting attention, and she certainly caught mine. There's something about a beautiful woman in deep contemplation that does it for me every time. I found myself following her from aisle to aisle, like a woman in a trance. A trail of musky perfume emanated from her as she sashayed down the rows, picking items off the shelves to check a price or read the ingredients. I would've sworn that she was completely unaware of my covert attentions, but after a few minutes she spun around, cocked her head, smirked at me, and said, "Look, honey, if there's something you don't see on the shelves of this here store, maybe you're just not looking in the right place."

The next thing I knew I was helping her carry her groceries up the five flights to her nearby apartment. And I'd forgotten all about my search for hot sauce.

Rosa's place was chock-full of the stuff that dreams are made of: sexy posters of k. d. lang, Madonna, and Selena on the wall; cushy pillows "casually" tossed across the red velvet couch; a faux-bearskin rug conveniently arranged before the fireplace; candy dishes filled with peppermints, lollipops, and other alluring treats; an impressive collection of votive candles; and adult magazines and videos positioned strategically about the room. This was a girl who clearly understood and operated on the Pleasure Principle—my kind of gal.

"Cherry soda?" Rosa called from the kitchen as she started unloading the groceries, her voice a mix of coy and sarcastic.

"Sure," I answered, but by the time the word was out of my mouth she was already drawing near, beverage in outstretched hand. I reached for the glass, but Rosa withdrew it with a teasing smile. Like a traffic cop she motioned for me to stand still, then advanced again, holding the cool glass to my lips, tilting a sip of sweet soda into my mouth. She did it with such authority, I was taken aback. I swallowed hard, then watched, eyes glued to her dark-blue nail polish, as she brought the glass to her lips, drained its contents, and set it down on the table behind her. A mesmerizing display.

"There now," she said with a smirk, "that wet my whistle. How about yours?" I wasn't sure what to say. I was still a little shocked by what she'd done, taking such a liberty with someone she had only just met. But I could feel my nipples beginning to pucker against my bra, and I couldn't blame that on the cold soda.

As if reading my thoughts, Rosa took a long, leisurely glance at my breasts, fixing her stare on them. I followed her gaze, and sure enough, my nipples were poking through my tight sweater like gumdrops. I was embarrassed, and would have tried to explain it away with some pitiful excuse—but before I could open my mouth Rosa had sealed my lips with hers and was pressed up against me, kissing me hard. Her mouth was a sweet mix of pink soda and blue lipstick, an intoxicating brew. Her tongue slipped between my lips, a hot little cherry bomb, sizzling and explosive. I closed my eyes and inhaled her musky scent, letting myself drown in sensation. As I ate the lipstick right off her lips, I began to feel my pussy throb under my short skirt. I pressed my pelvis against hers; I could feel her jeans against my leg, and the sensation made me swoon. I curled my fingers through her belt loops and held on tight, feeling her breasts crushing mine, her entire body pushing against me, creating the kind of friction that leads to one thing only: fire.

I thought we were going to do it standing up, and was relieved when she escorted me with confidence over to the sofa. My relief—and lust—increased greatly when she knelt between my legs and began licking my skirt with her beautiful pink tongue, like a kitten. The skirt was pulled taut against my skin, so I could feel the strokes through the material. It was meant to drive me wild. She knew I wanted her mouth on my pussy, but she wasn't the type to rush. She was going to make me wait—maybe even beg—for it.

The afternoon sun slanted into the room, catching us in its caressing rays. My body warmed to it, stretched out into the pleasure rippling through me. Very slowly her fingers began moving up and down my calves, along my panty hose. Her fingernails raked my skin lightly, then harder, until they'd made little tears in the hosiery on either calf. She pushed her fingers into the holes and made direct contact with my skin, then slowly ripped the panty hose to shreds with her nails, careful not to hurt my vulnerable flesh, but making her point in no uncertain terms. The sound of ripping material was delicious. Once the panty hose were dispensed with, Rosa began a more powerful form of massage with her strong, competent fingers. Inch by inch she moved up my inner thigh, all the way up beneath my skirt, until she came to my black silk panties. When her finger reached my mound, we both gasped: I was soaking wet. She smiled up at me, and knowing that she could feel in the wet black silk my desire for her—so palpable and undeniable—made me feel unbearably open and exposed. I whimpered with embarrassment and lust.

Rosa took this as a signal to bury her face under my skirt and begin nibbling at my panties. Her movements grew more and more intense, as if she were struggling to control herself. Her teeth grazed my cunt through the silk, and I pushed myself hard against her. Her tongue was tantalizingly warm through the heat-conducting material. In a moment I felt her grasp the underwear with her teeth and slowly pull it off me, all the while continuing to rake my bare legs with her fingernails, like a lioness within striking distance of the first warm-blooded meal of her adult life.

My clit started throbbing harder; I imagined it glowing under her tongue, a helpless firefly trapped in a jar. I

watched her head bobbing up and down on me, her eyes
blissfully closed as she worked my pussy eagerly. "*Áay, que
rica!*" she murmured as she started lapping at me with little flicks of the tongue. "You taste so good! Who needs groceries?" This was a girl who clearly loved pussy and knew
just what to do with it. She nibbled my outer lips, suckled
the clit, and stroked the entire area lightly with her tongue
until I could barely stand it. When her tongue forcefully
poked my hole and began fucking me that way, I reached
around behind her head and grabbed her braid, pulling
her toward me, urging her on. I could feel myself getting
hotter and hotter as the pressure increased. My cheeks
were warm and flushed; her lioness claws on my thighs
were sending me into outer orbit. But just as I was approaching the moment of truth, she lifted her face, leaned
back, casually wiped her lips with the back of her hand,
and purred, "Ah, *mi corazón,* you didn't think Rosa would
let you get off that easy, did you?"

I was so inebriated with desire I could barely think
straight, let alone fathom Rosa's question. Every cell in my
body was poised on that tiny clitoral island in the sea of my
pussy. I could scarcely believe she had stopped; the sensation of her mouth on my cunt was still reverberating, creating little waves of pleasure and longing. I moaned in
frustration as she rose, walked away from me, and began
pulling down all the window blinds in the living room and
lighting candles here and there. Within moments my afternoon with Rosa had been transplanted into a Gothic lesbian love den, full of shadows and mystery and flickering
yellow light.

Immediately upon creating this transformation, Rosa
was back, lying on top of me on the red velvet couch. As we
kissed I could smell my most intimate scent on her mouth

and chin mingling with the aroma of her perfume. Her breasts were again pushed against me, pliant and cushy. My hungry mound seemed to have a will of its own, and was grinding hard against her pelvic bone like there was no tomorrow. But was it her pelvic bone? It suddenly occurred to me that Rosa had a visitor between her legs, a suspicion confirmed a moment later when she sat up, unzipped her jeans, extracted a long, thick dildo, and began to stroke it seductively. The sight of her working that dick would have been a turn-on no matter what, but this was no ordinary dildo; it glowed in the dark, shining between her legs like a beacon. It was an exotic, otherworldly blue—vaguely metallic, like her nail polish. I suddenly felt as if I were being seduced by a Martian. But at that particular moment, my clit still rock-hard, I truly didn't care if she was from this galaxy or another.

"This little guy has your name on it, baby," Rosa whispered, cradling the mock cock between my open thighs. And then, grinning like an angel, she rammed it in.

I moaned in ecstasy and surprise. I was so wet that it slipped right in—a delicious sliding sensation echoing through my cunt. The walls of my pussy just closed right up around it; I wasn't about to let it go. But Rosa wanted to fuck. Rosa wanted to ride. Rosa wanted to take me places.

"Let the glow-in-the-dark rodeo begin!" Rosa cried in a fake Tex-Mex accent. "Yee haw!"

She rode me like a pro. The smooth rubber cock rolled in and out of me like a stallion in a hurry. She pushed in hard, pounding against the tunnel of my cunt, then pulled out again, real slow, pausing with just the head of the cock at my open hole as I strained to take her back inside me, throbbing with unbearable emptiness. She pressed all the way back in, kissing me softly on the mouth, nibbling my lips, then withdrew again, this time teasing my soaking wet clit with the dildo. She dragged the dildo up and down along the outside of my pussy as if buttering bread. Every time it touched my clitoris I almost flew off the couch, my hips thrusting up toward her, trying to get her to enter me again. Just when I thought I couldn't stand another moment without her cock inside me, she'd plunge back in, nice and strong. Her rhythm was perfect, keeping me balanced between overwhelming need and fulfillment. With every thrust I'd whimper with gratitude. With every withdrawal I implored her to penetrate me once more.

I wanted to come so bad I could hardly stand it. My cunt was quivering wildly, becoming wetter and more inflamed with every stroke of her glowing sword.

Meanwhile Rosa was also getting close to coming. Each time the dildo rammed into me, its flat, flared base pressed hard against her clit, bringing her closer and closer to her own orgasm. Watching her pleasure build drove me wild. Her eyes were closed; her mouth opened with every thrust as she let out a little moan of pleasure. Her body was hot; I ran my hands along her back and down to her ass, circling the cheeks through her jeans with my palms, then running my fingers up and down along the crack, that most sensitive and forbidden region. Rosa growled as I did this, and the fucking took on a more urgent rhythm. She was plowing into me, so smooth, so hot, so powerful—and our bodies were pressed together, nipples hard against each other, faces cheek to cheek, our warm breath and our moans mingling, becoming more humid with every thrust. She sucked my earlobe as we approached our moment of release. The exhaustion and animal motion were so compelling that all we could do was work it until our bodies could take no more.

At last Rosa let out a long, loud wail as she hurled her cunt—and the cock—against me one last time. I knew she was coming; the dildo thrust into me so hard that it released my own explosive orgasm. We writhed together, our cunts greedily pushing against each other to extract every remaining wave of pleasure that had built up inside of us. As the throbbing subsided we kissed again, our tongues wrapping around each other the way our arms and legs were now intertwined. We lay like that for a while, dozing off and on as the candlelight flickered on the walls and the afternoon on the other side of the window shades eased silently into night.

After a time Rosa looked at me and smirked in her devilish way. "Well, *chica,*" she said, "I hope this isn't premature, but all that food you helped me carry home is gonna go bad if I don't do something with it. I don't make a habit of cooking for strangers—but if I do whip a little something up, any chance I could tempt you into staying for dinner?"

"That depends," I said, lowering my mouth to her already hard nipple, "on what you're planning for dessert."

A Live One

BY GRETA CHRISTINA

*W*hat an asshole, Sheila thinks as she plays with her pussy. He's been popping quarters into the booth like they were rock candy. A smile wouldn't cost anything extra.

She smiles down at the customer through the glass, a sugary, seductive smile full of bubble and promise. He responds with a blank stare, the same blank stare he's been giving her for the past five minutes. His face is flat and listless, a cheap cement statue of a gloomy frog, with a trickle of hostility leaking through the stone set of his mouth.

She sighs and spins around, giving up, turning her face away. She sticks her butt in the window, bends at the waist, and runs her hand slowly over her ass. *The flicking brick-wall men,* she thinks, as she rocks her hips slowly from side to side. *I've never understood why they come here. I mean, I can give them the sight of a dancing naked woman, but I can't give them the joy of watching a naked woman dance. Don't they get that they have to bring that themselves?*

She licks her forefinger and runs it up and down her pussy as she gyrates to the thumping music. She catches

Tanisha's eye, and gives her the contemptuous look she can't give the customer. Tanisha rolls her eyes, gives a quick nod of sympathy, and turns back to Danielle. The younger girl is sprawled over Tanisha's lap; she squirms and rolls her hips dramatically, putting on an extravagant show for the two drunken sailors in the corner booth. Tanisha scowls ferociously and slaps Danielle's tight, round rump; Danielle gives a theatrical squeal of pain and fear and wriggles in delight.

I like a girl who enjoys her work, Sheila says to herself. She knows these two; they'll be doing the real thing later on tonight. They get a kick out of faking it for the guys, but they never do it for real for money.

She hears the window panel slide down behind her, and glances over her shoulder. Yup, he's gone. What a tragic loss to the human race. She arches her back, aching from bending over, and looks around dutifully for a new customer.

Sure enough, just as she finishes stretching, the panel in the other corner booth slides up. Sheila glances at Lorelei, who's on her hands and knees, busily spreading her pussy for a middle-aged man with a briefcase in one hand and his dick in the other. Guess the new one's mine, Sheila concludes. Conscientious as always, she shimmies over, squats in front of the guy, and smiles. "Hi," she hollers over the deafening synth-pop din. "I'm Chloe."

In response he pulls a pad and pen out of his pocket and begins scribbling. He holds it up to the window and smiles back. *Hi Chloe,* it reads. *I'm Henry.*

Her eyebrows shoot up, surprised and impressed. *Smart guy,* she thinks. *Inventive. And he actually wants to talk to me. Maybe this will be a live one.*

She tucks her legs under her like a cheesecake model

and runs an exploring hand over her torso. "So, Henry, you come here often?"

He writes furiously for a minute and holds the pad up to the window. *Yes,* it says. *That's why I brought this. I know it's too loud in there for you to hear me. . . .*

He flips to another page and scribbles some more. *But I want to be able to talk. This is the best I could come up with.*

He reaches into his pocket and quickly inserts a handful of quarters into the slot. She ducks her head and blushes; she knows she should know better, but she's always a little surprised when guys drop their money just to look at her. She licks her finger and runs it over her nipple, pinching it lightly. "So, you like me?"

Yes, he writes. *You seem . . . friendly.*

She leans back, spreads her pussy lips open for a teasing moment, then lets them close again. "I try," she answers. "So what would you like to talk about?"

You, he writes.

"Sure thing," she smiles. "What would you like to know?"

He thinks for a moment, then scribbles again. *What part of your body do you like best?*

Her eyebrows shoot up again. "Interesting question. No one's asked me that before."

Really? Nobody?

"Well, nobody in here, anyway," she says with a shrug. "But to answer your question, I'd have to say . . . my ass. I really like my ass a lot. Would you like to see it?"

He scribbles hastily. *Sure, I'd like to see your ass. . . .*

He flips to a new page. *But I want to see your face too.*

"You got it, bub," she says cheerfully. She leaps to her feet, spins around, flops over at the waist, and gapes at him between her legs. "How's this?" she grins.

He laughs and shakes his head. *That's really silly,* he writes.

"You're right," she answers. "I never understood that one either. Okay, let's try this."

She gets on hands and knees, putting her body in profile. She gives him a smoky look over her shoulder, tousles her hair, and growls. Tiger woman, she thinks. Queen of the Jungle. She shifts her leg to show him her soft, round ass, arches her hips into the air and grinds them around in slow circles. "How's that?" she asks.

Much better, he writes. *So what do you like doing with your ass, Chloe?*

She doesn't hesitate. "I like to get it fucked," she replies crudely.

Show me.

She puts her finger in her mouth and draws it out slowly, getting it nice and wet. An unexpected shudder goes through her body as she raises her eyes to meet his. His gaze trails down her back like gentle fingers, and she squirms and wriggles, pleased and flattered and oddly bashful. She reaches back with one hand, opens her ass cheek invitingly, and runs her wet finger up and down the crack. He gazes back at her face, solemn and anxious; she gives him a small, coy smile and waits.

Please?

She grins and licks her lips. She wets her finger again, teases her crack for a moment, then slowly slides her finger into her asshole.

A sudden rush of warmth and pleasure rolls into her head. She moans and slumps and closes her eyes, almost against her will, as she slowly pumps her finger into her ass. A small, tight spot in her throat begins to dissolve, melts down into her breasts and stomach; she bucks her hips up hard, bites her lip, and begins to whimper quietly. Her ass clenches tight around her finger, pulling it in deeper.

She opens her eyes suddenly, remembering where she is, and gives Henry a wild, intent look. His hands are pressed against the glass, clutching the notebook; his eyes are open wide, shining with lechery and delight. She shoves a second finger into her asshole and begins to fuck herself in earnest, hard and crude and a little rough, just the way she likes it. Her asshole grabs her fingers like a vise, demanding and insistent. She moans louder, throws her head back, and lets out a sharp little cry of bliss.

She collapses onto the floor, panting dramatically. She rolls onto her back, pulls out her fingers, and surreptitiously wipes them on the grimy carpet. "Oh, my God," she whispers.

He takes a deep breath and pulls away from the glass. *Jesus, you're beautiful,* he writes. *Thank you. That was wonderful.*

She stretches out and props herself up on her elbow. "You're welcome," she says.

Was it real? he writes.

"Mmmmmmm," she murmurs. "You bet."

Really?

She hesitates. "Well . . . yeah," she says uncomfortably. "More or less. I mean, it felt good. Felt real good, actually. But no, I didn't come, if that's what you're asking."

He smiles, nods, and writes for a long moment. *Thanks for being honest. I appreciate that.*

A softer song comes on the jukebox, a sweet, slow-dance love song with a low female voice. *So, do you like working here?* Henry writes.

The lie springs to Sheila's lips, the automatic lie ham-

mered into her by months of unspoken training. She gives
him a long, serious look, closes her lips tight, looks around
to make sure nobody is listening, and speaks.

"The truth?" she asks, leaning into the glass.

Of course, he writes.

"Well . . . here's the deal," she murmurs as softly as she
can and still have him hear her, as loudly as she can without being overheard. "Yeah, I do like it. The money's good
and the hours are flexible. I don't have to work forty hours
to pay the rent, so I have time to do my own stuff. And the
dancing itself is fun. I like to dance and I like my
body . . . and I like sex, I like being sexy." He grins and
waggles his eyebrows. "And the other women are amazing.
They're smart and sexy and funny, and they really take care
of each other. I just love them to pieces."

But . . . he writes.

It all comes out in a rush. "The flicking men," she says
bitterly. "They want it all spoon-fed to them. Pussy and
pleasure and all the rest of it. They think sex should be like
TV, but with hotter babes and no commercials. They just
wanna sit back and suck it down like baby birds. They don't
smile, they don't say hi, they don't say, 'Thank you' or
'You're pretty' or even 'Nice tits, baby.' They just stare like
dead fish. Not all of them . . . but a flicking lot of them."
She takes a deep breath, startled by her own anger.

He nods. *Men are assholes,* he scribbles.

She laughs heartily, her bitterness broken for the moment. "Thank you," she says. "So . . . what would you like
to see now? Anything special?"

What would you like? he writes.

She chuckles. "Why don't you take your clothes off and
dance for me?" she jokes. "Just for a change."

He scribbles seriously for a long minute: *Okay, I'll do that. But I'd better warn you, I'm not a very good dancer.*

He sets the pad on the bench, runs his hand through his hair, and slowly begins to unbutton his shirt. She stretches out like a cat and watches in awe, amazed that he took her seriously.

He unbuttons his shirt slowly, caressing his chest as he uncovers it bit by bit. She plays with her own body in response, moving her hand in slow circles over her belly as he strips off his shirt and shows her his thin chest. He begins to roll his torso in slow, hesitant, snakelike ripples. She can smell herself—the sharp, salty smell her pussy gives off when it wants something really badly. She watches hungrily as he runs his hands over his chest and slides them down over his hips. He begins to rub his dick through his jeans, squeezing it in rhythm with the slow music, and she draws a sudden, ragged breath. Her pulse beats hard inside her clit; she shoves her hand between her thighs and squeezes tight.

Suddenly he stops dancing and snatches up the pad and pen. *I feel silly,* he writes. *I feel like a dork.*

She shakes her head. "You shouldn't," she replies. "You look great. I'm getting totally wet watching you." She stares meaningfully at his crotch. "Now show me more."

He drops pad and pen, slumps against the wall, hooks his thumb into his waistband, and gives her a moody, smoldering stare like a model for designer jeans. She laughs and nods approvingly. He begins to move again, squirming and writhing against the wall. Slowly, teasingly, he unbuckles his belt, unzips his fly, tugs his swollen dick out of his pants and into the open air. He cradles it in his hand and gives her a wide-open look, proud and fearful and eager for approval.

She ogles his cock and licks her lips, drinking in his eagerness like water. "Very pretty," she says. "Very nice indeed. But I wanna see more. Turn around and pull them all the way down. Show me your ass."

He complies immediately; turns to face the wall, arches his back, and slowly pulls his jeans down over his slim hips. She whistles appreciatively as the fabric drops down to his thighs and his bare ass is revealed. He blushes bright red, presses his hands against the wall, and slowly bends over to give her a better look. She stares intently at his smooth, tight ass, relishing his exposure, sucking in the view like a starving woman. Her clit thumps hard, demanding attention; she begins to caress it in earnest, moving her finger in slow, tight circles. *I love a boy who does what I tell him,* she thinks.

"Now turn around again," she commands. "Let me see your dick. Let me see you jerk off."

He spins around to face her, jeans around his knees, face flushed, his dick twitching of its own accord. He jams his back against the wall, licks his hand like a dog, and begins to slide it up and down the shaft of his cock.

A sudden flash of longing stabs into her cunt, and she whimpers and spreads her legs wider. She opens her pussy lips with her fingers and thrusts her hips toward the glass, frantically and insistently, forcing her hole into the open, trying to show him as much of herself as she can. His eyes widen as they take in her sopping-wet cunt; he grips his cock with a trembling hand as she spreads herself apart and furiously rubs her swollen clit. Their eyes connect; they stare intently, flushed, shivering, mouths hanging open, eyes wide. His hand moves faster and faster; a shudder travels through his body, and he bites his lip, throws his

head back, and squirts into his hand. She sees his face con-
tort. She cries out hard, and comes.

They both take a deep breath and slump backward.
Sheila stretches back on the grimy carpet and clamps her
thighs around her hand; Henry collapses against the wall,
lost in quiet bliss.

Finally he pulls his pants up, takes a handkerchief out
of his pocket, and wipes the come off his dick and his
hand. Shoving the hanky back in his pocket, he picks up
the pad and pen.

Thank you thank you thank you, he writes.

"Jesus," she gasps. "You're welcome. Thank *you.*"

That was real . . . right?

She nods. "Yeah," she answers. "That was real."

The window panel starts to slide down. Henry scrab-
bles through his pockets and quickly drops another quarter in the slot. The panel slides up again; he spreads his
hand and shows her the contents with a sad, wistful smile.
One more quarter. He drops it in and shrugs. *How much
time do we have left?* he writes.

"About a minute," she answers. "A little less actually.
Shit. You'd better get dressed."

He pulls his shirt on and quickly zips his pants. *So is
your name really Chloe?* he writes.

"No," she replies. "Of course not."

What is it really?

She gives him a long, clear look. *Maybe I should make up
a fake real name,* she thinks. She likes this guy a lot; it'd
make him happy to think she'd confided in him. She gazes
at the floor, thinks carefully for a moment, then looks back
at his face and shakes her head.

"I'm not going to tell you that," she says. "I'm sorry."

Quite all right, he scribbles. *I understand. Thanks for not lying to me.*

"You're welcome," she replies.

They stare at each other awkwardly, somewhat at a loss for words. "That was wonderful," she says at last. "Really. You made my day."

He kisses his hand and reaches out to touch the glass. The panel drops down, sliding over his hand, clicking shut. "Come back sometime," she calls into the metal plate. She presses her hands against the window, drained and dazed and a bit forlorn, hoping that he heard her.

She feels a light touch on her shoulder. "Hey, Chloe," Tanisha says. "It's time for your break." She gives Sheila a light slap on the rump. "Nice show, girl," she adds. "Hell, you even got me going."

"Thanks." Sheila sighs. "Me, too. Sometimes I really like this job."

"I know what you mean, babe," Tanisha says as Sheila walks off the stage. "I know what you mean."

The Naked City

BY MARCY SHEINER

*U*ncle Mikey had a peculiar and, so the family thought, harmless hobby: Perched in his eighth-floor New York apartment, he whiled away the hours exploring the city through a pair of powerful and expensive binoculars. When I was little he'd let me look through them as he pointed out interesting architectural features on the city skyscrapers. That was probably one of the reasons I ended up studying architecture, an unusual choice for a girl in those days. On a clear day he'd take me up to the roof, from which we could see all the way downtown to the Statue of Liberty.

Thus I grew up thinking that city-gazing was a pastime as normal as bird-watching, and after Uncle Mikey died my aunt presented me with his binoculars. I was twenty-six years old before I realized that, when I hadn't been around to cramp his style, Uncle Mikey had found subjects for scrutiny that were far more entertaining than Lady Liberty.

One evening while casually running my binoculars up, down, and around the city, I was stopped dead by the sight of a young woman preparing to step into the shower. Feeling I was invading her privacy, I quickly veered my optics to the right—only to have them land on a window behind which a couple were locked in an amorous embrace, the woman's red sweater raised to reveal a plump breast. Shocked, I dropped the binoculars into my lap as the implications of what I was seeing dawned on me: Uncle Mikey had been a voyeur.

I shuddered, wondering if my uncle had been a pervert. From what I'd seen, he'd had a fairly normal relationship with my aunt, and I certainly never recalled him touching me in an inappropriate manner. Yet there was no getting around the fact that he'd enjoyed spying on people during their most intimate moments.

Slowly I raised the binoculars and focused on the couple who'd been making out. They'd progressed to the point where they were lying down, and therefore hidden from view. Moving my super specs to the left, I saw the young woman emerge, wet and glistening, from her shower. Fascinated, I watched as she dried herself off, vigorously bouncing her breasts with the towel. My God, why didn't she think to draw the shade? And how could that couple paw each other in full view of the entire city? Maybe Uncle Mikey wasn't the only sicko around—maybe the city was crawling with exhibitionists. Shaken, I drank a cup of cocoa, and carefully closed every shade and curtain before retiring.

The next day I couldn't stop thinking about what I'd seen through the binoculars. Surely what I'd done was immoral—and yet I couldn't wait to get home from work and "watch the movie," as I came to think of it. Although I felt somewhat guilty, and still thought of Uncle Mikey as something of a wrongo, I had to admit that I understood him. I canceled dinner with my boyfriend, Adam, and declined my friend Sally's invitation to go to the movies. I had to follow my curiosity, never mind about it killing the cat.

I set myself up for the evening, bringing pillows, blankets, and a bottle of wine over to my window seat. The city's lit windows twinkled against the darkening sky. As the night wore on, the prudent closed their curtains, while the more thoughtless—or daring?—remained exposed to curious eyes. I watched as mothers prepared babies for bed, teenagers copped one last feel before separating, older couples climbed into bed and turned out the light. Finally I lucked out—I hit upon a couple right across the street, a few stories down, whose window angle allowed me a panoramic view of their activities.

Completely naked, they lazily slithered over and around each other, unaware they were providing me with hot entertainment. I found them extremely sensual as they coiled their long, smooth limbs in an endless variety of positions. I was surprised to find that what turned me on the most was not his long prick gliding in and out of her inviting cunt, but the looks on their faces as they became more and more aroused. And when they came, their faces were utterly exquisite.

First her orgasm began, as her mouth opened wide; apparently she was making a lot of noise, which I unfortunately couldn't hear. Her eyes were half-closed, but I could still glimpse that peculiar look of ecstasy, so intense it bordered on suffering. As her head thrashed from side to side, I zeroed in on her partner and watched his face dissolve in a thousand emotions as he released his fluid into her. I could actually see beads of sweat forming over his thin mustache as he pursed his lips, probably making an "ooooh" sound.

At that point I abandoned the binoculars to tend to my own needs. I pulled my skirt up and slipped my hand in under my panties. I was soaking wet between my legs, and the moisture made it easy for my fingers to slip inside. I pulled them out and brought them to my nose to sniff the aroma. Then I reached in again and flicked myself in earnest, rubbing my swelling clit back and forth with my thumb. I like to finish off with my vibrator, which I had brought over to my window seat with a long extension cord. It hummed quietly as I pressed it between my legs. I had taken the precaution of turning off every light in my apartment so nobody could see what I was up to, yet I couldn't help but fantasize that somebody was watching me as I came.

A week went by, and I spent every night in front of the window. Eventually I selected a few main stars from the cast of characters in my vicinity; on any given night I could locate at least one couple making love, one bather, and one masturbator. I lost all interest in seeing Adam, who began to complain about my lack of attention to him. I didn't care; I was too absorbed in my new hobby.

One night as I sat munching popcorn and gazing through my binoculars, I heard a key turning in the lock. I froze. Adam had a key to my apartment, but had never used it without first telling me he was coming over. When he walked in, I nearly sobbed with relief that he wasn't a burglar or a rapist. But as Adam gazed around the darkened room, and I saw what he was seeing, I cringed in embarrassment. In this case one picture was indeed worth a thousand words: The scene revealed the sordid story of my week's activity.

I had just about moved into the window seat. Lying atop the bedding were my binoculars, vibrator, dildo, and lubricating jelly. The floor was strewn with candy wrappers, and an empty wineglass stood on the windowsill.

"What have you been doing?" Adam asked, bewildered.

I held my breath as he came over and picked up the binoculars. Slowly he raised them to his eyes and peered through. A low, throaty chuckle emerged as he moved them from window to window, pausing every now and then to observe a scene.

"This is some trip," he said softly. "How'd you ever get into doing this?"

"Well, see, my Uncle Mikey . . ." I began, hesitantly at first, then excitedly describing the scenarios I'd witnessed, pointing Adam in key directions. At first he roared with laughter, thinking this was a big prank. But when he came to the sensual lovers with the expressive faces he stopped laughing. The binoculars remained riveted to that one spot, and I watched the bulge in Adam's jeans grow and throb. Hardly believing what was happening, I knelt on the pillows, unzipped Adam's pants, and took out his pulsing meat. I pulled on it a few times with my hand, feeling it in its half-erect state. I love it like that, just before it gets hard, and I know I have the power to make it grow and stiffen.

I parted my lips to take him into my mouth. I licked and sucked, sliding his cock all the way down my throat, excited by the thought that he was watching my favorite couple fucking their brains out. When he came in a gush of liquid, I pictured the woman's open mouth, the man's pursed lips, and greedily swallowed Adam's come. In the back of my mind I couldn't help but hope that my couple had been watching us.

Quietly Adam stroked my hair. I looked up question-ingly.

"Whew!" was all he said, before lifting me into his arms and heading in the direction of the bedroom.

"Hey," I protested. "Where are you going?"

"To bed, baby. I'm gonna fuck your brains out."

"Oh, you are going to fuck my brains out, Adam, but not in bed."

"Not in bed?"

"Uh-uh." I pointed to the window.

"Really?"

"Really."

Adam hesitated, as if struggling with his conscience, then shrugged a "what the hell" and headed back to my lit-tle den of sin. I knew exactly what I wanted to do, and I choreographed the entire wonderful dance. First I lit a candle to give the corner a bit of illumination, just in case anyone might happen to be watching. Then I got down on all fours, facing sideways so that my entire body could be seen, but so I could still turn my head and see out. I told Adam to get behind me.

"Can you get hard again yet?" I asked. Adam usually needed at least a ten-minute respite in between erections.

"Are you kidding? This is too hot not to," he said, grabbing my hips and pulling me onto his cock. "Okay, girl," he whispered, "ride me."

And ride him I did. With Adam pulling me by the hips I slid slowly back and forth over his prick. I made lazy cir-cles to get it to touch me in all the right spots. I slammed vigorously against him, taking him to the root, causing his balls to slap against my labia. I turned my head to look out the window. Was anyone watching? I couldn't tell, but I imagined that someone, anyone, was. The thought of others observing me like this, so sexy, so juicy, my hair hanging down, my tits shaking, my ass up in the air just begging for pleasure, was the most exciting sensation I had ever known. Goose bumps crawled over my flesh, and my cunt contracted, slowly at first, then in wider and wider circles, suffusing my whole body with waves of pleasure. I shivered and moaned, my head dropping down. A few final thrusts and Adam showered my open vagina with another hefty dose of semen. Half laughing, half crying, we collapsed onto the pillows and kissed each other passionately.

I'll never know if anyone saw us that night, but I like to think they did. After that Adam made me give up my voyeurism, saying he thought it was unethical and maybe even illegal. I have to admit, though, that sometimes when he's not around I sneak a little peek at the passing show. Is it really so bad to enjoy watching people in the throes of pleasure? How did Uncle Mikey feel about it? I guess I'll never know. But I do know that I can't help but laugh now whenever I remember the closing line from that famous television series: "There are eight million stories in the naked city. This has been one of them."

Thumper
and the
Plaid Rabbits

BY BETH LEEZER

She walked up the aisle with cognac eyes, stopped next to him in the aisle, examined her ticket and the empty seat. Greg had no idea it was his lucky day until the red-head lifted her luggage into the overhead compartment, exposing herself. A strange greeting . . . but nice.

When the girl reached up, peach garters winked at him. Eye level with the silver clasps, Greg accepted the view with pleasured astonishment. The pussy curled in its silk cage was like flames reaching for him. He leaned forward to take in a fragrance similar to the Sonora Desert after a rain.

The naughty dress lowered as she closed the overhead cabinet doors. Without so much as an "Excuse me" she slid against his knees as she moved to her seat. The strict pleats of her skirt tried but failed to conceal the plump bottom jiggling within. It was a juicy ass, just like a well-fed girl should have. Tiny rabbits danced around the hem of the plaid.

Once seated, she looked left, studying the tightly

bunned blond head of the woman beside her until the woman glared back. To the right she scrutinized Greg while tugging a curl from a corner of her wire spectacles. Seven scattered freckles on a cute nose insisted she was innocent. Greg could not help but smile. Aisle lights faded on the midnight flight from Phoenix to San Diego. The plane took the runway.

Greg fantasized a slick pussy rotating atop his cock as the plane ascended toward the clouds. That "Weeeeeeeee!!!!" feeling in the bottom of his head during takeoff might mix with the sensation of a cunt slide-sucking his prick. With any luck it would freak out his brain, and he'd come until the pussy was sprayed white, the chair filled with goo, and him a babbling idiot.

Greg snorted at this unlikelihood and chanced a look at the girl, who had turned away from him. Beside her the woman in the bun had fallen asleep with a business publication in her lap. The redhead's legs were curled under, stretching her dress above her ass. She lay sideways against the back of the seat, her head perilously close to the padded shoulder of Ms. Executive. Greg blinked while his mind did back flips. He took a deep breath and wondered how her ice-cream skin would quiver if he rubbed it with his five-o'clock shadow.

Peach straps lined each cheek of that ass, and they pouted as if in prison. She had magenta pubic hair that didn't curl, lying like a horse's mane between her thighs. Greg desperately wanted a comb. This girl was testing him.

But why? Why him? What the hell could he do for her on a plane that was completely full? If he shoved his mouth in the crack of her ass and gobbled the marshmallow flesh, people would notice. The pulse pounded in his prick as his hand strayed to the armrest and pushed it slowly up.

The garters were old silk, the buckles antique, with etchings of flowers on the tarnished clips. Had she bought them used? How many pussies had that lace strapped down to be licked? Maybe years ago she had stolen them from the drawer of an older sister who'd bought them at a vintage shop and worn them thin. Perhaps the older sister's cunt was a golden red and glistened like sun-drenched wheat when it came, whereas the younger's was more of a dark, dewy velvet rose.

The girl did not move or indicate that she was aware of Greg's attentions, but he knew she was. She was waiting for his hands, which were beautiful. Greg was vain about them, had the nails manicured twice a month so the tips were white. Tanned and double-jointed, they were perfect for finger-fucking, nipple pinching, and of course caressing. He rested a forefinger on her left garter.

"Let's see," he said to himself, "if this girl really wants to play."

The finger slipped beneath the silk, and pulled it taut, like a bow. He heard her hold her breath, so he let go. The snap of silk against skin sounds softer than it feels, and as he watched, a red mark surfaced, marking her ass.

Uh-oh, he thought. Greg figured he could point to the guy in front of them if she turned around angry. Her back-side began to quiver. He gulped. She was moving, but not turning . . . no, not at all, merely raising that powder puff farther into the air, exposing a view of her crevice, which was clenching like a hungry mouth, open and shut.

Holy God, was it alive?

That was not a pussy. It was an exotic sea anemone. Glistening pink swirled before Greg's eyes. Its closing and popping open undid his manners. Without thinking, he shoved his finger into the puckering mouth.

"Hello, hello, hello," it said to him, soft as a cloud and slick as a squid. He rested his other hand on her ass cheek for support, because he felt faint at his own luck. He pushed in and out a bit just for the hell of it, enjoying the gooey sweetness, then got down to business.

Let's see, he silently asked. *Where are you, hmm?*

The tip of his finger brushed every crevice, all over the deliciously slimy interior.

"Where are you?" he whispered. "Come out, come out, wherever you are—ahhh, there she is. C'mere." His finger rubbed the little thing affectionately, like the chin of a reluctant cat.

The G spot.

It was a little uneven and tucked beneath a ridge under the belly button. It was prickly.

Her asshole was fluffy; all he wanted to do was slap on a little butter and some honey and eat this biscuit. It was rutting onto his finger as he teased the G spot. His pearl-tipped pinkie traveled the rim of the anus, exploring its sensitive ridges—pretending to plunge in, then not. So smug was he at holding her orgasm in the palm of his hand that he dipped his finger into her squishy pussy like a chip to be popped into his mouth. Then Mr. Cool realized *he* could not wait.

The pinkie baptized itself deeply into the ass, the forefinger fondled her clit without mercy. Two other fingers spun around inside to relieve the G spot of its torture.

She came with the quietest of jerks. Cream frothed onto Greg's wrist. Her legs did not stop trembling, even as he rubbed the moisture down her flanks to her curled toes. Greg merrily licked his digits and waited to see what would happen next.

It took a while for her to sit up.

Perhaps he should stop licking his fingers, or maybe extend his hand to share?

The dishevelment of the blonde with the business magazine wiped the smirk off his face. His redhead stood, her own fingers glistening. Her fox eyes looked meaningfully at what he recognized now to be the third porn of this party. The magazine was shredded across the woman's lap. Wetness darkened the crotch of her pants, and the zipper was down. The bun, which had been pulled firmly back, now stumbled around her shoulders in disarray.

Incredulous, he looked to the clever redheaded girl for confirmation, and she held up the prize fingers. In slow motion they glided wetly to his nose. He inhaled a full-bodied pussy aroma that was not the redhead's.

She whispered, "Meet me in the john." And left.

This is getting out of hand, he thought happily, while rubbing come into his nostrils. Who was he dealing with?

Aw, who cares, he answered, standing in the aisle, knowing his erection was trying to tear like Alien through his pants. He imagined the passengers' alarm if li'l Elvis actually did fight its way through zipper-land and hiss at everybody, shooting sperm everywhere. People would scream and faint; the plane would crash, because the captains would get it in the eye. . . . But nothing bizarre occurred, and Greg reached the bathroom with little incident.

He pulled off his pants faster than Clark Kent. Arranging his jeans on the toilet as a cushion, he sat and spread his thighs wide so his dick stuck straight up like a butter churn. The door handle clicked. He had left it unlocked, almost daring someone else to enter. She peeked in and observed his eager extremity. A little slyness flickered at the corners of that shapely mouth. A kisser like Veronica Lake's, he decided: wide hilly upper lip, and tiny round bottom one, perfect for framing the stem of a prick as the tongue caressed its vein.

Her glasses were gone, and Greg smiled at this mysterious female with the elegant cheekbones, suddenly understanding the predatory look in her eyes. This was no girl, this was a woman. She stepped in, immediately leaning into him, and without ceremony pulled up the bottom of her dress. He kept his fists clenched on his knees, unwilling to touch her yet.

The "Fasten Seat Belt" light came on outside. There were knocks on the door. Eyeing Greg, the redhead reached back and locked it with finality.

She pulled the plaid garment over her head, and two ice-cream-cone toppers spilled from the material, bounced free a few times, then lay still. Being naturally large, there was a nice swing to them when she arched her back. Their round architecture offered refuge and pleasure. They molded softly around his face. He inhaled and sighed, then took up like a pig at supper, slurping while she watched and played with his hair.

All the while an emergency was building up in his cock. It began as a glowing ball of sexual energy throbbing between his anus and dick. When she talked dirty, it grew. It remained at the base of his dick and felt about the size of an apricot, at first. But when she reached down and stroked his balls, cooing and sucking, the energy ballooned to cantaloupe size. Yet, for him, the most wonderful thing about sex was not launching that energy too soon.

Finally she placed one bare foot on the toilet paper rack, the other on a ledge. With thighs trapped in juice-darkened garters, she squatted onto Greg like an Indian mistress, slower than poured honey. He banged his head back against the wall in happy tension as his hands kneaded her buttocks. She was so leisurely about it, he felt he would go insane. It was like his dick was being stirred into something warm, like hot chocolate, or being mixed into somebody's dessert, with melting sugar, milk, and butter. Absolutely delectable.

She put him in a semi-liquid world each time she engulfed him, her nipples bobbing, boobs shining. His anus extended to the walls around them as if the walls were caving in. As the stewardess outside buckled her seat belt and opened a trashy novel, the redhead told Greg she wished there was time for an ass fucking. And would he like to squirt all over her meringue cheeks and rub it in like a lotion? Greg squeezed her waist and pumped her up and down, faster and faster. The plane was descending. His ears popped. That "Weeeeee!!!" feeling hit the back of his head. His eyes crossed. His balls rumbled.

Holy fucking damn, he moaned and let it go, lifting her off just before his spasms pumped out the sperm. It shot up from the base of his dick and jetted out the tip like machine-gun fire. Later he swore it was about two-hundred miles per hour. Everything he had erupted onto her stomach and breast.

She kneaded his dick to wring every bit of mellow from it, watching—too intently—the way his jaw quivered as he forced himself not to squeeze her thighs too hard. She admired the Adam's apple in his straining neck. She smiled at his wide-open eyes. It was charming that he did not know what to say.

Sweat made their hair dark at the roots. He luxuriated in her softness, while she licked jism from his fingers like lemon pie.

The plane skidded to a stop, forcing her to lean into him. Greg locked her in his arms.

"Tell me your name?" he asked, stroking her vanilla back.

She kissed the top of his head and whispered, "Don't ruin it."

"Not even a name?"

"All right," she said in his ear with a giggle. "Just call me Thumper."

She dressed, gave him a deep kiss, then backed out the door with the same sly smile she wore upon entering.

He just sat on the toilet and glowed for a while. When the stewardess jiggled the handle and inquired if anyone was left, he gathered his spent body together and sauntered back to his seat. Greg reached for his briefcase and spied a silver clip with a few peach strands stuck in the minuscule spring.

He put it in his pocket.

Outside, Thumper jumped in a taxi. She pulled out a cell phone.

"Hello, Helen? Sorry to call you at home so late, but I've changed my mind, we won't have to push back the deadline on my *Erotica* story, after all, because I just wrote the last page about five minutes ago. It's a new process of writing for me, exhaustive, but definitely satisfying," she confided, unable to suppress a grin as she watched Greg walk out the glass doors and hail his own taxi.

Five Miles
to Minooka

BY JENNIFER MILLER

ive miles to Minooka." The excitement in me doubled at the sight of the sign. Jade and I became friends over the Internet, both avoiding the real world. I think fate made us meet and become friends. We had both just gotten out of abusive relationships and needed each other's understanding to survive.

We lived about four hours from each other, so after talking a few months we decided to meet. Jade seemed very dear to me, and had become my closest friend.

She had found a hotel halfway between our towns and reserved our rooms. I was so nervous I hunted down a restaurant right off the highway, and sat for a minute to reapply my lipstick. I then headed for the hotel.

When I walked in I was completely taken by surprise: *This is a lovers' cove!* It was lit by candlelight, and a sensual aroma consumed the air.

I gave the hostess my name and she smiled and said, "The other half of your party is waiting at the table." A young, handsome waiter escorted me to the table.

Jade practically jumped out of her chair and ran to me. I had been so worried about how the first minute we met would go. We hugged, and kissed each other's cheek, as if we had been friends since grade school.

We talked about every major part of our lives, and even the minor parts of them. We were still talking about grade school when the cute waiter took our orders. We talked about old boyfriends and the trouble we caused.

When our food arrived we were still laughing about childhood like we were still kids. It was amazing—even though we talked online all the time, I never imagined this day going so well.

I was sipping on my drink when I felt her leg run up my calf. I wondered, *Was that an accident? Or is she coming on to me?* I kept questioning what happened, but my body was busy sending me signals. It didn't matter really how it happened, what mattered was I liked the feel of it. *Should I attempt to rub her leg? I will know for sure then if this is something . . .*

I looked deep into her eyes as we talked, so I could watch her reaction. I slipped my foot out of my high-heeled shoe. Slowly I ran the side of my foot up Jade's soft, well-defined calf. I watched carefully for her reaction. Her next breath was a little deeper, the corners of her lips lifted a little higher. I slowly caressed her calf.

No more food was eaten. We played "footsy," caressing thighs and massaging calves. The conversation didn't stop, and we had another drink.

I was in my business suit, and the skirt and jacket were just irritating at this point. Once I was back in my room I got out of my suit and started unpacking for the night.

Jade had found out about the entertainment in town. It sounded like we were going to a lounge with a live band.

There was still time to relax before I got ready, so I raided the mini-bar.

I don't know if it was the buzz the drink gave me, or the thought of Jade in the next room—but I had wonderfully warm sensations flowing through my body. Slowly I finished my drink and then started to shower.

The hot water was gently beating down against my skin. I could feel every drop, and every drop drove my body wild. I wanted to be touched, kissed, and held. Passion was pouring out of me, and it was coming from somewhere deep inside. I had never felt this kind of passion before. It was amazing; I could close my eyes and it was as if each drop of water was someone else's fingertips against my skin. When I was washing my hair, my hands became someone else's, Jade's, massaging and pulling at my scalp; my body became even more aroused. The anticipation of being with her tonight was starting to hurt. I wanted to be with her now.

When I got out of the shower I threw on a purple silk slip and started to do my hair. That was done in seconds; my hair is too short to spend much time on. Tonight I needed to look better than I normally did. I felt the need to impress Jade, even though we already knew and cared for each other. Now that there seemed to be a sexual underlining, the entire meeting ritual was somehow starting all over.

I was finishing my makeup when I heard a knock at the door. I went to answer it, before realizing the knock wasn't at the front door, but at the door adjoining my room to Jade's. Just the thought of her at that door excited me. I opened it, and she stood there in a terry-cloth robe, more attractive than ever. I felt a little insecure. She was so beautiful, and I am so average. But the look in her eye said something else. She couldn't take her eyes off me, and she stumbled over her words.

"Can I borrow your hairspray? I seem to have forgotten mine."

All I could do was smile and say yes. When I turned toward the bathroom Jade stopped me. "You look so beautiful in that slip." I started blushing; I could feel the burning sensation in my cheeks getting worse as I thanked her. "Is it silk?" I just nodded my head in answer. Jade then proceeded to lay her hand on my waist to feel the material. Only she didn't take her hand away.

I stepped toward Jade and kissed her. Just a small kiss, almost no pressure at first. That wasn't enough though; as soon as my lips started to part from hers, I went to kiss her again. This kiss was deep; I got chills up my spine.

We inched our way back toward the bed, kissing the entire time, Jade's hands never leaving my waist. I had a handful of her hair, and the soft terry cloth kept my hand from the soft skin on her waist.

We sat on the bed kissing and caressing each other; I was scared to think of the next step. I was more excited then I had ever been in my entire life. Jade leaned against me, laying me back onto the bed. I knew I couldn't have made the next move, and she stepped right in.

I closed my eyes as her lips brushed against mine. All the sensations became more intense when she started nibbling at my neck and ear. I could hear myself softly moaning, but I had no control over it. Jade moved farther down, taking my nipple into her mouth. The wet fabric between my body and her tongue gently scratched at my nipple.

The touch of her lips stopped. All I wanted was more, so I opened my eyes to see why she was backing off. Her shoulders were back; she was arching her back and lifting her breasts. The soft white terry cloth fell silently to the floor. Her body was amazing—the large soft breasts, the bronze of her tan skin, and the gentle curve of her waist—all perfect.

Jade crawled back on top of me, kissing me so deeply, so passionately. Her hand was gently pinching my nipple; her thigh started caressing my pussy. She went back to nibbling at my silk-covered breast. Her hand slid down my stomach, then down farther. Pushing two fingers deep into my body.

My body was so wet and warm; I could feel the pressure already in my stomach. I wanted her, and I wanted her badly. Her mouth moved farther down my stomach; as her hands ran up my thighs, I spread my legs open a little farther. Pulling my slip up enough to reveal my passionate V, Jade pulled my thighs up and spread them, to gently kiss my clit. All my body would let me do was moan. The touch of her lips made the rest of the world disappear.

Jade ran her tongue up my wet, swollen flesh; all I could do was cry out in pleasure. She thrust her tongue inside my body. My muscles started to contract, and she pulled away again. The sexual tension in my body was ready to be released. It couldn't build any more; at least I didn't think it could. When Jade pulled away, though, the climax I was reaching was all of a sudden nowhere near its peak. Jade was giving me little kisses all over my body, each one creating more gooseflesh. Between each kiss she would whisper something new: "I want to taste you badly." "Let me know you're ready to come." "Just looking at you makes me so wet." "Tonguing you is driving me wild." Each phrase making me moan, making my body ache—making me call out for more.

Jade started sucking on my clit and my body couldn't

contain it anymore. I started trembling as the orgasm rushed through me. I moaned so loudly and called out her name. *"Oh, Jade!"* I had a handful of her hair, holding her against me. Everything rushed out of me so fast, but the ecstasy seemed to be endless.

My body started to calm. I couldn't move, there was nothing left in me. Jade was just lying there, softly kissing my wet contracting petals.

She then climbed up to face level and put her arms around me. I wanted to please her, make her feel the same pleasure I just had, but when I turned toward her she just kissed me softly and said good night. I fell asleep in Jade's arms, never wanting to return home.

I woke the next morning to find the spot next to me empty. I looked around for a note, perhaps to explain her absence I found nothing. My heart sank, I couldn't believe that she would just leave without saying good-bye. I lay back down on the bed, thinking of a reason why she would do what she did. I couldn't come up with anything, other than the fact that I didn't have the kind of body she did. That maybe she regretted what she had done. Then I realized I was insane to feel that way. I mean I had one night with her, and it had been a wonderful one. So now if it was over, it was just time to go home. . . .

I gathered all my things and starting packing them up, putting a few things aside to get ready before I took off. I grabbed a drink out of the minibar while I packed. I wondered why I had brought as much stuff as I had—I was only going to be in this town for one night. Maybe in my head something else was going on when I packed; who knows. I mean I didn't even realize I was attracted to Jade until she rubbed her leg against mine.

After I finished packing I jumped into the shower. This

was bound to be a longer shower; the water was so hot and relaxing. I could hear nothing over the sound of the water beating down. I leisurely caressed my body with the soap, moving constantly, but slowly, to make the water strike down on different parts of my body, relaxing all my muscles. Eventually I shaved and washed my hair. I think I spent a good hour under the mesmerizing waterfall. I didn't even realize I had been in the shower that long, it was as if I was in a complete trance.

I gently patted my body dry and threw on the hotel robe. Surprisingly it was very soft. I was combing out my hair when I heard Jade call out: "Your breakfast is getting cold!" Instantly a smile consumed my face. Here I thought she had just left without a word, when she only went to get food. She told me why she had been gone so long: "I wanted to be back before you woke up, but I had trouble finding my way around this town!" My mind hadn't even contemplated that simple reason for her absence.

She kissed me on the cheek as I walked out of the bathroom. We sat down on the edge of the bed to eat. She had gotten donuts and coffee, not sure what I would like. I wasn't really in the mood for eating breakfast though; I had gotten so excited when I realized she was back, the only thing on my mind was Jade. I ate anyway—she had taken the time to buy breakfast, and it would have been rude to eat nothing.

When I finished eating, I moved behind Jade and wrapped my arms around her. She was still eating and I took advantage of it. I proceeded to massage her shoulders, sliding her hair over her right shoulder to expose her graceful neck. I didn't quite feel close enough though, so I slid my body completely along hers. You could see goose bumps form on her arms as my breath ran across her neck.

I ran my tongue up her neckline, then softly blew a cool breath across the wet spot. As my breath ran across that spot, she gripped my thighs and delicately moaned.

I kept rubbing her shoulders as I kissed her neck; nibbling at it in the sensitive spots. It was amazing how easy this was for me. I thought that once I started to touch her I would shy away, but there was no apprehension. I slid my hands down her sides, then onto her stomach. Jade took my hands and placed them on her thighs. Guiding them up and down the top of her legs. When she went to lead my hands up again I slipped my fingers under the edge of her skirt and pulled it up.

My fingers slid between her faintly opened legs, tenderly rubbing up the heat of her panties. I could feel the moisture of her body through the material, and it excited me all the more. Jade reached up and ran her fingers through my hair, and with her other hand held me against her. I suckled her soft skin and nibbled at her earlobe. My fingers were caressing her clit. I felt like the entire scene was right out of a movie, but it was real.

I turned to her and guided her back onto the bed. My leg was uncomfortably stuck underneath her. I knew she had to have felt cramped as well, but when our lips locked, being uncomfortable didn't seem to matter anymore. We were in a passionate kiss when I cupped her breast. Jade just felt so right in my arms.

I pulled myself on top of her, sliding my leg from underneath her. I was kissing her when I slid her arms over her head, holding them against the bed. Then I slid my fingertips down the length of her arms, gently caressing the sides of her breasts. She was so beautiful lying there. Slowly I started undoing her top, exposing her ample breasts. Jade pulled herself up from the bed so that I could slide her shirt off. Our lips never parted for more than a second.

Jade pulled at the tie of my robe, looking deeply into my eyes. I stood and let the robe fall off my shoulders, not worried about how I looked. Jade sat up and kissed my stomach, and a wonderful tingling sensation ran down my spine. My head fell back as she gently bit at my nipples.

Jade wrapped her arms around my waist and pulled me back down on top of her. Her bra fastened in the front, so I quickly undid it. I pressed my breasts against hers, rubbing up and down. The slight heat from the friction between our bodies was so erotic. Jade said she was about to come; I couldn't believe it. We had only been messing around at this point, but my body was very excited as well.

I wanted to taste her; I wanted to know the feeling of her passion on my lips. I slid down to her waist, kissing her torso in a teasing way. I undid her skirt and slid it down. She had this beautiful pair of white lace panties on. I almost didn't want to remove them, but then slid them down her legs. Jade said I didn't have to do it, if I didn't want to, but I did want to, I almost felt like I needed to, it was an experience I deeply wanted.

I ran my hands up her thighs, spreading her legs. I kissed her inner thigh, then moved a little closer in. Leaving a little kiss as I moved up. Then I ran my tongue up the center of her body. Jade was so wet; feeling how badly she wanted me excited me more. I sucked her clit for a moment, and then looked up at her. She moaned softly as her eyes were held shut. I pushed my tongue as deeply as I could into her, as she played with her nipples. Then I proceeded to insert two fingers inside her, pushing them in and out, playfully licking her clit while I fingered her.

Jade's body started throbbing as I kept going. She was

going to climax. She held me tightly between her legs. I moved from the lips to the clit, tickling and thrusting my tongue against it. She moaned loudly as she reached her peak, and her hands fell to her sides. Jade lay there breathing heavily. I had given her the same passion she had brought out in me.

I looked over to the clock and saw it was just short of checkout time. Sadly, I showed Jade the time. She sat up next to me on the bed and said we would get together again. I kissed her softly and agreed.

I finished packing and suggested she do the same, but she had already packed up and put all her things in her car.

We kissed each other when we exited the hotel, promising to spend time together again soon. I got into my car and drove off, with a feeling deep in my heart that I would not be seeing Jade again.

Carnal Club

BY ERIN PANNELL

I've never been much of a barhopper. In fact, I don't even like going to bars. Spending an evening with people crying in their beers over love gone wrong isn't my idea of a good time. But, after my divorce became final, a couple of my friends, Mark and Kelly, insisted that I go out for a celebratory drink. I agreed with the stipulation that it would only be for an hour. Little did I know how much could happen in just one short hour.

That evening, when I followed them into the Carnal Club, it was like I had walked into a dream. A thin veil of smoke dropped a filmy curtain around the crowded dance floor and filtered the lights around the bar. Music thumped a seductive rhythm. The air hung thick with sexual tension and hot sweaty bodies bumping and grinding under strobe lights.

Energy sizzled around me as I found myself getting caught up in the moment. I shook my shoulders in time to the music and followed Mark and Kelly through the crowd.

While they went to dance, I took a seat at the bar and

scanned the people around me. Everyone talked, laughed, and danced anywhere they could find a spot. This was so unlike the clubs I used to go to with my ex.

While I was remembering the sleazy dive he used to take me to, something caught my eye. Over by the front door, I spotted a couple in their mid-twenties pressed together so tight that it was hard to tell where he ended and she began. In slow, languid movements, his hands boldly explored every swell and curve of her body. His lips feathered kisses from her mouth, to her neck, and over her shoulder, stopping shy of her tits. Carefully, he inched her back until her body pressed against the wall, and then he wedged himself between her legs.

My cunt grew wet as I watched him grind against her pussy. His slender hips rolled and thrust as his tongue licked a seductive path to the valley between her tits.

Suddenly, I longed to feel a hard erection between my legs. Nothing could compare to a hard cock rubbing my clit—no vibrator, no sex toy, not even fingers.

My clit throbbed in rhythm to the music as I watched him cup her tit and pinch her nipple through her shirt. The tender flesh puckered under his touch and pressed hard against the thin material of her dress. As if he had done it to me, my nipples tightened in response.

The girl reached down with one hand and stroked his cock through his jeans before cupping his ass and pulling him close. Now, his rhythm picked up, faster and harder.

I shifted a little more and spotted the taut bare flesh of her hip and thigh as he pumped his dick into her. I didn't know what shocked me more—that he was fucking her right there, or that no one seemed to care.

My first instinct was to look away, but watching them turned me on so much I couldn't. He glided his hands to her bottom and lifted her up so that she could wrap her legs around his waist. His long fingers dug into her thighs as he thrust into her. Pure ecstasy covered her face. Eyes closed and lips parted, she clung to her lover as he brought her to an all-consuming orgasm.

Then, he rammed himself into her a few more times before slowing his rhythm and lowering her to the ground.

By this time, my cunt dripped with desire. I needed to feel a long hot shaft inside me. At this point, I knew that I either had to find someone fast, or find a distraction to take my mind off my soaking wet panties.

I turned my attention to the dance floor and searched for Mark and Kelly. There, off to the side by themselves, I found them rocking their bodies in time to the music.

Kelly's short black dress clung to every curve of her body. Lights flashed a hypnotic rhythm against her long slender legs, tiny waist, and full chest as she ground her hips, simulating sex with Mark. Her tits bounced and swayed as she moved. Not only did I find myself admiring her great body, but I also couldn't take my eyes off her rock-hard nipples.

When more people joined the dance floor, Mark and Kelly were thrust even closer together. Not that they minded. As her nipples brushed against his chest, his erection ground against her pelvic bone. Suddenly, I found myself wondering what it would be like to have a threesome with them. I closed my eyes and fantasized about sucking on Kelly's clit while Mark fucked me doggy style. I imagined the sweet smell of her cunt mixed with my own as I lapped at her swollen lips. Then, we'd come in a chain reaction—Kelly, then me, and finally Mark.

When I opened my eyes, a man joined Mark and Kelly on the dance floor. Lean, with ropes of muscles rolling down his arms, his slender hips cozied up to Kelly's tight ass.

My gaze roamed over the stranger's body, devouring every inch of him. From his thighs, to his crotch, to his narrow waist, I couldn't find a single flaw on him. Then, when my gaze locked onto his beautiful clear-blue eyes, my mouth dried. He was watching me watch him.

He kept me locked in his sights as he scooted closer to Kelly until their hips melded together. As he worked his cock against her ass, Mark slipped a hand under her skirt. Just by the expression on her face, I knew he was fingering her. And watching my best friend get off with two guys sent a white-hot heat straight to my cunt.

When one song faded into another, the man sauntered like a jaguar over to me—sleek, sexy, and oh-so-dangerous. My heart raced into overdrive, anticipating what this stranger had in mind for me. Without saying a word, he cupped my face in his hands and captured my lips with his. His tongue glided over mine, softly at first before exploring the depths of my mouth. My pussy lips swelled as he teased every erogenous zone along my neck and shoulders. As he worked his way down to my tits, I glanced over to the dance floor. Just like I had been watching her and Mark, Kelly was watching me. After she had given me a mind-blowing show, I wasn't about to disappoint her.

I spread my legs as an invitation for him to step between them, which he gladly accepted. With his large hands, he eased up my skirt, then ripped off my panties in a fluid movement. I moaned when I felt his huge dick nuzzle against my pussy. The scratchy fabric of his pants sheathed his hard cock as he humped against my hard bud. I shifted just enough so that Kelly could watch him pinch my sensitive nipples. She slowly nodded her head as if telling me she liked what she saw.

Whether it was the heat of the bar, the alcohol, or the gorgeous man in front of me, I couldn't be sure. But, without any hesitation, I eased back against the bar so that I could slide the edge of my stool and feel the tip of his cock glide from my ass to my clit. He knew exactly what I wanted. With deliberately slow strokes, he worked his cock against my ass and then my cunt while he nipped one of my nipples between his teeth. I gasped with the sensation and grabbed his cock. He was wider than I had anticipated. But the thought of him entering my swollen pussy caused my clit to distend even more.

I closed my eyes as he unfastened one button after the other until both of my tits were freed. A wicked smile tugged at the corner of his mouth as his eyes devoured the creamy flesh and barely pink nipples of my tits.

Like an animal, I ground my clit against him. I nearly screamed with desire. Never had I wanted a man in me so bad.

With his long fingers, he parted my swollen lips, before sliding one finger inside of my warm soft hole. "Oh, yes," I panted. "I love it."

With that, he added another finger, then another. I'd never been three-fingered before, and the new sensation stole my breath.

As I humped him, my heavy breasts swayed as if begging him to touch them. He sucked and nibbled one tit while his warm thumb and forefinger squeezed the other with gentle pressure. Even though I knew I could come like this, there was one thing that I needed more than just an orgasm.

I rose and led him to the dance floor. Once we found a

spot, I stepped in front and turned my back to him. I reached behind and pressed his cock against my ass. Through the material of his pants, I felt a spot of precome. With me as his cover, I eased down his zipper and freed his dick. A film of warm precome coated the velvet. Hungry for his taste, I slid my fingers over the tip, then licked them clean.

As if on cue, Kelly and Mark joined us. They mirrored our position, with Kelly facing me. Since Kelly and I were the same height, our tits were conveniently at the same level. Kelly must have noticed this as well because she moved so close our nipples brushed against each other as we moved. A spark of electricity zipped through me the second her hard nipples made contact.

"Grab her tits," Mark said to me.

Without any hesitation, I cupped both my hands under her breasts, then dragged my thumbnail over her nipples.

Kelly tossed her head back. "Oh, it feels so good."

"Suck it, baby," Mark demanded.

Kelly and I shared a knowing smile as I leaned over and pulled the strap of her dress down. Her pebble-hard nipple looked like a delicious piece of pink candy. At first I licked it until it glistened under the pulsing lights, then I sucked it between my teeth.

She gasped and pulled me closer until my face was buried in her tits. I nibbled and sucked as the stranger behind me hiked my skirt up over my hips. Then, I felt the heat of his cock pressing against my cunt. Reaching between my legs, I eased his eight-inch cock inside me while the curve of his shaft rubbed against my ass.

"Is he fucking you?" Kelly panted.

I released her gorgeous nipple and answered, "Oh, yeah."

"Mark's fucking me in the ass. It feels so good."

I kissed her mouth and tasted the sweetness of her tongue as it mated with mine before I returned to her nipples. Then I ran my hand up the soft inside of her thigh to her swollen folds. Just like my lover had done to me, I teased her clit with my fingertip, as then glided one finger after another inside of her. She grabbed my arm, urging me to her cunt deeper, harder, and faster.

My lover reached around and stroked my hard clit with one hand while he pinched my nipple with the other. Kelly took charge of the other. Between the two of them, I was on the verge of total ecstasy.

Just like in my earlier fantasy, we came in a chain reaction: Mark, Kelly, me, and then my lover. The aroma of sex, sweat, and raw carnal lust enveloped us. Exhausted, we all leaned against each other, with Kelly and I hugging in the middle. When Mark and my lover caught their breath, they went to the bar to order drinks, leaving Kelly and me on the dance floor. As we hugged, I gave her another kiss while cupping her tits in my hands.

Kelly traced my nipple with her fingertip as she said, "I always hoped this would happen one day."

"Me too."

When my hour had ended, I left the club with an invitation to Mark and Kelly's for the next evening, and with a new lesson that a lot can happen in an hour.

Kathy,
My Darling

BY SHARON BUSH

*A*wakening in midday, Kathy climbs into the shower. Lukewarm water wraps its arms around her, massaging the contours of her velvetlike body. The setting sun shines through a skylight window, casting a natural glow on the fine, translucent frizzies on her arms and buttocks.

She spreads a bar of moisturizing soap over the thickness of her abdomen and lathers the light brown, lustrous hairs of her pubis. As she parts her outer lips to reveal the spare tongue in her pink palace, Kathy looks up and into the electronic eye of her video camera. She inserts a finger into her vagina, pumping the light crimson flesh until the soothing overhead spray rinses clean her orgasm.

After drying off, she transfers the camera from its voyeuristic position on her vanity and takes it into the living room, where she deposits the newest addition to her collection of narcissistic videos.

When she is not at the television station, most of Kathy's time is spent pining for Ben's lost affection and running errands. While purchasing groceries one Tuesday morning, she is handed a coupon for a complimentary sampling of the Rendezvous Restaurant's world-famous dry ribs. It is an offer she finds difficult to refuse.

Among the sparse lunchtime crowd at the restaurant is Carmelita, WHEG-TV's vice president of entertainment and news programming. Kathy eyes her superior like a pubescent female would admire the fullness of any total woman.

As her glance lingers, Kathy remembers the day when she first saw a woman's body. She had just finished her weekly swim class at the YWCA. The locker room was segregated. Anyone under age twelve was isolated to a small, partitioned area of the room. As usual, the two showers were occupied, with nearly eight giggly girls waiting in a queue for their turn.

With her patience evaporating as quickly as the beads of water on her shoulders, Kathy decided to venture to the adult side of the room, where she could hear only one stall being occupied.

"Do you always bathe with your clothes on?" a voice rang out.

Startled, a bashful Kathy glanced up at a smiling face. "No, ma'am. It's just that there are no curtains over here," explained an embarrassed Kathy.

"The chlorine is harmful. It'll age you faster than the Arizona sun," the woman exclaimed.

Maybe she has a point, Kathy thought to herself as she sneaked a look at this squeaky clean woman who seemed to be no more than twenty-five years old. "I get it," said the woman. "You're shy. That's all right. I'll give you your privacy. But you'd better hurry because the rest of the adults will be in here in about five minutes. See ya!" The woman turned her back to Kathy and continued to dry herself.

When she left, Kathy quickly removed her swimsuit and enjoyed her shower.

While bathing, ten-year-old Kathy could not help but compare her body with the woman's. She looked down at her tiny, budding breasts and wondered whether they would ever grow to resemble the woman's bountiful set of mammaries that jiggled with the slightest movement. Kathy could not wait to grow up. Her teen years seemed to drag. Her girlfriends matured much quicker than she and that only added to her inflated sense of insecurity. "Let me see it!" one friend would tease during a slumber party. Reluctantly, Kathy would lower the bottom half of her baby-doll pajamas to reveal little, if any, development.

Like wildflowers springing up overnight, it happened. It was her fourteenth birthday when Kathy reached inside her panties to discover she was not a birth defect after all. There it was. Her prayers had been answered. And Kathy has been fascinated by pubic hair ever since.

She remembers the first time she saw a man's pubic hair. It wasn't until she was in college. Although she had convinced her girlfriends that she was deflowered, it was not until her twenty-first birthday that she decided to lose her virginity to her boyfriend, Ben. He had rented a room at a cheap motel and had decorated it with an assortment of colorful balloons. "Pick a balloon, any balloon," Ben instructed. "Pop it and follow the directions on the inside."

Choosing an exceptionally large yellow one that stood out among the others, Kathy pricked it with a hairpin and the prompt caused her eyes to grow wide. "What's it say?" asked Ben.

"Suck my dick," Kathy read.

"Well?" Ben asked as he stood in front of her. Kathy undid his jeans and lowered them to the floor.

To her surprise, the only thing he was wearing underneath was his manhood, which gained in size by each blink of an eye. Kathy kissed his navel, rubbing her nose against the fine line of curling hair that ran from it down to the huge mound of hair surrounding the erect muscle that Kathy knew would soon invade her body. The hair felt soft against Kathy's face and the scent of his sex aroused sensations in her body that she had yet to discover.

Wrapping her lips around the crown of his cock, Kathy's tongue fondled every inch of its curvature. Holding her head snugly between his hands, Ben slowly pushed his dick deeply inside her mouth until he could practically touch her pharynx. "If your mouth feels this damn good, I can imagine how your pussy must feel," Ben groaned.

Pushing Kathy back onto the bed, Ben grabbed the crotch of her shorts and pulled them aside. Spreading her lips, he thrust his tongue inside her pussy, lapping up all the secretions that continually escaped her cavity. Kathy whimpered in ecstasy.

"Now for your birthday present," Ben announced. He bounced to his feet and ran into the bathroom, returning with a video camera which he placed on a bureau positioned opposite the bed. "What are you doing?" Kathy asked as he turned on the camera.

"Making a memory," Ben answered laughingly. "Your own private movie."

"So what's the name of this private movie?" Kathy quizzed as Ben removed her clothes and began kissing, licking, and sucking her.

"Kathy, My Darling," he replied as he stuck his swollen cock gently inside her moist, tight pussy.

The following morning, a sore but happy Kathy stumbled her way toward the bathroom, stepping over nearly two dozen now deflated balloons. Inquisitively, she tore open one and read the instructions inside it.

She ripped open another one. Then another. To her astonishment, each balloon contained identical instructions: "Suck my dick," they stated. "Suck my dick." Kathy smiles each time she remembers that experience. She unwittingly finds herself again flushed as she stares at Carmelita's legs. Her knees slightly parted, Kathy can see a trace of white panties every now and then. She admires Carmelita's tanned thighs and wonders for a fleeting moment whether they taste as good as they look.

"Hi, Kathy! It's good to see you while the sun is still out," jokes the raven-haired beauty, who is dining alone. "Would you care to join me, that is, if you're not expecting anyone?" Kathy changes tables and she and Carmelita engage in a pleasant chat.

Over the next few weeks, the relationship between Kathy and Carmelita grows into one of common admiration. One Sunday night, Carmelita phones Kathy at work and requests to take her to a Monday matinee movie. Since Carmelita has foot the bill for several luncheon dates in recent weeks, Kathy counters in a reciprocal gesture and offers to prepare dinner for her.

The aroma of baked lasagna floats throughout the apartment like a spirit. As Carmelita relaxes on the sofa sipping a glass of white wine, Kathy remembers that she had to pick up a fresh loaf of garlic bread. "I'll be back in about fifteen minutes. Make yourself at home," Kathy says as she slings on a light jacket.

During her wait, Carmelita flips on the television which Kathy has left neglectfully in the VHS mode. She immediately identifies her subordinate in the video. Carmelita watches motionless as Kathy reclines on the chaise longue that faces a mirrored wall. The camera, perched on a tripod, gazes over her shoulder like a tutor critiquing a performance. Void of expression, Carmelita observes Kathy's image as she spreads her legs, displaying a labia that resembles the erotic juncture of a fuzzy hemispheric peach. Kathy buries a finger into the sensitive opening, gyrating her hips to a climatic zenith. As she throws back her head in fulfillment, the natural lubricants from her cavity are spread over her buttocks like a coverlet of morning dew. The video fades to black.

Carmelita turns off the television, returning to her position on the sofa. Lacking emotion, she stares at the black screen and then down to nearly a dozen videotapes, each titled *Kathy, My Darling*.

Kathy returns and Carmelita decides not to disclose what she has witnessed.

In a couple of weeks, Carmelita phones Kathy requesting to stop by her apartment on her next day off. Kathy agrees and the two meet on a Tuesday afternoon.

While Kathy is out of the room, Carmelita picks at random a videotape from Kathy's autoerotic collection and imagines its contents. She returns it to its original position.

Upon Kathy's reappearance, Carmelita proposes an offer. "The station is revamping its newscast and I want you for the five o'clock anchor position," the executive reveals. "You have an outstanding resume and your looks are easy on the eye." Kathy corrects her posture, amazed by what she is hearing. "I need to know how much you want the promotion," Carmelita continues.

"Oh, Carmelita, I want it. I've worked so hard to reach this level," Kathy gushes. Carmelita sits next to Kathy.

"I want to make it happen for you," Carmelita says as she brushes away strands of hair from Kathy's freckled face. They stare at each other, eyes fixed. "You're so beautiful," Carmelita compliments in a low, hoarse voice. She rakes gingerly the tips of her fingernails across the side of Kathy's blushing face. Kathy does not wince or pull away. Rather, she enjoys the graze of Carmelita's gentleness. "I have a confession to make," Carmelita reveals. "While you were out, I turned on the television and watched one of your videos. I had no intention of invading your privacy.

"The tape was already in the machine. I know I could have turned it off, but your loveliness mesmerized me." Kathy stands up, flushed with embarrassment.

"Don't worry about it," Carmelita comforts. "What you do in the privacy of your home is your business. It won't have a single bearing on your professional objectives. If you don't mind, I would like to see more of you."

Carmelita rises and inserts into the VCR a selection from the *Kathy, My Darling* series. They both watch, and within a minute, Carmelita begins to disrobe.

She pulls off her sweater, exposing a pair of small, firm breasts. Her ebony nipples are erect with vehement anticipation. She slips off her slacks, exposing G-string panties partially covering a thicket of black pubic hair. "Come to me," Carmelita begs.

Kathy remains puzzled. "I'm not a lesbian," she says with conviction.

Carmelita smiles and tells her that neither is she. "I like to consider myself a sexual being.

"Do you like my body?" she asks in a submissive manner. Kathy's eyes scan Carmelita's physical composition, stopping at the narrow triangle of silk masking the woman's bush. "You may touch it if you'd like." Carmelita takes Kathy's hand with care and holds it closely between her caramel-colored legs. Slowly their lips meet and

Carmelita's tongue searches for Kathy's. Retiring to the bedroom, Carmelita methodically strips her fledgling, muttering a series of raptures as she slides her hand inside Kathy's panties, penetrating her moist, soft opening. Her thumb rubs across Kathy's upright clitoris. Kathy closes her eyes and clasps Carmelita's large, round buttocks. They tumble onto the bed, entwined like a winding vine of jasmine.

Carmelita rises and walks into the bathroom. Kathy follows, magnetized by curiosity and an insatiable yen for endearment. Carmelita draws a bath and Kathy climbs into a tub of fragrant water, resting on her knees. Carmelita positions herself behind her and proceeds to shampoo Kathy's tresses, sensually massaging her scalp. Her graceful fingers tour Kathy's lily-white frame, searching for the dandelion-soft arena of her sex.

Kathy sighs hedonistically, rising and turning to a pyramid over Carmelita, allowing beads of water from her pubic hair to drip upon the face of her paramour like a light sprinkle on a spring day. Carmelita licks the remaining droplets, inserting her tongue in and out of her lilac-scented vagina.

After their bath, the two return to the bedroom for a continued escapade of eroticism. This time Carmelita finds herself on the receiving end. Kathy reaches for the strawberry-flavored liquid she once oiled over Ben's body and anoints Carmelita's in a full-body rubdown. The esthesis of Kathy's roaming fingers impels Carmelita to a state of total relaxation.

They kiss tenderly, embrace lightly, and fall asleep like two pieces of fine china atop a cushion of carnal felt.

They are awakened in the morning by a music alarm. Carmelita stretches for the phone, calls the station, and tells her secretary not to expect her today. Still in bed, she switches on the television to monitor her station's programming.

Kathy is in the kitchen preparing brunch. At eleven o'clock, she brings to Carmelita a tray of red grapes, rolled deli ham, scrambled eggs, and hot croissants. They toast each other with mimosas blended from the champagne Carmelita brought with her the day before.

Following brunch, Carmelita invites Kathy to engage in a game of hide and seek. "I've hidden a grape on me and your assignment is to locate it," she teases. "But there's one stipulation . . . you can't use your hands to retrieve it." Kathy examines Carmelita's body, discovering the grape inside her vagina. She nudges it with her nose. The scent of Carmelita's saturated pubis excites her. Using the tip of her tongue, she feels the grape, but pressure on it only pushes it in deeper.

Kathy opens wide the jungle that protects Carmelita's dark lips and thrusts her tongue inside. The sensation sends Carmelita into a quivering frenzy. Kathy grips Carmelita's sexy behind and tilts it higher. With Carmelita in perfect position, Kathy's tongue recovers the grape.

But rather than end the game, Kathy continues to tongue Carmelita's love canal until the vixen slumps from an explosive orgasm. Kathy licks the secretions from Carmelita's inner thighs as though they were her last meal. Gently inserting her thumb, Kathy slams her love hand against the opening, leaving a splattering of sexual sap like spilled molasses on the bedsheet. As Carmelita rests in absolute gratification like an odalisque waiting for her next sexual adventure, Kathy's gaze grazes the admirable workmanship of God's creation. The tips of her fingers feather the fine curvature of Carmelita's voluptuous perimeter. She praises the evenly hued texture of her softness.

Moving to her stereo, Kathy selects from a stack of CDs a recording of New Age music that flows throughout the room like light whispering winds.

Returning to her newfound interest, Kathy kisses Carmelita's delicate feet, taking each toe into her mouth. With every kiss, lick, and touch, she realizes the power she possesses over Carmelita and exults in it. She crawls over the woman, pecking soothingly along the way. As she rubs her long, satiny legs against Carmelita's, with breasts pressed against each other, their lips lock. Carmelita is at her mercy and Kathy knows it. Before leaving the room, Kathy watches Carmelita as she sinks into a catnap.

Kathy realizes how easily a lightning rod for mutual ecstasy can be created by the simple flicker of a finger or the twitter of a tongue.

Upon Carmelita's awakening, the two make love off and on all day. When it is time for Kathy to prepare for work, Carmelita attempts to persuade her to stay home. "I'll cover for you," convinces Carmelita. Kathy relents and makes mental plans to give Carmelita a night she will not soon forget.

"You enjoy my videos, don't you?" asks Kathy as she pulls playfully at the long, thick hairs of Carmelita's pubis. "Then you'll just love a live performance, won't you?" She rises from the bed and sits on a chair directly across from Carmelita. Kathy proceeds to apply aloe to her own body, starting with her uplifted breasts. She raises a long, slender leg, divulging a crotch that appears to have been honey-glazed.

"Let me kiss it, Kathy," Carmelita begs.

"Not yet," she answers as she lusters the mound to a

near shimmer. Kathy introduces a moist finger to her vagina and masturbates to an earth-moving climax. She returns to Carmelita and makes love to her for hours on end.

Intoxicated by lust and a compelling desire to establish a long commitment with Kathy, Carmelita vows to give Kathy whatever she fancies. "Anything?" Kathy probes.

"Whatever you desire," Carmelita replies in a guttural voice. Kathy kisses her hard on the lips and they make love some more until Carmelita again falls asleep.

"It's time to get up, Carmelita," Kathy whispers. "I have a present for you!"

"What?" Carmelita murmurs as Kathy kisses her ear. "You've given me more than I could ever dream. Now my life is fulfilled. I have a promising career and, the best of all, I have you."

Kathy purrs. "Look behind that tree over there."

Camouflaged behind it is her video camera with its red light on. "What's that?" Carmelita asks.

"I'm making a memory," Kathy answers. "It's your own private movie."

"What's it called?" Carmelita questions.

"Whatever you want to call it," Kathy remarks. Carmelita smiles and lies back on a pillow, falling into a slumber.

Minutes later while Kathy watches her new lover nap, the doorbell chimes. Artfully sliding out of bed so as not to disturb Carmelita, Kathy tiptoes to the door.

She peers through the peephole. There is no one there. As she cracks open the latched door and peeks out, she is startled. She unlatches the door, opening it wide to reveal a bouquet of helium-filled balloons with a huge yellow one in the center. It is anchored by a soft, cuddly stuffed animal. Taped to it is a card.

As she reaches down for it, goose bumps rush over her body in a torrent. Opening the card, her heart is silenced as she reads, "Hi . . . Kathy, my darling."

Mmmm . . .
French Food

BY A. LEE HALO

For nearly an hour, I studied the last couple in the cafe. They laughed quietly, not seeming to care about the world around them. Minute by minute, his hand crept farther up her knee. I thought of how warm it must be up there. He whispered something that made her look down at the floor, smile, and giggle. The way her blond wavy hair fell in her face reminded me of Alison.

When she raised her eyes, she stared back at me, licking her lips at the sight of my growing bulge. She turned her face to his. They kissed, their tongues darting in and out of each other's mouths. She placed her right hand on his jewels and squeezed them. I imagined Alison jerking off that asshole she ran off with. Did he make her laugh like that? Did she let him touch her like that in public? I slugged the remaining wine in my glass.

Her legs opened slightly, then snapped shut, trapping his hand inside. She closed her eyes and parted her mouth in longing. I remembered how stroking Alison's clit made her squirm. How she became deliciously wet. How loudly she'd moan when I lapped up her syrup.

The ponytailed waitress passing by didn't even glance at them when she briskly dropped the check onto their table. She ran up the metal staircase, her footfalls echoing. I watched her tight little ass disappear and then refocused my attention.

He was still up her skirt with one hand, and kneading her breast with the other. He whispered something else. She then threw back her head, clenching her teeth. I thought I heard a low moan. After he withdrew his hand, I saw his fingers glistening. I could smell her pussy from across the room and got so hard, I thought I'd tear through my jeans. I took another big gulp of wine.

"Okay! Okay, we closed, eh!" boomed the big French chef storming from the kitchen. His voice startled everyone, even causing me to choke. I barely noticed the couple getting up after he slammed his fist on their table.

"I said good night, you no understand! Now, leaf!"

I must have been really hacking away because the next thing I knew someone was hitting me hard on the back.

"I'm all right, really, I'm okay!" I turned to see who was attempting to save me and saw the pixie face of the waitress with the tight ass. I was surprised such strength could come from such a petite woman. For an instant, I wondered what else about her would surprise me.

"You okay?" she asked, sincerely concerned and looking hard into my eyes.

"Oh, I'm much better now." I grinned. The chef locked the entrance and approached us, shaking his head. It was time to leave and I didn't want his fist to slam on my table.

"That man and woman! No shame, eh," he grumbled, throwing his hands up in disgust. I abruptly stood up, only to have him push down my shoulder. Although I was much taller than he, I could see him slicing through a round of beef with a single blow.

"You stay," he said, his voice softer. *"S'il vous plaît,* an aperitif? On the house. My niece Chloe and me, we see you in here almost every night."

It was true. Although I wasn't at the cafe every night, I was there often, not being able to bear being alone in my big loft and bored with the bar scene. Chloe and I knew each other, but only by face. She was the head waitress and always darting around the cafe. He introduced himself as Jacques.

"I'm Joel." I offered my hand. He shook it hard.

"So, you have no woman anymore, Joel." Wasn't that observant of him?

"Chloe and me, we watch you come in all alone." She nodded. So, little Chloe's been watching me, eh?

"You've been such good customer. Stay."

While I appreciated the hospitality, I was already a little drunk and wasn't sure if I wanted him to catch me ogling his hottie niece.

"Oui, stay!" Chloe chimed in for the first time. "You must. Uncle insists, it would be an insult." Her delicate fingers undid the first two buttons of her jacket.

"Well, I would never want to insult your uncle," I conceded.

He laughed heartily and walked to the bar. Chloe and I looked at each other. A bead of sweat crawled down her neck, disappearing under her jacket. I imagined how that little drop would taste on my tongue. How I'd lick its salty trail between her firm breasts. Jacques returned, placing two full glasses in front of us.

"Chloe will keep you company. I must finish downstairs and lock up."

"Uncle, let me help you."

"No!" He held up a hand in protest. "No, I do alone! You stay until customer leaves!"

Once Jacques split, we started to really talk. Chloe pulled up a chair and straddled it. Her white trousers took on a tinge of pink from her skin. Even though her pants were loose, I could tell she had shapely legs. When she removed her barrette, she shook free her dark silky hair and let it cascade to her shoulders.

Chloe explained that she had just graduated from culinary school in Paris and was being groomed to start a new family restaurant. I listened and watched as she undid another button, revealing another inch of smooth skin. I was getting harder than a day-old baguette.

"People get such pleasure from eating," she said. "I like to give people this pleasure." She tilted her head to the side and ran her finger up and down the wet stem of her glass.

"What about your lost lover?" she asked.

I told how we met on a photo shoot. How the day she disappeared, she left nothing but a note and a mattress.

"Oh, Joel, I'm sorry." Chloe started to stroke the top of my hand. Her complexion was porcelain perfect. Her lips were so full, so soft. Her green eyes sparkled in the candlelight.

"I want to kiss you." But before I could even make a move, she cleared the table with a quick sweep of her arm, sending everything to the floor with a crash.

"Chloe! Are you all right!" Uncle Jacques sounded like he was halfway up the basement stairs, holding his huge butcher knife, ready to lop off my meat!

"It's fine! I dropped the bottle. No problem, I'm cleaning it up," Chloe called back while giving me a look full of heat.

"My fault!" I added.

I grabbed her by the jacket, pulled her toward me, and thrust my tongue in her eager mouth. She threw her arms around my neck and sucked on my tongue. I wanted to devour her.

I dragged her around the table, and sat her on it directly in front of me. She opened her legs and I stood between them, pulling her against my crotch. She wrapped them around my waist and started grinding her crotch into mine. I put my hands up her jacket and felt the softness of her breasts, the stiffness of her nipples. She pulled my shirt out of my pants, slid her hands up my chest, then started digging her nails into my back. I kissed her lower and lower down her neck until I reached the hollow of her throat, where I lingered with my tongue. Her legs tightened around me.

Suddenly, she tore open her jacket and the buttons went flying everywhere. Her nipples were so pink, her breasts so creamy. I dragged my tongue down between them, making a spiral until I reached the bull's-eye of her right tit. I felt her nipple get even harder when I gnawed on it while pinching the other.

"Bite them, bite them harder. *Oui!*" she whispered loudly. For an instant, I thought of her uncle just downstairs. But when she unzipped my fly and wrapped her hands around my thick sausage, I could only think of her. When I touched her pussy through her trousers and felt how wet she was, I couldn't wait to get inside.

I tore off my shirt, and before long we were completely naked. Pretty soon, that little round table was way too small for what I wanted to do to her. With her legs still tightly around me, I carried Chloe to the metal staircase.

I took a seat on a step and just stared, admiring her exquisite breasts, her long elegant arms, her bright eyes. I ran a finger down her delicate strip of pubic hair, down to her lips, and made small circles. I felt her clit swell. She started to drip with her sweet nectar. I spun her around and had her sit on the stair. Chloe gasped from the cold of the metal. I'd warm her up in no time. I rubbed my rock-hard shaft against her moist folds. We were both starting to breathe harder. The smell of her cunt was so sweet and so strong, I had to bury my face in it. She had the most delectable pussy! And she sure liked me licking her! She thrust up her hips every time I stroked her with my tongue. Then I started to use my finger too, sending it slowly in and out of her hole, while I sucked longingly at her hard clit.

"Oui, oui," she cried in that loud whisper. I grabbed her ass and pulled as much of her steamy cunt as I could into my mouth. She grabbed the banister. She arched her back. She cried out and her sap flowed all over my face.

"Are you sure you're all right up there?" Uncle Jacques yelled from down below.

"Yes." Chloe laughed, trying desperately to catch her breath. "We're just having a grand time."

Under which table did I leave my pants? Of course I forgot to look for them as soon as Chloe slipped my dick in her tender mouth.

"Mmmm," she purred. "I can tell how good you'll taste." With each flick of her tongue, I felt a surge all the way down to my toes. Back and forth with her head, then around and around with her tongue. She slipped my balls into her hot mouth. Then she went back to sucking fast. It was getting impossible to hold it in any longer.

"I want to taste you now!" That's all she had to say. I exploded harder than any champagne bottle could.

"Mmmm!" I looked down at her face and saw come on her chin. She wiped it away with her finger, which she licked clean. I sat down next to her on the stairs and again admired her beautiful nude body. Chloe saw I was ready for more action and smiled.

She climbed onto me with her tits dangling in my face. She lowered herself down onto my cock, then glided up and down, slowly, steadily. I wrapped my hands around her narrow waist and helped her move. Faster, harder, deeper she ground herself into me. When I couldn't hold out any longer, I plunged my cock in hard. She bit my shoulder and didn't come back up.

I felt her muscles ripple and held her tight. With a single thrust, she ground her pelvis into me and we both came.

"You kids finished the wine yet?" I could hear a door closing and knew Uncle Jacques was in for a big surprise. Chloe leapt up and ran behind the bar, her buns glowing in the dark. She turned and winked at me, laughing while I scrambled for my clothes. I threw my shirt in my knapsack and zipped my leather jacket all the way to the collar.

"You smile so big, you must be really drunk, eh. Ha-ha-ha-ha!" Jacques was now wearing a sports jacket and led me to the door. Chloe was soon standing behind him, wearing a light blue wool sweater, her beautiful hair again in a ponytail.

"Now, Joel, we must say *bon soir.* Come again soon?"

"Thank you, I definitely will! That was the best meal I've had in a long time, and such delicious wine." I meant it.

The two stepped outside with me. As Jacques turned to lock the door, Chloe kissed me on both cheeks. Then in a voice pitched low for only me, "Come eat me . . . with us . . . again soon," said Chloe, running her tongue over her lips.

"Of course," I replied. I love to eat French.

Bruised Daffodils

by Deborah Hunt

*W*hile standing on a London underground platform, I impatiently flicked a pen cap between my teeth, my map marked with haphazard lines. An innocent act, my playing with the pen cap, but it was enough to catch the attention of a bystander.

I stopped what I was doing and glanced at him. His gaze was on my mouth. He did not look away. He stood with another man. They wore expensive business clothes, I noticed, and I idly wondered if they were Dutch or German by their blond hair, blue eyes, and imposing builds.

A train stopped at the platform. I squeezed inside a packed car, my panty hose bristling against the tweed of someone's suitcase. I smelled the scent of rain on my skin. Fooled by the warm morning, I'd left behind my coat and umbrella and got caught in a spring shower. My clothes were still damp. My blouse stubbornly hugged my skin, revealing the white lacy bra I wore beneath.

As the train took off, I held on to a bar above me, realizing my breasts were eye level with a man seated across from me. He adjusted the crotch of his pants as he looked at me. I tried to adjust my blouse, but only succeeded in hardening my nipples with the tug.

Looking away from him, I remembered yesterday afternoon when I had been coming up the stairs at the underground station. A man had come up behind me on the steps and caressed the inside of my legs. His hand slid up my skirt, brushing my inner thighs. At the top, I broke away and spun, but he had disappeared in the crowd.

After it happened, I hurried to my room, where I found the cotton crotch of my underwear was damp.

It seemed odd that I had to come all the way to London to get damp panties from a casual grope in an underground station, but then I hadn't thought about dating in ages. I had been so caught up in work and school that I hadn't even given myself the chance to think I was desirable.

I smoothed my hands over the curves of my hips and looked at the shape of my body. I tried to imagine how the men in the subway saw me. My hips were full, my breasts smallish, but they were large enough to cup and squeeze together to make cleavage. My waist was thin, and my limbs were lanky. They could be either graceful or awkward at times.

Lying on my bed, I inched up my skirt to my waist and pulled down my panties. I opened my legs and touched the inside of my thighs where the man had caressed me. My skin tingled where his fingers had touched. I lowered my fingers to my pussy and dipped one finger inside to get it wet. On my clit, I made the small wet circles that had gotten me off so many times. My pussy was throbbing. I tried to bring myself to passion, but it was no good. I needed something more.

The blond man who stared at my mouth was nearby. His continued gaze at me was intense and mischievous in this light. His hair was cut short, but it looked as if his bangs wished to be tousled over his forehead. The back of my neck felt suddenly warm. I clenched the pen cap in my hand, flicking it with my tongue. The train approached my station and jerked to a halt. I squeezed off the train car. The air smelled stale. The sounds of people running to the platforms and the rumble of the escalators echoed behind me as I made my way out.

At street level, I paused at a fruit and flower stand. A handful of wilted, bruised daffodils had been left in the trash, some of their petals still yellow and vibrant. Thinking they would brighten my budget-rate room, I reached to take them when I felt a presence behind me. I turned.

The blond man stood there. His friend was gone. He reached around me, his breath on my neck for a moment as he took the flowers. His elbow grazed my breast.

I looked into his eyes. They shone with interest. I noticed they were the same color blue used on Delft china. I kept walking, hearing his footsteps coming behind me with the rustle of the flowers against his coat.

At the next street, he overtook me. He hooked his arm in mine and pulled me into a darkened doorway. The closeness of him was overwhelming, the scent of daffodils on his clothes. I looked down.

His trench coat was unbuttoned to his waist and I saw the breadth of his chest. His shirt collar was rumpled as if he had recently removed his tie. Ever so gently, he took my head in his hands and pressed his forehead to mine. His skin was heat.

"Where can we go?" he asked.

I hesitated. My body prickled with alertness. The dampness was back between my legs. I wanted him.

Without much decorum, I led him to the YWCA. Men weren't supposed to go beyond the reception area, but he walked by the desk and entered the elevator with me. In my small room, I put down my things.

He laid the flowers on the bed. Unbuttoning his trench coat, he sat on the bed. His legs were longer than his torso. He motioned me toward him. I stood between his legs. He turned me around by my waist and stood.

I was floating as he stroked my neck, moving my hair to the side to kiss me behind the ear. His hands were burning holes in my skin. He sighed the way a man sighs when he finds the perfect cigar or lover, and he pulled my coat off my shoulders and dropped it to the floor. He returned to my waist and untucked my blouse from my skirt. Roughly, he handled my nipples through my bra. I responded. I reached back and fondled him, his hardness roughly pressing against his pants.

Slipping off my blouse and bra, he tossed them to the bed. He molded my breasts and sucked them. With a slight jolt, I realized his tongue was pierced as he licked them. I pulled back, surprised, but he began to work his jewelry. He pressed the ball on the top in circles against my tightening nipple. I arched my back in intense pleasure.

Letting go of me, he unbuttoned his shirt. His left nipple was pierced as well, but this was a small steel ring hanging through his flesh. As he took off his shirt, I saw tattoos on his arms. Pinup girls. An Oriental woman in a Japanese background of flowers graced his left biceps. A space-age girl sitting on a smoke-filled sphere tantalized his right.

Seeing my gaze on his skin, he turned and showed me two lovely women on his back in a boudoir scene with satin pillows in a Victorian setting. I gasped at the beauty of his women. I noticed buried in his chest hair a tattoo of a Dutch flag.

"You're as beautiful and mysterious as my girls," he said.

He knelt and tugged off my shoes, skirt, and panty hose. I gazed down at his back, seeing a spot with swirling black lines on his shoulder blade. An unfinished woman, I realized. I longed to trace the uncolored skin with my fingertips, but he stood and took my head in his hands. He pressed my lips to his pierced nipple.

"Bite it," he said.

At first, I thought he wanted me to bite his nipple, but he raised his nipple ring to my teeth. I knew what he wanted: his metal against my teeth. I bit and pulled the ring with my teeth like I had with my pen cap, flicking it with my tongue. He groaned with pleasure, running his hands through my hair, holding me close.

The moment I slid my tongue so it poked through the center of the ring and looked up at him, he could take it no more. He unzipped his pants. He wore no underwear. I half-expected his cock to be pierced, but it wasn't. Still, I stroked it with my left hand, while tugging his pants down with my right. From his wallet, he pulled out a condom. I ripped open the foil with my teeth and held his cock for him as he put it on.

I traced his skin where tattoos were on his biceps, marveling at the smooth texture. It felt unlike any skin I had touched before. He pressed me to the bed, the daffodils beneath me. He spread my legs and went for my clit. He buried his tongue toy deep inside me for a moment and then began to lick around my clitoris in fine circles. I felt a curious sensation building inside me. It was the pressure of his jewelry. He used long slow strokes with his tongue, flipping the underside of my clit at the top, the warm steel a sharp contrast to his soft tongue. I gasped, never having realized how sensitive the underside of my clit was. It felt as if it were swelling to a mini hard-on. Then he took my clit beneath his tongue and rubbed my bulging nub with the ball on the top, meanwhile shoving the tip of his tongue into my hood.

I grabbed his blond hair and pulled his head closer to me. With both hands I spread my thighs wider. I was on the verge of a climax. I wanted more. I started to pull his head toward my stomach to get him on top of me. He stopped and stood up. He motioned me to the edge of the bed. Still standing, with my legs wrapped around him, he pressed his cock head to my pussy.

He fucked me with deliberate slowness, watching every movement as he pulled in and out of me. My legs felt as if they were going weak. I unhooked them and he lifted my ankles to his shoulders without missing a beat. I slid my hand to my pussy, feeling my engorged clit and his cock sliding in and out of me. Everything was so wet. I played with my clit. He watched, his gaze riveted on my fingers. My foot slid near his mouth. He turned his head and sucked in my toe between his lips.

His mouth was warm, wet passion. I pulled my toe out, reveling in the suction noise. He ran his tongue along the backside of my toes, his jewelry playing each toe like the keys of a piano.

My climax was coming from the center of my body. Pinching his pierced nipple, I used his ring to twist it. He cried out in ecstasy. A shudder of pleasure passed through his body. I went over the edge. I could feel every pulse of his cock inside me as he came. My orgasm was so fierce that my ears buzzed and my fingers tingled.

As our breathing calmed, I felt him pull out of me. He knelt before my pussy once more and gave it a sweet kiss. An electric shock went through me. He smiled and rubbed his tongue toy on the inside of his teeth, the noise exactly like when he was eating my pussy. A chill of excitement went through me.

He lowered his head.

He was an exotic creature. The women on his skin stared up at me with gorgeous, content eyes, moving on his skin in rhythm as he rocked me to my second orgasm. I clutched him as I cried out, my fingers grazing the unfinished tattoo, and I imagined myself tattooed on his skin, brazen, sexy, and marvelous.

A Vengeance
of Vixens

BY LISA LaROCK

I met Pam via the worldwide web on an Internet chat relay and developed a friendship with her over the course of many months. I didn't have many female friends, but for some reason I felt so comfortable about Pam right from the beginning. We were relatively the same age, enjoyed the same activities, and were both involved in an "online" relationship with a mysterious man. It wasn't long before we began to share secrets, including our intimate thoughts and desires. Even though Pam had made a few scoffing remarks about bisexuality, I could sense that there was something different about her. There were actually a few times when I tried to visualize Pam masturbating in front of her computer while we conversed. One day Pam asked me about the man with whom I was involved online—what his real name was, his birthday, and about the relationship. When I answered her questions truthfully, there was silence between us for five minutes. Then she dropped the bombshell: Apparently we were both being played with by the very same man. I did not want to believe it.

I disconnected myself and stayed away from the computer for days. I did not answer my e-mail, nor the phone. My mind raced so that I could not sleep at night, and the mere thought of eating sent ripples of nausea through my stomach. I was finally able to confront the truth: Not only had I lusted wildly after this man for months, I had really fallen hard for him. After spending some time thinking about the whole bizarre situation and connecting all the pieces, my fury and need for revenge took over. Abounding with a newfound energy, I phoned Pam and began a wonderful brainstorm with her. "So, are you in?" I questioned my friend.

"Yes, I'm in. But how do we go about this?" Pam asked.

"I want to shock this man," I purred. "But I also need to get him out of my system."

"I know what you mean." Pam sighed. "God, he really knew how to make me wet. . . ."

Even through the silence over the phone, I could hear Pam's breath wavering. "MMMMmmmm . . . yes, he had a way of making me cream without even fingering myself," I murmured. For some strange reason, this conversation had taken a twist that was really turning me on. I had many bisexual desires, but I couldn't believe that I was talking to another woman this way.

"Lisa, have you ever been attracted to other women?" Pam asked.

My hand slipped into my bikini briefs, feeling the moisture already there. "Yes," I quietly told her.

"I bet you have a nice pussy," Pam murmured. "I bet that it is so beautiful that if I had it sitting in front of me right now, I'd lick it good."

My fingers began moving with a steady rhythm over my clit. When I slid a finger into my wet, tight vagina, I sighed shakily. The dialogue was kept brief, but the breathing on either end became increasingly intense.

Within minutes, I had released myself to a hand-stroked orgasm and filled the receiver with heavy moaning. Pam repeated with a similar response, although I was certain that I could hear wonderful, wet pussy sounds in the background. After we had regained our wits, the decision was made to carry out our deliciously wicked plot within the following few weeks.

Meanwhile, Roger had been logging on to his computer each morning. He hadn't heard from either of his "girls" for several weeks, and it was frustrating. BOTH couldn't have dropped off the face of the planet, could they? Sure, he could wander off into the porn rooms and gaze at the picture buffets before him, but these two hot ladies made him really horny.

He felt slightly guilty about deceiving them, but he was just so damned insatiable. Other men would kill to be in his shoes—he still had "the stuff." After another hour of hopeless messaging and waiting, he shut down and collected messages from his secretary. There were a few messages from clients, one from his son, but there was one last message that REALLY caught his attention.

It was from his wife: She wanted him to meet her at a hotel in exactly one hour. In capital letters and underlined was the word "URGENT." He washed up and changed clothes, all the while curious what his wife could possibly want with him. Their sex life was satisfying and regular, but so vanilla. Could it be a change? Roger hopped into his car and drove to the designated hotel.

To enact our revenge, Pam and I had agreed to meet at the airport, and we quickly chose a hotel. Our attraction was immediate . . . and we talked excitedly about a plan of attack. We found the hotel, paid for a decent room, and began talking excitedly about out plan. Although we had discussed in detail what we would do to Roger, we both knew that some things would happen spontaneously. Like right then, when Pam put a warm hand upon my smooth thigh. I sighed and closed my eyes and savored the touch. I reached over and felt Pam's cheek before kissing her deeply on the mouth.

We began to caress and explore each other's breasts. Before long we were comfortable and warm, and we began to display our lingerie to each other, commenting on each other's beautiful physique, then slipping off our panties to show each other our most intimate regions.

We were both so equally aroused and curious. We positioned ourselves so that we could both explore and taste one another's mounds.

I felt Pam spread apart my delicate, pink pussy lips and dart her exquisite tongue against my clitoris.

The sensation was much like electricity passing through my body. I had never before been this close to a woman. I glanced at Pam's pussy, waiting just inches from my face. I could smell her musky woman scent, and her clit was swollen and glistening with her wetness. I stuck out my tongue and hit the sweet knob; Pam responded with a soft moan of pleasure. Tongues flickered, slashed, and fucked until we both wiggled and climaxed with muffled cries. With incredible timing, there was a knock at the door.

It was Roger knocking at the door, his mind racing with the possibilities. He was totally unprepared for what followed: When the door opened, it was NOT his wife standing there! I stood before Roger with a satisfied smile upon my lips, watching his surprised reaction. "OHHH, baby!" he exclaimed pleasantly. "What a surprise this is!"

He entered the room and wrapped his arms around me. I recognized the scent of his cologne from the doused stationery he had sent me. Another figure quietly approached us from a darkened corner.

Pam cleared her throat. Roger pulled away from me abruptly. His jaw dropped and his face became ashen. "How long did you plan on keeping us on a string? Did you think we were just two stupid pieces of tail?" Pam blurted. For the first time since we had known him, Roger became silent.

"Boy, are you ever in trouble now," I scolded and shook my finger at him. Pam and I, feeling confident in our lingerie, approached him quickly and pushed him onto the bed. Roger was bewildered. He wasn't sure if he should be afraid or enticed.

"Yes, be afraid, be very afraid," Pam told him.

Quickly and roughly, we ripped away his tie, his shirt, his shoes, his pants, and all his accessories until he was completely naked. His cock was already rock-hard with excitement; both Pam and I noticed, but we were transformed into sisters on a mission. We handcuffed Roger's hands to the bedpost and tied his feet in the same manner.

We then stood before Roger at the foot of the bed and began arousing each other in ways that he had never seen in real life. I could feel his eyes as I suckled and licked Pam's gorgeous hard nipples. Pam knelt down before me and began licking my pussy with enthusiasm, almost as though Roger wasn't in the same room—nor, for that matter, on the same planet. Roger's cock pulsed with frustration. There was an agonized expression on his face.

"Ohhhh, girls," he whined. "Don't do this to me. . . . Please, help me out here!"

We continued our own pleasuring, pretending to ignore the pleading man. "Please, do something with me, and I promise, I'll do anything!"

"I think he's on to something, Pam," I mumbled. "I think we should teach Mr. Man here something about what it feels like to be used."

"I definitely agree with you," Pam stated. She crawled between Roger's bound legs and held his cock inches from her face. "And besides, look at how hard his cock is. We can't very well let that go to waste, now can we?"

I joined my friend, gently nudging her over to give me some space.

"Oh yes," she murmured. "Look at that precome right there on the tip. . . . Which one of us is going to get that?"

"There's more where that came from," Roger said. "Now, please . . . don't fight . . ."

As Pam held the cock in her hands, I bent forward and gathered up the sweet fluid with my tongue. I turned to my friend and darted my tongue into Pam's open, luscious mouth. How erotic it was to share a kiss as well as a treat.

Roger shivered and sighed with delight. Pam slipped her mouth around the swollen cock head and fastened herself there with a hard suction, while I licked and slithered down the shaft toward his balls. Roger raised his hips slightly when Pam slid her mouth over his cock. My eyes widened at how deeply my friend was able to take his cock into her mouth. I worked on stimulating his balls—taking one into my mouth at a time, rolling each around with my wet tongue. Occasionally I would drift down even farther and lash my tongue against his asshole.

It was too much for poor Roger to bear as we girls worked in unison: sucking, licking, mouth-fucking his prick until he let out a deep groan and spewed the first shot of creamy come down Pam's throat. She swallowed quickly and removed herself from him and nudged me from any further action.

Roger looked bewildered. "What the hell?" he stuttered. His cock pulsed madly; his silky jism continued to cascade from his slit.

"Please, don't leave me like this, girls! I'm begging you!"

I reached over and licked Pam's earlobe. "Are we ready for step two?"

Pam nodded in agreement. We briefly probed each other's sopping, dripping cunts—each knowing how aroused we were and how badly we needed to climax. I took a blindfold from my luggage and tied it securely around Roger's eyes, completely disabling his vision.

"Just don't hurt me." Roger shuddered. Pam climbed over Roger's head, placing one slender leg on either side of his neck, and lowered herself slowly. She parted her swollen wet cunt lips with her fingers and sat her hot sex right upon Roger's mouth. He mumbled gratefully and began a slow circling motion with his tongue all around her. Pam's pleasure was obvious.

I moved inward like a hungry leopard, ready to attack my prey. I climbed onto the bed and squatted over Roger's waiting, throbbing cock. The moment that I had been waiting months for had finally come. Many sleepless nights had passed from wanting to feel his member deep inside me. Now, finally, I could feel it enter me, plowing the sides of my slippery vagina.

My moist hole was so very tight from the lack of sex. Roger groaned at the warm, wet muscle tightening and sliding around his cock. I began to pump myself in a fluid motion up and down the length of his cock, increasing my efforts and speed but backing off before I got too close to my orgasm. There was one more thing that I needed to take from him, before it was too late. I reached down, grabbed his cock firmly, and slid my passionflower off of his rod. I noticed how slick his cock was from my juices. I wiggled and positioned myself for the kill.

I directed the head of his prick against my asshole. Just the touch of it against my puckered rosebud sent shivers up and down my spine. Slowly, I began to put my weight upon him, and the wet tip of his cock popped easily into my hole. Pleasure burned throughout my body unlike anything I had ever known. I lowered myself upon him completely—his entire cock filling my hottest and tightest region.

Pam watched me, her own pleasure rising even more as she saw Roger's cock buried in between my firm buttocks. I began to rock slowly and Pam bent forward, still enjoying Roger's love feast on her pussy. Pam was drawn to the beautiful, bestial action before her. She began to lick my honey-covered clit as Roger's manhood entered and retreated from my asshole.

I couldn't help but moan as I felt Pam's tongue running wildly around my pussy lips, vagina, and clitoris. The three of us became a single unit of licking, sucking, fucking, writhing, and moaning . . . each bringing the other closer to physical liftoff, each feeling every nerve inching toward an explosive point of no return.

I was the first to reach that erotic height. I cried out and shook, my love juices dribbling all over Pam's tongue and Roger's pump-organ. As my orgasm subsided, Roger threw his hips up mightily and let out a muffled roar. I could feel his seed rumble up inside of me, shooting into the farthest areas of my heat. The sex fluid began to seep onto my buttocks, and another tremble of pleasure overtook me. I removed myself from Roger and moved closer to my female friend. Roger's tongue continued to flicker and drive into Pam's burning, sopping holes, his movements becoming quicker and harder, with more purpose. Joining forces, I began tickling Pam's clit with my tongue. I could feel Pam's clit respond with pulses. Pam's breathing became deeper, faster, louder. Two madly lashing tongues were enough to drive her into a series of convulsions as she began to fuck Roger's tongue and grab my head, grinding into our faces.

"Ohhh fuck, that's it!

"Yesss . . . I'm coming!" she screamed.

Her orgasmic fluids slid over our mouths. I had never seen a woman cream like that before, even in erotic films. When the breathing relaxed and brain cells fell back into place, Pam and I looked at each other with a satisfied smile. We rushed to get dressed and gathered our luggage.

"Hey, don't leave me like this!" Roger exclaimed. This time we did not detect an ounce of sexual tension. As we opened the hotel-room door, we took one last look at the naked man bound upon the bed. I went over and undid Roger's blindfold, then bent down and kissed him on the cheek.

"Goodbye, Roger," I said plainly.

"It was a blast, Roger," Pam exclaimed with one last wave, and she blew him a kiss.

As we walked down the hall with our heads held high, we could hear Roger's loud, unwavering protests of love and affection. Before we left the hotel lobby, we proceeded with step three, the final step of our wonderful plan. We phoned and left a message for Roger's wife, instructing her to come to the hotel, room 303, where her husband was waiting anxiously for her.

After booking into a different hotel, Pam and I showered together, dressed up, and went out to paint the town.

We danced and laughed, drank and flirted. I had one of the best nights in my entire life! When we returned to our room, although exhausted, we still managed to pleasure each other one last time before drifting off into a deep slumber. After all, revenge is tiresome work.